DEEP END
OF THE
LAKE

A Lake Surrender novel

Carol Grace Stratton

*If you're in the deep end of the lake,
you'd better know how to swim.*

LPC Books
Imprint of Iron Stream Media

LPCBooks
a division of Iron Stream Media
100 Missionary Ridge, Birmingham, AL 35242
ShopLPC.com

Cover design by Elaina Lee

Library of Congress Control Number: 2020952489

ISBN-13: 978-1-64526-277-0
Ebook ISBN: 978-1-64526-314-2

Praise for *Deep End of the Lake*

Deep End of the Lake continues the story of Ally Cervantes, a character readers came to love in *Lake Surrender*. The single mother of a defiant teenaged daughter and an autistic son, Ally struggles to bring her family to a place of wholeness and restoration. In this sequel, author Carol Stratton offers an engaging tale of family relationships, forgiveness, romantic love, and ultimately faith in God. For fans of *Lake Surrender*, Carol's newest offering is a must-read!

~ **Ann Tatlock**
Award-winning novelist, blogger, and children's
book author

Deep End of the Lake, sequel to *Lake Surrender*, is a joy to read. The realistic characters capture you emotionally with both their troubles and their joys. The difficulties faced by divorced protagonist Ally Cervantes, who is raising a rebellious teenager along with a son on the autism spectrum, are believably and sensitively portrayed on each page. I was totally caught up in this story as Ally's engagement to Will seems to be in jeopardy, and she is forced to deal with her own insecurities. Lovely story with a satisfying ending. Five stars!

~ **Elaine Cooper**
Author of *Scarred Vessels* and *Love's Kindling*

Deep End of the Lake grabbed me from the start. Carol Grace Stratton has a wonderful way with words, a wonderful way with a story, and creates fascinating characters. I loved *Lake Surrender*, so I was eager to read the sequel. It was well worth the wait. Stratton weaves complicated emotions through the book that will resonate with readers from all walks of life. I love that she dwells on the life of a family with a special needs child, but so much of what she feels is what all moms feel. The scenes dealing with the teenaged daughter are just as real. The romance is sweet and tender. The setting impacts the characters and mood. *Deep End of the Lake* is sure to keep you turning pages and leave you wanting more.

~ **Norma Gail Holtman**
Author of *Within Golden Bands*

Settle in with a cozy blanket to read Stratton's sequel novel *Deep End of the Lake*. You'll feel the chilliness of a Michigan winter in the descriptive prose and shiver with the concern and worry of raising a teenager. Your heart will flutter as Ally, once divorced, contemplates remarriage and settles into her new life far from California. Stratton captures and catapults us into any woman's romantic side, along with our emotions as mothers, especially mothers of special needs children. But most of all, Stratton show us how God guides us on our journey—particularly when we're in the deep end.

~ **Suzanne Ruff**
Author of *The Reluctant Door*

Acknowledgments

I am grateful to all those who have pushed me to sprint over the finish line with this story. *Deep End of the Lake* is covered with a lot of invisible sweat and tears. Thanks to Elaine Cooper, Barbara Hall, Debbie Callaghan, Debbie Sousa, Ann T., Denise W., Jeanne Romack, Kathy Wickware, and many other dear friends who cheered me on when I wanted to call it quits. I think of Hebrews 3:13—"But encourage one another daily, as long as it is called 'Today.'"

To Denise Loock at Iron Stream Media/LPC, who did a great edit of the story and helped me create a stronger novel. Thank you.

Finally, thank you to my family, especially my uncomplaining husband, who endured many frozen dinners because of his absent-minded wife who burnt meals while deep into writing.

This story is dedicated to all those parenting and
stepparenting children with disabilities.
They are the real warriors, the unsung heroes in our culture.
Many struggle in pain and sorrow.
But one day in heaven, their praises will be sung:
"The King will reply, 'Truly I tell you,
whatever you did for one
of the least of these brothers and sisters of mine,
you did for me.'"
Matthew 25:40

CHAPTER ONE

The gray-blue waves of Lake Surrender lapped against the shoreline, hitting sand and dune grass, like a playful puppy kissing its new owner and then scampering away. Ally Cervantes dipped her toe into the inviting water, tempted to take advantage of the unseasonably warm September day. Autumn in northern Michigan brought rain and cooler weather, so this might be her last chance for a swim. Besides, the kids were still at school, and she didn't want a vacation day wasted—a delicious escape from the hustle and bustle of the newspaper office. She loved being a reporter. Still, a day without computers, phones, and deadlines was a rare treat. She relished the quiet, broken only by a squawking gull and the faraway drone of a lone motorboat. Ah, freedom—like the tattoo on the nape of her neck that said, "Free bird." She instinctively touched it and laughed, remembering her impulsive trip to the tattoo parlor after her divorce became final.

Ally tipped her head toward the noontime sun and sighed. Kids, fiancé, work—they all needed more of her attention. Her boss's words flitted through her mind for the thousandth time: "Get your act together, Cervantes." *Yes, but how? So many things I still need to take care of—the wedding, the kids, succeeding at this new job, and making my relationship with Will work. Some days the pressure is too much.*

The chill soaked her body as she inched into the water, trying to avoid water plants. The deep end of the lake meant murky waters created by a muck bottom and tangled weeds.

Townspeople called it a haphazard obstacle course for boaters. The growth also meant caution for swimmers. Aunt Nettie always warned her and the kids to be careful.

But Ally's mind, freed of worry, clicked into relaxation mode. Reaching the five-foot depth, she shoved off from the marl, the mud mashed between her toes. "Squishy-wishy," her seven-year-old son, Benjie, called it. The marl was her least favorite section of the lake but convenient to the cottage and easy access for a quick swim.

She dipped her arms into the water. Left, right, left, right until she found a rhythm. *Maybe I'll head out to Party Bar.* The sandbar was the perfect place for sunbathers, kayakers, and the occasional teen beer bust. She turned over onto her back to float for a moment. *After today, my leisure days are behind. Between working at the paper, planning a wedding, and parenting both a teenager and a special needs child, my free time is nonexistent.*

After a brief rest she pushed on a few yards farther, her arms aching. *Man, I'm out of shape.* Her swim-team years were long gone. She stretched her head back toward the shore, shocked she had already swum half a mile from the beach. She floated for a minute, then switched to an easier sidestroke as she mopped up the lingering rays of sunshine. The moment, etched in her mind, would pull her through the long, overcast winter ahead.

"Hey, watch it." A booming male voice interrupted her thoughts. She looked to the right. A bass boat sped toward her, the driver cupping his hands in a warning shout. She tucked her legs to her chest as the boat roared by, missing her by a couple of yards.

"Didn't expect floating bodies out here." The fisherman tipped his canvas hat as he made a sharp turn away from her. She bobbed up and down in his wake like a beach ball.

"Didn't expect a bass boat to run me over," she shouted after him. Her body shook from the near miss. The close call had sucked out any enjoyment of swimming alone. *And I'm too near the largest drop-off in the lake anyway.*

Ally propelled her body with powerful leg kicks back toward the tiny beach near her aunt's cottage. Then she spotted a brilliant greenish orange shell in the water. A painted turtle and its five-clawed feet paddled toward her. Living in northern Michigan still hadn't made her a wildlife lover. She dove deep under the water to escape its path, but as she ascended to the surface, her foot tangled in a mess of weeds. She pushed with her other foot to release it, but her foot didn't budge.

So these were the Snags. Her heart rate increased as she fought them. *I'm like a fish caught in some horrible net.* Over and over townspeople had cautioned her about a rare freshwater plant that only grew in this end of the lake. Freshwater seaweed. Locals called this area the Snags. She'd laughed, thinking they'd been exaggerating. How could a bunch of plants ensnare her?

Again and again, she yanked her foot, but the seaweed's tentacles held fast. Arms flailing, she jerked her body, twisting and turning it as underwater fingers clutched her tighter and tighter.

Her lungs burned as what started as a relaxing day morphed into a nightmare. Her mind spun. Was this the end, her life swept away into the bowels of a Michigan lake? Her lungs were set to explode. *Get to the surface, get to the surface.* Adrenaline pulsed though her body as she tugged her foot this way and that, frantic as a cornered animal.

This couldn't be the end. She wasn't ready to go. She wanted to marry Will. She wanted to see her kids grow up. Kylie, only thirteen, was figuring who she was and Benjie, well … he'd always need her. She grit her teeth and fought the weeds. But her strength waned.

From somewhere deep inside her, she called out, "Lord, save me … don't let me … please." Her thoughts jumbled together, and her inability to think straight showed she was seconds from drowning. Then one phrase tumbled inside her brain: "I've got this, I've got this."

She floated in and out of consciousness as a brute force yanked on her limbs. With one strong jerk, it untangled her foot from the demonic plants. Then the world went black.

Sunshine warmed her face as Ally drew up her eyelids, trying to see through blurred vision. *Where am I?* She no longer felt water surrounding her. Instead, land cradled her body. Eyes closed, she coughed violently as lake water spewed from the sides of her mouth. Her hands touched the soft cloth underneath her, and when she opened her eyes, she lay on the beach in front of her aunt's cottage. Someone had freed her from the water and plopped her on top of a bright red beach towel, one she'd never seen. A cool breeze blew over her wet bathing suit, and she shivered, only partly from the wind.

Ally grasped the edges of the towel and wrapped it around her body as her arms shook. Her legs did not have enough strength to push her body off the ground. Finally, through sheer willpower, she forced herself to sit up and jerked her head to the side, puking water onto the sand until she had nothing left to bring up. She cradled her head in her arms for a moment, then eyed the lake that harbored such terror beneath its calm surface.

She pinched her waterlogged arm and it hurt. She was alive! But how? Who brought her back to the cottage? How on earth did she end up here? She scanned the lakefront and the road alongside it. No boats, no cars. And no one was at home at the cottage. An eerie sensation shot through her, and she gulped, still tasting the fishy aftertaste of lake water. Something, or someone had rescued her. But who? What?

Her frantic prayer for rescue flashed through her mind. It must have been a miracle. How could she believe any different?

అ

Twenty minutes later, Ally looked up from her beach towel. The school bus rumbled down the road and stopped at the cottage. The door shot open with a mechanical swish, and Benjie hopped out. He stood on the edge of the cottage yard, moving his head back and forth, searching for her. Ally knew someone always met the bus, and Benjie was a creature of habit. The worried frown on his face told Ally something was amiss. She called out to him.

"Honey, I'm here." She tried to raise her voice, but it barely carried to the street. With her remaining strength, she waved her hands back and forth. The bus driver honked to acknowledge her. Since the six-year-old's home was her last stop, the driver put the vehicle in park, climbed down the stairs, and held his hand till she had deposited him to the other side. "Hurry," she said.

Benjie picked up speed as he reached the beach. Ally caught his arm and pulled him onto the towel. His blond hair, bleached white from the summer, shone in the sun as he flapped his arms in excitement.

"No, we're not going swimming. But I need you to help me. Calm down." It was all she could do to get out those words. She took his hands in hers and stared him in the eye. "This is very important. Mama is hurt." She took a deep breath to stave off lightheadedness. "I need you to help me."

Benjie closed his eyes, concentrating. Then he opened them. He shot her a solemn look and nodded.

"Let me lean on you." She stood and put her left hand on her son's shoulder. "You can do it. You're strong. We'll cross the road together, but slow." They stood at the side and waited until two cars passed. "Now we can cross." The two hobbled across the road and into the cottage. Ally reached for the arm of the couch in the family room, and her aching body collapsed onto its pink-and-green flowered cushions. She forced her eyelids to remain open.

Benjie left and clambered up the stairs. A few minutes later, tiny fingers tucked a blanket around her shoulders. She opened her eyes just long enough to see Benjie's Spiderman bedspread covering her. She reached for his hand and squeezed it. "Good boy, you're a love. Now get out your new puzzle, and see if you can put it together." She kissed her fingers and patted his cheek.

Ally fell asleep. Her dreams swirled in her mind, a Mix-master of torment. At one point, she found herself back in California surfing in the Pacific Ocean, before a rogue wave knocked her over. The undertow sucked her under the water as she sputtered for breath, unable to fight the Pacific's mighty strength. The ocean then spit her out onto her aunt's Lake Sur-render beach. Ally gasped and panted for air. When she raised her head, Will, her fiancé, and his ex-fiancée, Sarah, stared at her. What's she doing with him? Ally wondered.

She woke with a start, hyperventilating. *Where am I?* A cartoon show droned in the background. *That's right. I'm home with Benjie, and he's watching television.* What a horrible dream. She reached for her phone on the coffee table to call Will.

"Enjoy your vacation day?" The sound of his voice cracked the barrier of tears she'd been holding back.

"I am now. I had a near miss … a fight with the Snags and they almost won. Almost."

"What do you mean?"

"Let's just say I shouldn't be here talking to you. Technical-ly."

"Al, I'm coming over right now."

৵

"Where have you been?" Derrick eyed her with annoyance.

"Mom stayed home today, so I acted as if I got on the bus and then snuck over here to your house." Kylie ran toward the cherry-red car.

"What do you think?" Derrick leaned over and grinned at her. His inky hair poofed on top of his head, adding an inch or so to his six-foot height. Kylie smiled, amazed that an older guy liked her.

"Are you kidding? It's lit." She ran her hand over the Mustang's fender, sleek and smooth to the touch. "Perfect time to cut class."

She clambered into the convertible without opening the passenger door. "Anyway, probably the last day before nasty weather comes in."

"Don't mess nothing up. My dad can't find out I'm hauling around babies."

Kylie smiled and gave his shoulder a friendly shove. "Jerk. Not a baby. People think I'm fifteen 'cause I'm tall."

He glanced at her. "Are too. You've never even vaped."

"Did you bring it?"

Derrick waved the artificial smoking device in front of her. "Yep, got a girly flavor. Found some they still sell at the bait shop." He started the engine, put the gearshift in neutral, and pushed hard on the accelerator.

Kylie glanced at him. *Must be trying to impress me.*

"Let's head to Blackwater Lake." He took his foot off the brake, backed out of the driveway, and they shot down the street. Three blocks later, he turned onto one of the back roads. "Shortcut," he shouted, gripping the steering wheel as the tires squealed around the bends.

"Woot Woot!" Kylie shot her hands in the air, allowing the breeze to rush through her fingers. They bumped along the road, the dust flying into the interior of the car and into their faces. After a few turns, Derrick pulled into a small blacktop parking lot that butted up against the edge of the lake. After he turned off the engine, they sat and watched the leaves dancing across the pavement.

"Wait for it." Kylie searched for her phone in her pocket but remembered she'd left it on the mudroom counter. No epic selfie today. "Darn, I wanted a photo, but my phone's at home."

"No way. I don't want you posting anything." Derrick tossed his head, scowled, and pulled the key out of the ignition.

"You don't have to get mad." She climbed over the top of the passenger's side and followed Derrick, who headed toward the edge of the lake by the boat launch, the sun outlining his thin profile and long legs. He is cute *and* he drives. Her friend Emerald couldn't top this setup.

"So when do I get to try it?" Kylie inhaled an imaginary puff, then giggled.

"Hang on, I have something better than swimming and vaping." He winked at her before walking away from the ramp toward a clump of willow trees fifty yards away. When he got there, he squatted and pulled out a shabby red canoe, tucked under a tarp.

"Hey, haul your butt over here and help me." Kylie ran toward him and took the other end of the boat. Together they dragged it back to the launch. "Seems shallow here. Better place to slip this in."

"Whose canoe?"

"Ours right now. Have a problem with that?"

"No."

"My friend's parents always hide the canoe under the trees. Was out here a few summers ago."

"Aren't we sorta stealing?" Her stomach flopped like a fish out of the water.

"*Borrowing.* You afraid?" He shrugged. "They'll never know."

Kylie nodded. They maneuvered the boat into a few inches of water, and she jumped into the bow.

"Not so rough. Jeez, haven't you ever been in a canoe?"

She bit her lip. She didn't want to appear clueless. Why hadn't she taken that canoeing course at camp last summer? She picked up a paddle inside the boat while Derrick pushed off from the shore. He stepped into the stern, sat, then grabbed his paddle, and dipped it into the cool water. The sun created ripples of shimmer. When she was young and her family came to Lake Surrender for vacation, Mom said she always thought the ripples were lake fairies doing their last dance before the leaves fell. Right now she didn't need to think about fairies but maneuvering this boat. She plunked her paddle in, trying to match Derrick's strokes.

"I took a class at Camp Lake Surrender last year on water safety, but they didn't talk about boats," Kylie said.

"You mean where your stepfather is the director?"

Kylie's hands gripped the paddle tighter. "He's not my stepfather yet."

Derrick raised up his hand in surrender. "Hey, sorry. But isn't that camp lame?"

"Sort of." Two Canadian geese flew above them, headed south for the winter. The pair paddled without speaking until they reached the middle of the lake. Kylie figured it must be deep because she couldn't see very far down.

She glanced down at the boat's bottom and saw a puddle of water. "Hey, something's wrong. We're taking in water."

Derrick shrugged his shoulders, unconcerned. She wondered if the canoe had sprung a leak. What if it sank, and they had to buy the owners a new one? Her stomach churned, and she wished she had brought a snack. How much did Derrick know about canoeing anyway? Not only that—they didn't even have life jackets.

Biology class didn't sound too bad right now.

Kylie turned and squinted at Derrick, the sun reflecting off of the water. "Hey, shouldn't we be getting back?"

"Put your oar in the water and paddle. We aren't even halfway across the lake. I thought you could hang out for more than an hour."

The excitement of sneaking off with an older guy evaporated in the early afternoon sun. An uneasy sensation grew in her stomach. Yes, she'd have bragging rights if she hung out with Derrick, but she wasn't sure he was that great. She bit her lip. Kylie stared down into the water, but the lake bottom wasn't visible. That explained why they called it Blackwater Lake.

Must be ten feet deep or more. A long slimy object moved in the lake, and she squinted to see what it was. She stretched her arm out the side of the boat. "Hey, what's that—a snake?" She stood. "I'll just …" The canoe rocked.

"Are you nuts? Sit down or we'll …" He waved his paddle at her. Too late. The vessel rocked and bobbed, each time at a more dangerous level until the right side found the tipping point. Kylie toppled into the lake. Her head went under, and she came up coughing water.

Derrick let out a few words that would have flipped out her mother and followed her into the lake, paddle and all. Fortunately, the depth was only five feet. They both touched bottom. Derrick blinked and shook his head of the excess water, the dirty water droplets spraying Kylie. He grabbed the overturned canoe, heaved it, and flipped it upright. "I'm pushing this back to shore." Kylie trudged through the water behind him, her wet clothes glued to her shivering body.

Derrick turned around. "You're something else. Let's forget this whole thing."

"What about vaping?"

Derrick stared at her. "I'm going home. You coming with me, or do you want to walk?"

CHAPTER TWO

Derrick stopped at the drive-thru window of a fast-food joint and ordered cheeseburgers before he let Ally out so she could walk the few blocks home.

She jumped out of the car. "Hey, sorry about the canoe. Guess that's one way to learn what not to do in a boat," said Kylie.

Derrick tossed her beach towel at her. "Hope you don't get caught."

She pulled the towel tight around her shivering body. "See ya." Kylie headed toward her aunt's cottage, entered through the side door, and walked into the mudroom where she found her phone. Good. Mom hadn't heard her come in yet. She'd better change her clothes fast.

"Where have you been? It's almost five o'clock." Will's voice boomed as his black eyes surveyed her.

Kylie jerked her head up. *Jeez, who does he think he is, bossing me around?* Will stood in the doorway, glaring at her, his arm wrapped around her mom. *Wow, she looks weird.* Mom had turned five shades paler and her red hair, usually bouncy, fell in straggly waves around her face. Her five-foot-eight frame drooped in exhaustion. Kylie tightened the towel around her middle. "At the lake. I got a ride home with a friend, and we stopped there for a sec." *Hmm. That sounded believable.*

"Your mother almost drowned today," said Aunt Nettie, who stood behind and peeked over Will's shoulder, her gray curls bobbing up and down to emphasize her point.

"Mom, what happened?" Kylie lunged at her mother and threw her arms around her neck. Ally swayed.

"Careful," Will said. "We took her to the emergency room, and she checked out, but she'll need a few days' rest." He walked Ally back to the family-room couch, an ancient flowered thing.

Kylie found an oblong throw pillow and positioned it under her mother's neck before scooting next to her on the couch. "But how?" Tears crept into the corner of her eyes. She could have lost her mother today while she was cutting school. Shame burned inside her chest. Guess she wasn't such a great daughter after all.

"I made a stupid mistake and swam out alone to the Snags, the place I always warn you not to go to. Dumb. I miscalculated my strength and went too far. When I turned back, I dove below the surface and got tangled in the weeds."

"The Snags?"

"Yes. I panicked, then blacked out. When I came to, I found myself stretched out on a towel on the beach. I can't figure how I got there. Someone rescued me."

"Who?"

"I haven't a clue, but God answered my prayer. Guess your mom will be around a little longer to nag you."

"I'd call it a miracle," Aunt Nettie said. "I'll make some coffee." She scurried into the kitchen.

"You're okay now?" Kylie grabbed her mother's hand and held it in her own shaking hand.

"A few days rest and I'll be fine. Heck of a way to get off work for a few days." Her mother mustered a weak smile, but Kylie didn't think she looked fine. Her eyes weren't focusing well, and her hands shook as she picked up the coffee mug Aunt Nettie brought to her. "Where have you been? You're supposed to be here to meet Benjie's bus," said Ally.

"Sorry, I was late hanging out with a group of girls. They had a water fight and dumped me in the lake." The shame grew hotter inside of her—from candle flame to campfire.

"You need to tell us where you are and if you can't meet your brother's bus. We depend on you. We called you a few times from the hospital and even left a message on the landline," said Will.

Her shame turned to irritation as Kylie pushed her lips together in a tight line. Will was really starting to bug her.

"Oh, nobody checks that old thing. I don't get why you are making such a big deal about it."

"Better start." Will shot a questioning glance at her. Did he figure out she'd cut? To her relief, he flashed her a grin. "Why don't you help Aunt Nettie? She's making some sandwiches for dinner in the kitchen."

Wow, saved by sandwiches. Dodged a week's grounding.

❧

Ally grabbed Will's hand as they walked to the pier off the end of Surrender's main street. He wore her favorite blue plaid shirt, a color that emphasized the summer tan lingering on his face and neck. His eyes, steady, searched her face as his hand brushed across her cheek. "Why don't you stay away from the lake for a while? No more close calls, Al."

"Yes. Have been thinking things over."

"Near death experiences do that to you."

"Yep."

"So shoot."

She stroked his arm. "Benjie ran off during recess."

"Oh no."

"Happens a lot."

"I figured that." They strolled in silence until they reached the Polar Bear Ice Cream Shop. "Do you want two scoops of Mint Chocolate Chip?"

"Yes, please," said Ally. Will paid for the ice cream, and she took the cone he offered her, licking a wayward drip. "Here's the deal …"

"When you say, 'Here's the deal,' I figure it will be serious."

She put her hand on his shoulder. "No, really, I want you to understand what you're jumping into by marrying me. Because of his autism, Benjie will live with us for the rest of our lives. We will always have him. He has limited choices."

"So what if he doesn't date, marry, or even hold a regular job. Don't compare me with your ex. I'm not Bryan."

"I know." She found his hand and laced her fingers through his. "I want to make sure you know there will *always* be three."

Will lowered his head and ran his hand through his hair. "I've thought that over. Al, all couples have stresses, and, yes, we have stresses other couples will never have to handle. But people who love each other as much as we do trust each other to work together."

"My life's complicated."

"Complicated works." His eyes narrowed as if to say, "Give me some credit."

"I'm not an easy match."

Will grabbed Ally's shoulder and gave her a shake. "Stop that right now. You're the best thing that's ever happened to me. I can't imagine life without the three of you. I'm happy with a package deal … get it?"

She made the okay sign. Peace soared through her heart, his words a soothing ointment for her battle scars. "I don't deserve you." She reached over and nuzzled his cheek.

"Glad you realize that. Now let's enjoy the sunset. I love you, and that isn't changing. Here, hold this." He handed her his cone and took a couple running steps down the sidewalk before doing a forward flip. He turned around and bowed.

Ally's jaw dropped. "When did you learn that?"

"I have plenty of hidden talents."

"Will, you're a riddle wrapped in a mystery inside an enigma."

"Oh, so now we're quoting Winston Churchill? I doubt he was talking about love." Will did another flip, then walked back to claim his ice cream. "And I can whistle. Helps me when I'm doing maintenance work at camp." He pursed his lips together and demonstrated. "Also keeps me brave when I referee two teen girls fighting over their favorite male staff member. You'd be surprised how often that happens."

"You are pretty cute."

"No comment." He took her hand and swung her around so she was face-to-face with him. "Speaking of camp, the cook's position is still open. Remember, the place where you worked last year?"

She crossed her hands in front of her in mock indignation. "Yep, where the boss kept hitting on me and the crazy assistant cook almost got me arrested?"

"I did not hit on you. You kept gazing at me with those forlorn green eyes and what was a guy to do? Nothing like a girl with a problem to summon my inner knight in shining armor." He knelt on one knee.

"Wait. Didn't you do that already?" She giggled.

"Please come work with me, my love."

She shivered. The night had suddenly grown cooler. "Don't pressure me."

"It's a great way to influence the next generation."

"I'm making an impact at the paper. People like my stories."

"Yes, they're good. But then readers skim over them and throw them in the kitchen trashcan."

Ally bristled. After a year-and-a-half absence, she had returned to the profession she loved—publishing. Was he blind to that?

"I can't believe you said that."

"Jeez, babe, I was joking." He took a strand of her hair and wrapped it around his finger. "Hey, we're on for tomorrow, right? I need to talk to you."

"About what?"

"It can wait. You're the most curious female I've ever met, which will get you in trouble someday."

"And makes me a great local reporter."

❧

That night Ally tapped on Kylie's bedroom door. "Can we talk?"

Over loud music her daughter answered, "Do we have to? I'm writing an essay for English class."

"Yep."

The door jerked open, and Kylie greeted her with a sour expression before sprawling out on the bed. "Is this going to take long?"

Ally scanned the room. No evidence of any paper being written. She cleared a pile of clothes off a chair, still shaky after her near-death episode. "You doing okay?"

"Yeah, why?"

"Lately you've acted bummed and disconnected from the family. What's going on?"

Kylie fingered a notebook she'd been writing in before putting it down. "Everything's different now, Mom. You're gone so much for work and then you hang out with Will."

"And what's wrong with that?"

"I want our old family back—you, me, and Benjie. Will hogs you and besides …"

Ally let out a loud sigh. *Well, at least she was talking.* "Will doesn't hog me, but when you date someone, you need to get to know each other. Yes, I love Will, but that doesn't mean I love you any less, sweetie. I get that this is hard to understand, but God sent Will into our lives to be a part of our family. Give Will a chance. He may become one of your best allies."

"Ha."

"Come on, Kylie."

"You can't make me love him, and I never will."

❧

Tuesday, Ally sat on a kitchen stool sipping a second cup of coffee and enjoying the partial quiet. Aunt Nettie had taken Kylie to school and then headed out to her part-time job at the Painted House, where she painted whimsical designs on furniture. Only Benjie slurping his cold cereal and the neighbor's leaf blower interrupted the silence.

Her phone binged. A text message from her boss, Russ, at the *Surrender Sentinel*, asking her to write an extra article this week.

She moaned. "All I want to do is take a nap," she said to J Bean, her Jack Russell terrier, who searched for toast crumbs under the kitchen table. Her stress level rose as soon as she texted back "Yes." She couldn't return to the book publishing industry, but she still wanted to be a part of the writing world. She booted up her computer and searched online for ideas about an educational article, a section that was lean this week.

Ally scrolled through several school websites. A blurb on a junior who ended up on a national talent television show, a kindergartener who trains pets, and a teacher raising money for her son's cancer treatment. Nothing jumped out at her. She lowered her eyelids and reached back into her memory to the day she lost her book editor's job. Her boss, George, had pulled up in her driveway after work that sunny California day in March as she lounged on her front porch, relaxing after a long day. He walked to her porch and pulled up a chair. At the moment, it had seemed like a social visit, but when he started spewing "downsize" and "shrinking industry," she knew he had stashed a pink slip in his coat pocket.

Ally would not allow that to happen again. She'd prove to her editor, Russ, that he needed her at the paper by putting in extra hours. She had only worked at the *Sentinel* a few months, so she always volunteered to take on extra assignments. But lately guilt taunted her about the amount of time work took her away from Will and the kids. Yet she loved the job. *And wasn't she supposed to use her talents to help others?* Still, she wondered if she was hopping back on the too-much-work treadmill she'd left in California.

While she opened up a Word document and typed preliminary questions for the teacher doing a fundraiser, she glanced over at Benjie, the milk in the spoon dripping down the sides of his mouth. Half of his cereal had ended up on the table in a lopsided ring around his bowl. He had graduated from strictly Cheerios to milk and cereal. *So grateful for small victories, Lord.*

Ally turned away from her laptop and flicked a couple of Cheerios back in the bowl. "Thankfully, it's Teacher Workday, and you didn't have to go to school. Which reminds me …" She swallowed a laugh as Benjie bent over and tried to spear a random Cheerio on the counter with the tip of his tongue.

"Let's talk squirrels. You know, what happened yesterday." She leaned in close and took his face in her hand, tilting it toward her. "Listen to me. No more chasing squirrels. Your teacher said that's why you ran off yesterday." Ally reached for the cereal box and poured him more Cheerios. *Man, this kid could live on cold cereal alone and be happy.*

He looked up, his eyes widening. He nodded. "Squirrels bad."

"Well, they are for you."

He finished his cereal, slid off of the kitchen stool, and catapulted to the family room to organize his rock collection. Roads or piles, both fascinated him. He never tired of them. "If you're obedient this week, I'll pull the dominoes down from the shelf, but no more squirrels." Early that morning, she'd stored his dominoes in the kitchen pantry as punishment for wandering off at school. She hid them out of sight more for her sake than his, knowing that if he saw them, he'd have a meltdown. Next to his rock piles, he loved dominoes, especially when he played with Will.

"No squirrels," he said from the next room.

Ally shoved a cereal bowl in the dishwasher while Benjie laid a trail of stones from the family room into the kitchen.

She stared at his project. How many times had she watched him build theses roads? Hundreds? Thousands? He might be building them into his teens and twenties. Was this his life? A wave of sadness gripped her. Things would always be the same with her boy.

CHAPTER THREE

Two weeks had passed since Ally's lake accident and Benjie's squirrel incident. Home early, she changed from her work clothes into a saggy gray sweatshirt and matching pants, then crashed on the sofa, letting the week's stress seep out of her aching muscles. She flung off her shoes and massaged her throbbing feet, vowing to never wear that pair of flats again. Gone were the days of haute couture and spike heels when she met a client.

J Bean, her Jack Russell, barked. Will tapped on the front door, pushed it open, and peered in. "Hey, lazy butt, I've been up, dressed, and working at camp since seven this morning. Is this what I have to look forward to after the wedding? Pajamas in the late afternoon?"

"Ha, ha." Her heart still leaped when she took in his solidly built frame that had grown buff over the last few months from remodeling Camp Lake Surrender. She ran to give him a haven't-seen-you-for-three-days kiss, one to remind Will she'd missed him. Then she socked his arm playfully. "Keeping it real, Camp."

"Got anything to drink?" he asked and headed to the kitchen for a pop. He opened up the refrigerator and grabbed a Vernors, his favorite. "How 'bout you throw on street clothes, and I'll take you for a ride? Fall colors are almost gone."

She nodded. Ten minutes later, they sailed down one of their favorite country roads, the wind whistling past Ally. She tipped her head out the open window as the sun warmed her face. Sugar maples snug against the edge of the road cast a ruddy, luminescent shine on the horizon.

"Good to have a break from the office," said Ally.

"Forget about the paper. Right now it's just us." He reached over with one hand and slid it against her cheek. She touched the familiar territory of his callused palms and fingers, and even the missing tip of one of his pinkies lost in a boating accident. His hands told of hours spent chopping wood, remodeling cabins, and repairing roofs—symbols of Will's dedication as a camp director at Camp Lake Surrender and his commitment to the kids who spent summers there.

"You gave me a scare last week."

"I know."

They drove in silence for a few minutes as his truck plowed over leaves beyond their prime, pressed into the asphalt, the result of endless tires passing over them daily. The effect gave the road a padded appearance.

"Mother Nature preparing her bed for the winter," said Ally.

"Huh?"

"The road."

"Oh, yeah." He cleared his throat and popped a cough drop into his mouth. "Remember, I said we needed to talk?"

His voice sounded hesitant. "Shoot."

"Yeah … um … I'm not sure Kylie approves of the wedding." Will clenched the steering wheel as the road took a hard right before it straightened. A handful of scarlet foliage tumbled down from a maple tree, showering the pavement in front of them. "So last week when you covered the American Legion Festival, and I toted her to that school play …"

Ally reached over and squeezed his arm. "I appreciated that."

"No problem. Part of my upcoming role as stepdad." He glanced over at her. "On the way home, she let me know I didn't live up to her father's standard."

"What!"

"She dropped a few comments like 'you need to be more chill.' That translates, 'Don't check up on me.' Evidently, I'm stricter than her dad was."

"True."

"And I'm not as funny. She said things like 'My dad loved to joke around with me,' and 'We had special code words for things,' and 'He was real good at lip-synching Disney songs and doing car karaoke.'" Will turned his head and rolled his eyes. "Hey, I can be funny too."

Ally clenched her fists together, glancing at the floorboard as she searched for words. *Why did Kylie have to say those things?* "After the divorce, she took his side. He was always the cool parent. And when he died, Bryan became a hero in her eyes."

"I don't fault her for that. I'm glad she has happy memories of him. He is her flesh and blood ... which I'll never be." Will stared at the windshield, then turned his head and tapped the brake pedal to slow the Suburban down to avoid hitting a doe. "Seems she thinks I'm trying to replace him."

"I'm sorry she treated you that way."

They bumped along, headed west through the back roads. Normally, a ride in the fall woods cheered her up, but Will's comment didn't put her in a jovial mood.

Ally surveyed the road as the SUV turned the bend for her first view of Elk Horn, another one of their favorite lakes. "I'll speak to her. I guarantee she'll have a change of heart. I have to work tomorrow, but then it's the weekend and we can talk."

"And if she doesn't?"

"Don't worry." She slipped her hand into his hand resting on the seat beside her. "It will take time."

He raised her hand to his lips and kissed it. "Probably. And changing the subject, not that you'll listen to me, but stay out of the lake for a while."

"So you won't hire me as a lifeguard at camp?"

"I still have openings in Remedial Swimming. But all kidding aside, I want you around for a while." He turned his head toward her, and his right eye crinkled into a wink. "You put the 'hot' in my chili."

It felt good to laugh. "See, you *can* be funny. Lame but funny. Guess it's better than 'You put the grounds in my coffee.'"

❧

Friday morning Ally angled her car into a parking space in front of the paper's office, her head throbbing from an early morning fight with Kylie over a pair of jeans. *I didn't wear pants that tight in school.* Oh, the joys of mother-daughter fights.

She strolled into the rambling building, mentally rolling up her sleeves for work. She loved the white-clapboard 1930s house that served as a newspaper office for the *Surrender Sentinel.* The office consisted of one open room with five desks scattered across the floor. An opening on the back wall led to the kitchen; on the right wall, a door led to the editor's office.

"Great game last Friday." Ally gave a thumbs-up to Clay Carter, the twenty-something sports editor, transplanted from South Carolina. He nodded in agreement without glancing at her, his fingers not missing a beat as he typed out a piece. She brushed by Janice Bevington, office manager and assistant editor, deep into a phone call about pricing ads for the paper. How the transplanted Englishwoman with her precise accent ended up in northern Michigan was anyone's guess. Maybe she'd take Janice out to lunch one day and hear her story. But so far Ally had hit a brick wall in befriending the older woman, who ran the office like clockwork, doing payroll, copyediting, and selling ads. Ally prided herself on being professional. But as far as connecting with Janice—wasn't happening. What was it with her? She struggled with a feeling of distaste even now. Why? She should share a camaraderie with Janice, an outsider like herself. Ally vowed to try harder with her.

Janice put the phone back in its cradle and nodded at Ally. "I understand you had an eventful day at the lake ..."

"You mean my near drowning?"

"Yes, that. You're a mother and need to be responsible."

"Thanks for the tip." Man, this woman sure knows how to lecture.

"And you seem tired. Dark circles under your eyes. You might try some concealer."

Now she's giving me makeup advice? "Try juggling kids, a job, and planning a spring wedding." Ally felt her temper rising.

"Family's a good thing, especially kids." The word *kids* caught in Janice's throat.

"Didn't mean to suggest otherwise."

"My Martin passed several years ago. Wish I'd had an aunt to stay with," said Janice.

"She's been great. Say, is Russ in?"

A gruff "yep" came from Russ's office.

"It's all clear. You can go in," the office manager reassured her.

Ally smiled. Janice always acted as the self-appointed gatekeeper for guarding their editor's time.

Originally a first-floor bedroom, Russ's office jutted off the newsroom. The wall-to-ceiling dark-walnut paneling made her fingers itch to give it a new paint job, along with an organization of his entire desk. Between piles of manila folders stacked a foot high on the right side of the desk, and two computer monitors on the other side, she didn't understand how he could accomplish much. But through sweat and plain hard work, the paper got out each week, a minor miracle in her eyes.

As Ally entered, Russ removed his reading glasses, the dollar-store kind that always broke. The fifty-something man raised bushy eyebrows that matched his salt-and-pepper hair, and a smile lit his round face. "Welcome back. How are you feeling?"

"Pretty good but still kind of shaky."

"I'm so sorry about your scare. And glad you're back. We all missed you. We're slammed this week." He handed her a sheet of paper with her weekly assignments.

She scanned it. "Five articles? Uh, no problem." She looked up at Russ, who was studying her with a questioning expression. *Now what did I say?*

"Good." He crossed his arms. "Word count is eight hundred for all articles except the hardware store opening, which should be at least a thousand. We'll feature that on the front page, and I want a fantastic photo, Cervantes."

"Big issue this week?" Ally felt that old knot tightening in her stomach.

"Yep. Sure you can handle—"

Ally gulped. "Absolutely, I'll get them done."

"This isn't the book publishing industry—not like the fancy-schmancy San Francisco company where you used to work. We have tight deadlines. Every week."

Ally bit her lip. Why did he have to bring that up? "Five articles by next week. I promise."

Russ leaned over his desk and eyeballed her, his thick eyebrows raised like two furry barbells as he unwrapped a stick of gum. "I have the utmost confidence in you."

"Thank you." Ally never felt sure if he was threatening her or teasing her. She shut his office door behind her, jaw clenched. She'd write the best hardware-store article the paper had ever run. A piece of journalism so fresh that readers would rush down to the store with a lengthy list of items for a dozen do-it-yourself projects. She'd been polishing her writing skills and had gained several tips from an online writing conference to help make the piece shine—well, as much as a hardware story could shine.

Striding back to her desk with newfound inspiration, Ally felt a hand grab her arm. She stopped. "Meet me in the kitchen," Janice said.

She stood face-to-face with Janice in front of the sink. Ally stepped back so as not to inhale the potent perfume cloud that surrounded the woman.

Janice's voice lowered to a whisper. "I'd be careful. Russ has plenty of stringers who'd love to have a full-time job, and interns he could hire for free."

"What?"

Janice pulled a container of strawberry yogurt out of the fridge and dipped a spoon into the creamy mixture. "We've been receiving all kinds of résumés from students graduating in December with journalism degrees. I remember from reading your résumé that you studied English literature, so technically journalism isn't your background. Trying to give you a heads-up. I know you need the money because you have a wedding to pay for."

Ally studied the woman's expression, trying to decide if she was meddling or genuinely trying to help. She gave her the benefit of the doubt.

"Thank you."

"This office has a revolving front door. We've hired and fired as many people in the last three years as an Englishman has umbrellas." With one hand, Janice pulled out a red rose teapot from the kitchen's cabinet, placed it on the counter, and, with the other hand, poured boiling water into it from an electric kettle. Then she spooned loose-leaf tea into the steeper, screwed on the lid, and dunked it into the porcelain pot. A picture of efficiency.

"I must try that Earl Grey someday. Smells wonderful." Ally went back to her desk. *I can't give Russ any reason to think I'm goofing off and make him doubt my commitment. Better step up my game.*

She returned to Russ's office. She found him tipped back in his chair at his favorite angle—one that defied gravity—as he talked on the phone with a local politician about an upcoming election. Judging by his red face, Russ wanted the mayoral candidate to be more open about his platform. When he saw Ally, he signaled her to stay and ended the call.

"I'll expect the articles eight hours before deadline so I can check them over." He stood and put a hand on her shoulder. "Oh, and sorry about your son. Glad you found him."

"How did you know that?"

"Small towns have big eyes and bigger mouths."

Back at her desk, Ally sorted through a pile of messages and made a number of phone calls. As soon as she set the receiver down, the phone rang. Seeing Janice was on the other line, she took the call.

"Why can't you folks stop throwing the paper in the bushes?" the caller said. Ally drummed her fingers while she wrote the address, then typed an email to the circulation manager. She didn't have time to do Janice's job. Unfortunately, the unwritten rule at the paper was whoever wasn't on another line had to drop what they were doing and answer the phone.

Another call. "We need the paper to send out a crew to cover the fall concert tonight at the high school. We'll be featuring Jorge Esperanza, our teacher exchange from Spain, playing selections from Mozart and selected patriotic songs."

"Lord, give me patience," she whispered, then stifled a groan. The old Ally would have shot back, "Yes, we'll be out with two cameramen and three reporters; I'll notify the crew right away." But lately she'd tried to corral her snarky comments. Hadn't she learned, if nothing else from her new faith, to watch her tongue? Ally swallowed her sarcastic retort and said, "I'm afraid it's too late to cover that concert, but please send us an email with the details, and we'll put the information in our briefs."

By the third call from an irate reader disputing last week's editorial on repaving Maple Avenue, Ally was ready for a nap, and her phone said it was only ten o'clock. As a book editor, she hadn't had weekly deadlines. She commuted to San Francisco daily, where she set her own hours and took well-known children's authors to lunch at the Boulevard Restaurant. Ah, the life. Some days she fantasized about being back in the city, the cable-car bell clanging as it chugged past quaint Victorian houses shrouded in fog and overlooking the bay. She'd left California a year and a half ago, but it might as well have been a decade ago.

She and her family had summered often at Aunt Nettie's cottage, but she never thought she'd be living permanently in northern Michigan. She'd grown to love how life ambled by in the small town. She only wished life would amble a little more in the newsroom so she could finish her articles on time instead of constantly answering the phone.

Determined to make headway on an upcoming assignment, she sent out an email asking an apple orchard owner when she could interview him, then called two other people for appointments. *No one seems to be answering phones today.* The knot in her stomach twisted tighter, like a mop being squeezed in the wringer of a custodian's bucket.

Finally, the phones quit ringing, and the office remained quiet. *Too quiet.* Ally plugged in her earphones to listen to Lady Antebellum on Pandora as she researched apple orchards in northern Michigan. She tried to determine which apple orchard had been established first in the area and which type of apple made the best cider, but her thoughts kept drifting back to her conversation with Will. It wasn't easy to blend the family. One thing was certain—her marriage to Will would never work with Kylie wedged between them.

CHAPTER FOUR

That afternoon Ally jumped into her green Audi and headed down her favorite road, Mission Point, to interview the owner of the McDermott's Apple Orchard. Her car started making a new clunking noise, and she prayed the Audi would last through the wedding. As she breezed by Lake Michigan, a small patch of sun shone on Little Traverse Bay to her left, a long triangle of crystal aquamarine. Decades-old cottages lined the right side of the road. Stone structures, gray clapboard dwellings trimmed in white, and Queen Anne beauties stood on fading green lawns as the wind whipped trees and bushes. She wondered if she and Will would buy one of them someday. *Oh, a girl could dream.* She pictured Will, Kylie, Benjie, and herself crossing the road to the beach on the west arm of Grand Traverse Bay to swim. Heaven.

Ally pulled into the orchard's gravel road and waved to Gus McDermott. Seated on a green John Deere tractor, he towed a wagonload of school kids to the front of his produce stand. Behind the stall, he had built an enormous store with a small restaurant frequented by lunchtime locals.

"Hey there, been expecting you. I'm ready for the big interview." Gus stuck out a typical farmer's hand, tan and callused "Come on inside."

Ally followed him into the store—past glass gallon-jugs of apple cider and displays of Rome, Red Delicious, and Granny Smiths—to his small office. Gus offered her a chair next to the desk where she could write her notes.

She glanced at her phone, hoping she could wrap this up in a half hour. She had to return to the office and finish two other articles. Ally pulled out her long, thin reporter's pad and clicked her pen open. "You have a wonderful business here. What made you go into the orchard business?"

"I enjoy it."

"Is there any trick to running a small business like this?"

"Nope."

Ally tapped her pen against the wooden desktop.

"Any new products you've added this year?"

"Nope."

She clicked her pen and studied her notes. What question would prompt this man to talk more? "So what makes your apple dumplings so popular?"

"Use lard."

"Lard?"

"That's what I said."

Ally stifled a groan. She tried shooting him a few more questions but received more one- or two-word responses. How was she ever going to fill her eight-hundred-word quota? She tried another angle. The "give me your sage advice for success" usually started people talking.

"What tips would you give to a person who'd like to go into this field?"

"Gotta like apples. Apple cider, apple pie, apple dumplings, apple fritters, apple butter."

Apples, apples, and apples. He stood and cracked his knuckles, making a loud pop. "Say, miss, I need to go back to the barn."

Ally held out her hand and shook his. "Thank you, Mr. McDermott." She stuffed her notebook into her purse, clicked a photo of the business owner next to several bushel baskets of apples, and thanked him for his time. As Ally stepped up to the counter to pay for half a dozen apple dumplings, a tall, thin woman with short ebony hair glided by. She grabbed the arm of a tanned man dressed in jeans and a black blazer one size too small. Slicked-back hair emphasized his tall forehead and dark, thick eyebrows. Was that Janice—with a man? *I didn't know she dated anyone. Hmm, this could be interesting.*

Instead of heading back to the parking lot, Ally moseyed around looking at the arrangements of apple butter and applesauce grouped in towering pyramids. She picked up a jar— Aunt Nettie enjoyed good apple butter—and sneaked a better view of the gentleman. The couple, seated, looked at their menus. Ally slipped behind a pole and peeked out cautiously.

About forty, the man could have stepped off the label of a Sangria bottle. Suave and gorgeous. When he spoke with a Spanish accent, Ally concluded he was probably Jorge Esperanza, the exchange program teacher.

Ally leaned closer, hid behind four stacks of baled hay, and hoped no one would see her sleuthing. Cocking her ear to the side, she picked up the train of the conversation.

"Yeees, I looove de Americano food, especialmente el hamburgesa, how you say, hamburger?"

"I looove your accent," said Janice. She leaned in closer to Jorge.

Ally couldn't see Janice's face but imagined she was flashing her best smile. Must be a first date. Janice must be at least five years older than Jorge. Maybe ten. Whatever, she was on the hunt.

"Jorge—can I call you Jorge?—you know the arts are important, and we have a jolly good music program in the district. What we need is more visual arts." Her voice raised a notch and sounded more strident. "I've had this plan for an art center for years. I've rallied the art community and was counting on funding from the town's art grant."

He spoke too low to hear his response, but Janice replied, "That's very perceptive of you. Students in America don't know art history. This town needs an art renaissance, but that won't happen if the music department wins the grant." She crossed her arms. "Maybe I can persuade you to come over to my side."

Ally caught a few snatches of Jorge's reply. He didn't sound convinced. Janice suddenly looped her handbag handles over her shoulder. "Oh my, I didn't realize how late it is. Waiter, please bring me a to-go box." She stood and spit out her words. "I hope I've made it clear to you. I have to win this grant."

Ally ducked behind a life-sized cardboard cutout of a farmer juggling five apples. She had been wrong about it being a date. Janice was on the warpath. If she had her way, she'd convince the town to use the grant for her proposed art center instead of a music center. She was a bulldog.

Janice stood and walked right past her before she turned around. "Ally … what are you … why on earth are you hiding behind that cardboard cutout? Spying on me?"

❧

That Sunday evening, Ally raced into Spumoni's in downtown Traverse City to meet Will for dinner.

"Good to get some alone time," she said as she slid into the seat across from Will, catching her breath.

"Slow down, babe."

"Sorry I'm late; my interview ran long, and I had to submit two more articles."

"Why on Sunday?" Will's frown cinched his eyebrows closer together.

"Looks like they have some new items on the menu. This place is amazing. I mean, from the watercolors of Venice, the music from Aida, and the waitstaff that speaks Italian. I see why the locals joke that you don't have to visit Italy if you've been to Spumoni's."

"I suppose we should save our money, but I wanted to do something fun," said Will.

Ally squeezed his arm as he browsed the menu. "Just being with you is fun."

"Ditto." He turned on the broad smile that made her fall in love with him. "I'll be good and order the veggie plate. Cheaper."

"No, order your favorite, seafood linguini. Me, I'm hungry for spaghetti."

"Did you see how much the seafood linguini costs?" Will waved the menu. "No way."

"Wedding's still seven months away."

"And I can't wait." He touched his finger to her nose. "I'll never tire of those mysterious eyes." He took her hand, pulled it to his lips, and kissed it. "Ah heck, I'm not much of a poet."

She closed her hand around Will's fingers and studied them. "The only imperfect part of you, Will."

"Got you fooled." He leaned forward and tucked an unruly lock of her hair behind her ear. "Love that crazy hair." His eyebrows suddenly lowered. "I'm worried you're working too hard."

"We're a small paper and understaffed, but I'm fine."

"And I know you love writing …"

"I'm crazy about it all—editing, writing, the whole industry."

"Just think, if your publisher hadn't downsized, you'd still be in Cali, commuting to San Francisco every day."

"I love the local scene here, reporting on events and all the feedback from our readers. Lake Surrender's a unique community."

"I wish that boss of yours would hire another reporter."

After the server brought bread and salad, and took the rest of their orders—they splurged on their favorite dishes after all—Will crossed his arms, leaned back in his chair, and resumed the conversation about her workload. "I'm afraid Russ is overworking you. He has a reputation for burning out reporters."

Ally waved her hand in the air to dispel his worries. "I will not burn out."

"Says who?" Will wiped a breadcrumb from the side of her mouth. "I'm selfish. I'd like my future wife to hang out with me."

"I love that you want me around." Ally looked down at her plate and played with her Caesar salad. "But there's something else eating at you about this job."

Will tore a chunk off the loaf in the breadbasket and dipped it in a small red ceramic plate holding a mixture of olive oil and herbs. He took a bite, swallowed, and then cleared his throat.

"I miss you working at camp."

"Are you mad that I chose the newspaper job?"

"I want you to do what you feel you're called to do. But I loved having you around." Will put down his fork. "You don't have to prove anything to anyone about your abilities …"

Ally felt her cheeks grow flush. "I know."

He picked up his spoon and drew an imaginary letter on the tablecloth. "Isn't it enough to help me run the camp?"

"I love camp. But I want to use my talents and abilities."

"What's wrong with your culinary skills? You've come a long way since burned chili and soggy scrambled eggs."

Ally chewed on her lower lip. "Ha, ha. But when you lose the job you love, you owe it to yourself to see if you can make it in the business again."

"Aren't you and I enough?"

"Yes, of course, but—" She blurted out the words a little too quickly knowing he wanted to hear them. And she couldn't love anyone more than she loved Will. Still … Ally stabbed a piece of lettuce. She stuffed it in her mouth, then toyed with the croutons, setting them to one side of the plate. The server brought their entrees, and they ate in silence. Ally realized she hadn't eaten lunch that day. No wonder she had no energy. Before she knew it, the entire plate of pasta was gone. She put her fork down. "Will, I don't want to fight."

"Me neither."

"Let's forget this whole discussion."

"About your job? What did I say?"

"Nothing, but *I* might say words I don't mean. Let's call it a night."

He shot her a puzzled stare, then caught the server's eye to have him bring the check.

◈

Kylie greeted her mother at the front door as Will drove off. Her eyes showed annoyance, a look perfected over the ages by all teenagers. "Mom, where have you been?"

"You know, I had a date." Ally trudged into the family room and dropped her purse on the coffee table, before crashing onto the sofa.

"Will?"

"Honestly, Kylie, who else?" Sometimes she wondered what planet her daughter lived on.

"Figures."

Ally's forehead pounded, and she rummaged inside of her purse for a pill. "We can hang out now if you like. I'm all yours."

"Wow, aren't I lucky."

"Wait, I thought you wanted to hang out."

"Too late now."

"Stop playing games. Anyway, I'm too tired to fight right now," said Ally.

Kylie scowled as she gathered her papers together. "I can see I'll never have my mom back if you guys get married."

"That's ridiculous." Ally picked up one of the homework math sheets Kylie had scattered over the table. "Looks like you didn't accomplish much."

"Yeah, 'cause you were probably doing kissy-face with Will while I needed help with math."

Kylie smashed her lips into a big blob and made loud smacking noises.

"That's not funny. Are you deliberately trying to make me mad?"

"Why don't you stay home for a change and be our mom?"

Ally's voice raised a few decibels. "You are crossing the line, young lady."

Kylie stuffed her papers back into her backpack and gave her a long stare that could have frozen a pan of boiling water.

She put her hand on her daughter's shoulder. "Listen, let me help you with your math."

Kylie turned away and stomped upstairs.

Ally clenched her fists, swallowed a load of white fiery anger, and pushed back tears. Trapped between Will and her daughter, she didn't want to choose sides. Why couldn't Kylie see their lives would be so much better with Will? But instead her daughter acted like a complete stranger. What had happened to Kylie? And was she really that bad of a mother? Right now every angle of her life pulled at her. She wanted Will and Kylie to bond, but she sure couldn't make it happen.

❧

Ally clicked into her work email on Monday morning, deleting unnecessary messages and starring other inquiries for future articles. The music therapist who worked with kids suffering from social anxiety might fit the bill for an upcoming arts feature. Another email from a storeowner suggested she could write about his new business that specialized in food for dogs with severe allergies. *Hmm, maybe I could pick up samples for J Bean.* She loved that guy with his tipsy ears and the tan markings that dotted his white coat. Lately he'd become her confidant—something she needed badly.

"Weekly meeting in five minutes," Russ hollered from his open office door. As an old-school journalist, he never bothered with email reminders when his booming voice worked just as well.

Ally, Clay, and Janice gathered around Russ's desk with pad and pen in hand.

"So, wanted to go over a few things," said Russ. "Double-check names. We can't have the basketball coach's name misspelled. It's James Smithfield, not Smithfeld. Make sure you use this order when you write: location, month, date. Don't switch it around. I don't have time to correct all these careless errors, Cervantes. Pay attention."

"I thought I …"

"Get it right."

Ally chided herself for such an obvious rookie mistake.

"And, remember, this isn't a fiction magazine—it's a newspaper. Shorter is better, so cut out extraneous descriptions and flowery language. Think of it as cutting all the fat off a quality steak and offering the customer more real meat." Russ stroked his chin. "Hey, that's clever. Have to write that one down." He laughed and tipped back his chair, balancing himself by holding the edge of his desk. Ally held her breath, fearing a crash. It wouldn't be the first time.

He took a sip of coffee, likely Folger's Instant. The joke around the office was Russ wanted his drink fast and was known for his undiscerning taste. She wished he'd at least spring for a Keurig machine, but he hated to spend anything extra on unnecessary equipment.

"All right, folks, I think that's all, except turn in a list of your sick days to Janice by Wednesday." He nodded at Janice, who stood.

"I'm serious, staff," said Janice. Her long red fingernails flashed as she waved the spreadsheet around. "We will schedule vacations a month in advance. Remember that, people."

Back at her desk, Ally punched in her password to retrieve a voice message on her desk phone. Kylie.

"Hey, Mom, you forgot to turn on your cell phone, and you need to come to school this afternoon to talk to my English teacher. It's no big deal. Come by school at three thirty today."

Ally fiddled around in her purse and found her phone. She texted her daughter, but Kylie didn't answer. Hmm. Kylie hadn't had trouble in school when they lived in California. What was going on?

CHAPTER FIVE

Lakeshore Middle School, Home of the Cougars, the sign in front of the brick building proclaimed.

Ally arrived five minutes late to meet with Kylie's English teacher. The phone interview with the new pet food company had stretched out longer than she intended, with the owner supplying too many details of his life story. She slipped into Room 54 as Mrs. Brooks, an older woman with perfectly styled short gray hair, looked up from her desk.

The teacher extended her hand. "So glad you could come on short notice. I wanted to talk to you about your daughter's missing essays. Three of them."

"I know. I've been after her." She hated the lie, but she didn't want Kylie's teacher to think she was a delinquent mother. Ally wracked her brain about which specific assignments. How had she missed checking up on those?

"Kylie seems distracted and disinterested in class. Is there a problem at home I should know about?"

"She's adjusting to a few family issues. I'll talk to her and make sure she turns in her work. Thanks for letting me know."

Mrs. Brooks leaned over the desk. Her many silver bracelets jangled as she patted Ally's hand. "I understand she lost her father last winter."

Ally stepped back. She hated pity. "We're making it, but thank you for the concern."

Mrs. Brooks nodded and handed her a sheet of Kylie's assignments. "It's close to midterm, and I'd hate for her to fall further behind." She directed a sympathetic gaze toward Ally. "Your daughter evidently isn't happy here." She handed Ally an essay titled, "Ten Reasons I Hate This Town." "Does she need extra help to adjust to her new school? Maybe we can pair her with another student who …"

Surely the essay was one of Kylie's dumb jokes. *She doesn't seem that unhappy at school.* "I appreciate your concern." Ally picked up her purse. "We'll be in touch."

"I hope so. I'm sure you could help her. I understand you're a reporter at the *Sentinel*." The teacher raised her eyebrows. "Say, I'd love to have you come speak to my class next semester."

"I'll plan on that." Ally produced a slight smile and mentally made a note to put it on her growing to-do list—along with tutoring her own daughter.

❧

Before she returned to the *Sentinel*'s office, Ally stopped at the drug store and purchased a birthday card for her sister, Georgia. She and Auntie Nettie had kept Ally sane after her cross-country move a year and a half ago. Georgia, who had also moved out of California, was a mere phone text away. Aunt Nettie—well, her aunt's encouragement—had kept Ally going after her split from Bryan.

While Ally flipped through the cards, her phone rang.

"I was going to call you," she said to Will.

"Wasn't sure how you felt after last night's date."

The silence stretched out for an uncomfortable moment as Ally searched words. "What do you mean? How do *you* feel?"

"Al, you've seemed so agitated lately. We need to think through our relationship."

She took in a quick breath. "What are you saying?"

"I want to take a break from us and figure out some stuff. I've been thinking about this for a while." Her palms went sweaty, and her phone almost slipped out of her hand. Will's words reverberated with such force, she wondered if they had broadcasted over the store's intercom. *"Price check on Aisle Three … let's take a break."*

"I'm leaving for a few weeks to help my brother, Chip, the one who lives by Dad in Milford. He wants me to help him finish his basement remodel. Remember, they had that flood?"

Flood? Need a break? What was he saying? The words blurred in her mind. Part of her wanted to scream, "Don't go." She finally recovered her voice, hiding deep in her throat. "When will you be back?" To her surprise, her words came out calmly.

"Right before Thanksgiving."

"Will, you have to understand my need to prove to myself what I can do. And about Kylie …"

"Let's agree to not see each other before Thanksgiving. I'm giving us some space."

A rock tune droned in the background as she tried to process what he'd said. She wanted to shut out reality, run away. She didn't want this conversation. They were coming unglued. "Can I see you before you go? Do you want the ring back?" She hated the desperation in her voice.

Another interminable pause as he exhaled on the other end. "I'm not breaking up with you, but I need to sort things out. Can you understand that?"

"I guess." Ally forced herself to swat down her rising emotions. Her eyes burned with tears.

❦

Will slipped on his running shoes parked by his front door and yanked the shoelaces tight before tying them. He had to get out of the house, or he'd bust. He zipped up his gray hoodie and shot out of his front door, hoping the physical exertion would improve his frame of mind. He frowned, his eyes darting toward the darkening sky. Even the crimson sugar maples, which lined his road with color, couldn't cheer him up.

He clenched his fists as he pounded the road. He threw his weight and worry into each step, listening to his feet thud against the pavement.

After two blocks, Will pulled out his phone and dialed Ally.

"How do I say this? I miss the old Ally at camp. You always made me laugh, and you pulled me out of my funk when I broke off my engagement to Sarah."

"She was too serious for you. She's a great person, but her heart's in Mexico with those orphanage kids," said Ally.

"Enough about her. We need to fix some things. Come to an understanding. Otherwise, I can't do this marriage thing." Will heard a choking noise on the other end and scrunched up his eyes. "Are you …" he said.

"I'm fine. Got to go."

Will ended the call and passed his neighbor's mailbox with yesterday's *Sentinel* lying forlorn on the damp ground by the road. That darn paper. He kicked it back onto the lawn.

But more than the paper, Kylie is trying to pull us apart, and Al can't see what's happening. He took two deep breaths, his lungs burning, his feet hitting the pavement hard as he flew down the country road for another mile. Drops of sweat dripped down the back of his sweatshirt, and he shivered in the chilly evening temperature. He pushed himself farther than he usually did, past the Parker's Dairy Farm and beyond to the Blueberry Café. Pounding the asphalt, he looped back to head home before the sun set.

An image of Sarah popped into his mind. He'd known her since high school. *Don't want to go through another long, drawn-out relationship. No, cut it short if things go south.*

He raised his arm and wiped his dripping forehead with his sleeve. He continued his run, skirting around a dead squirrel in the road before picking up his pace for the last leg of his route.

He loved Ally and was weary of spending the long northern winters alone. He was sick of eating frozen Chinese food out of a cardboard dish and greasy fries from McDonald's. He was tired of going to bed alone and waking up alone. He wanted her next to him. He needed Ally's humor and companionship. And more. Even now he could imagine holding her in his arms, kissing her forehead while she blew back an errant strand of hair. He closed his eyes. Yes, he'd start with the forehead and work his way down, kissing her eyelids, her lips, and then her neck. He caught himself. *Whoa, I've got to stop thinking about her. Why torture myself?*

Back at the house, Will showered, changed clothes, and crammed a few items into a duffel bag. He stowed his Carhartt coat, toolbox, and the bag in the Suburban before jumping into the driver's seat. He took one last glimpse of his gray stone cottage in the rear-view mirror as he gripped the steering wheel. Would it always be a bachelor pad?

❧

"Looks like Mother Nature collected a few rays of summer and saved them for late fall," Russ said as he peeked through the blinds of the front office window. Sunbeams radiated through the bare tree limbs, and through the window of the old clapboard house. The building had been the *Sentinel's* home for years, wedged in the middle of an old residential neighborhood.

He turned from the window, strode to Ally's desk, and slapped a folder down. "Need to talk to you about this school board meeting tonight. Here's the agenda."

Ally thumbed through the stapled sheets. She pointed at a topic Russ had highlighted. "What's this?"

Russ shook his head. "Questions have been raised about how much this new teacher exchange has cost the district. A few parents want to know how the district affords the program when contracted teachers received a pay cut."

"What's the program called?"

"Hands Across the Water. The school district is paying for Jorge Esperanza to teach for two years at the high school while one of our teachers works in Esperanza's school in Seville, Spain. Mr. Esperanza is teaching Spanish in the middle school and is the high school band director. On weekends, he teaches classical and flamenco guitar to interested locals."

"Sounds innovative."

"Yeah, noble concept, but his salary and living expenses add an extra burden to the budget. Some feel the program is academic fluff and steals money from the town's rainy-day funds." Russ leaned over Ally's desk. "You might shoot an email to people after the meeting for quotes to add to your piece. Could have fireworks tonight!" He sported a wicked grin she'd seen before. He loved controversy because it sold papers. "They're also planning to talk about that grant funding program."

"The one Janice always talks about?"

"Yep."

"I'm on it." Ally formed an "okay" sign with her hand. "I'll make you glad you hired a book editor. You won't be sorry."

"Hope not."

Back at her desk, she sent up a silent prayer for Russ to keep her on staff. She knew she needed this job desperately. What if it didn't work out with Will? If she broke up with Will, she would still have three mouths to feed.

&

Promptly at 8:00 p.m., Jack Johnson, president of the school board, opened up the meeting at Forest High School. Ally pulled out her notebook and hit Record on her phone as he covered a fundraiser for the choral group to go to Florida the following spring and a new required course, Civics 101, for seniors. If she took notes and recorded the interview audibly, she wouldn't miss any details. She'd learned that the hard way when her phone battery decided to die in the middle of a meeting. When the president sat down, the superintendent, Dr. Stuart Goodman, a self-assured school official, opened up discussion for those interested in commenting on expanding the teacher exchange program next year.

A middle-aged woman with hair in a tight bun received permission to speak first. She said, "I think it's irresponsible to use that money for programs as frivolous as paying for a teacher from another country when we have plenty of educators here. We need to return to basics, and that means staying out of debt. Lord knows Michigan still hasn't recovered from the recent recession."

Another middle-aged man, wearing a "Let's Get Stoned" tee shirt, stood. "I disagree. Aren't we all tired of being considered a backwater town? Our goal is to help students become global citizens." Several heads nodded in agreement.

An older gentleman stood, walked over to the wall, and pointed to the American flag hanging on it. "I'm a patriotic American. None of this global nonsense."

Next up for discussion was the town's grant program. Janice strutted to the podium dressed in a black-and-white herringbone suit. She stood out like a woman wearing a prom dress in Walmart.

"This fabulous town shouldn't sell itself short. With all the beauty around us and our school's art budget cut to the bone, we desperately need an art center. I have researched this project for three years and have come up with a plan to turn the old railroad depot into a thriving art center." She pointed to a large artist's rendition of the center, displayed to her left on a standing easel. "I have all the financials here, and if anyone wants to examine them, they are welcome."

Dr. Goodman thanked her and then pointed to Jorge Esperanza. "Next month Mr. Esperanza will present the case for the music department. Please stand up." Jorge stood and waved. "As you know, Mr. Thomas and Mr. Esperanza have exchanged places this year, but Mr. Esperanza supports Mr. Thomas's vision for a music education center with the grant funds. He is standing in for Mr. Thomas.

As the meeting concluded, Ally reviewed her notes and checked with two board members for quotes. She had packed up her laptop and had one arm in the sleeve of her coat when Dr. Goodman appeared in front of her.

"Hi, I'm Emerald's dad."

"Yes, hi."

"I'd like to preview what you write about me before it's published this week. Mere protocol." His tall figure loomed over her as he stroked his neatly trimmed beard.

"Oh, I'm sorry. We rarely allow those we interview to preview articles. Did you want to clarify anything in particular?"

"I understand you are a recent hire. Check with Russ and we can talk tomorrow." He took off his glasses, polished them, and put them back on. "On the lighter side, I'm glad the girls are friends."

"Yes, they have been hanging out a lot at school." She didn't know how Kylie felt about Emerald. One day her daughter liked her; the next day she hated her. Who could keep up with teenaged girls and their friendships?

CHAPTER SIX

Back home, Ally heard Aunt Nettie flip off the eleven o'clock news and scoot up the stairs to bed. With the house quiet, she sat at the kitchen table, sipping a mug of coffee. She put down her mug and flipped open her laptop to study her notes on the town's budget. But her eyelids became heavy. Finally, she closed down her computer and headed to her bedroom. She pulled her phone out of her jeans pocket. She had one text message from Will. "Getting lots done. Praying. Future in God's hands."

Tears welled up in Ally's eyes. With the burden of meeting a high mortgage payment for their California home and the stress of raising an autistic child, she and Bryan had both failed to give their marriage much attention. Could she make a second marriage work? Will's decision to leave town had thrown her completely off-kilter. *Oh, Lord, help me find my compass. I seem to make a mess of things.*

Sensing a pair of eyes on her, she looked up. Clad in Spiderman pajamas, Benjie stood in the doorway. He held a long wooden box with a sliding lid and wore a sly grin.

She walked over to him. "Why are you up? It's way past your bedtime." Benjie didn't answer but handed the box to her.

"Yes, dominoes. Too late to play. You should be asleep." Then she realized what Benjie was trying to tell her. He only played dominoes with one person. Will. And Will hadn't been here tonight. Tuesdays were domino nights.

"You miss him, sweet thing, don't you?"

Benjie nodded.

"I suppose I can play with you tomorrow."

"No." Benjie stomped his feet. He had formed a habit of domino trails with Will. They had created a tradition she'd hate for Benjie to give up—change was so difficult for a child on the spectrum. No one but Will would do.

"If you stop stomping, I will tell you something."

He put his foot down and started to pick it up, but decided against stomping it again.

"Now that's an obedient boy. What I want to say is that Will is going to be back in this many days." She flashed ten fingers twice. "If you can wait that long, he will play with you. Promise."

Benjie broke into an enormous grin, and his eyes danced with happiness.

"Love you." Ally kissed her fingers and put them to his lips.

He returned the gesture.

"Hug?" She opened her arms. Sometimes he gave her one, sometimes not.

"Hug," he repeated and leaned his body into hers. She scooped her son into her arms and headed for his room.

❧

Next morning at the office Ally checked her email. First up was a note from Dr. Goodman. No surprise there.

> "Thanks for coming to the meeting. I hope the paper will be on board with the recent projects the school district is planning. Our state ranking is high and we'd like to keep it that way.
>
> I also want to say I'm sorry about the picture my daughter circulated. We've spoken to her, and she will apologize to Kylie. Hope that clears up things.
>
> Regards, Stuart Goodman"

Ally reread the second paragraph and scratched her head. She hadn't a clue what Dr. Goodman was talking about. Kylie and Emerald had probably had words, one of those stupid middle-school fights.

She gave her article a final run-through, looking for typos and grammatical errors. After adding two more quotes, she emailed it to Russ along with a question: "Russ, is it protocol for Stuart Goodman to preview anything we write about the district?"

The answer came back in a flash. "Are you kidding? Goodman thinks he can control the town. Ignore him. In this town, you'll learn soon enough who has an agenda and who doesn't."

Wonder why he'd say that? Sheesh, Russ sure has a lot of opinions. Oh well. She gave the piece a last glance, then filed it to the paper's server, along with a headshot of the superintendent. One article down, four more to go.

Ally slipped into the office kitchen to freshen her lukewarm coffee. Janice stood at the long tile counter.

"So how did you think the meeting went last night?" Janice inquired as she poured a generous amount of cream into her cup. "Do you think they'll keep the teacher exchange program?"

"There were more positive comments than negative." Ally opened the refrigerator for a leftover coffee roll she'd stored on the top shelf.

Janice leaned down to stir two exact-level teaspoons of sugar into her cup before lifting it to her lips. She wore a hint of a smile on her face—a rarity for her. She took the phrase "stiff upper lip" to heart. "I thought the audience responded positively to my art center project."

"Jorge didn't seem too interested."

"Well, if he thinks he's getting that grant to teach a bunch of elementary school students how to play the clarinet, he's mistaken."

"What's wrong with playing the clarinet?"

Janice glared at her. She put the cream back in the exact spot on the refrigerator shelf she always did. "I'm certain to win the grant."

Ally studied the woman as she stirred her tea. Janice was precise and accurate. Her eyebrows rose in perfectly sculpted high arches, and her scarlet lipstick never smudged. Even the outfits she wore announced a woman who spent a great deal of time pairing them with the perfect accessories.

"Say, how long have you lived here?" asked Ally as she bit into the roll.

"Dearie, I'm an old-timer at the paper. I moved here in 1998 with my darling and now deceased husband, Martin. We had visited my cousin who lived up in the Upper Peninsula, and, when we drove through Lake Surrender, we loved it so much we made it a permanent residence. I worked for a fashion magazine in London, so Russ was happy to hire me as a copy editor and office manager. You know, so few understand publishing." She waved a red-nailed hand in the air. "How about you?"

Ally put her coffee mug on the counter. "I lost my job as a children's book editor in San Francisco more than a year and a half ago. That, coupled with a divorce and losing my house, forced me to find a place where I could afford to live. I'm sure you remember we've been living at my Aunt Nettie's."

"You've said."

"My family vacationed here when I was growing up—lots of good memories here. In fact, I played with Will Grainger, my fiancé, as a child. The town seemed a good place to land after my divorce, and I ended up working at Camp Lake Surrender as a cook."

"You're telling me you went from being a book editor to a cook?" Janice clucked her tongue in disbelief. "Rather barmy. That must have been a big change, flipping hamburgers for a bunch of children."

Ally clenched her fists. Oh, how she wanted to tell this woman off. Two years ago, the old Ally would have folded her arms and snapped back with a clever retort, like "*Gourmet* magazine says rustic cooking is the 'new wine tasting.'" But these days, she attempted to control her tongue. Choosing her words carefully, she said, "Yes, a wonderful change. I fell in love with camp life—and the camp director."

"So I understand. Will Grainger seems to have a sterling reputation around here, I'll give him that. Also hear he's easy on the eyes, as you jolly well know."

Ally had never used the word *sterling* to describe Will. He *was* the most genuine man she'd ever known, and, yes, he *was* very handsome in an outdoorsy way. A few of the female counselors at camp had crushes on him. One even mailed him cookies after she returned to college. "He's an amazing guy." As she said it, her heart sank. Would this amazing guy become her husband?

Russ slipped in to warm up a leftover McDonald's breakfast sandwich in the microwave, crowding the miniature kitchen. "Did you know my wife started guitar lessons with the exchange teacher, Jorge?" he said.

"Yes. She takes guitar lessons right before I do on Saturday mornings," Janice said.

"You're learning guitar too?" Russ raised his bushy brows. "My, a woman of many talents."

"I try to expand my horizons. I've always wanted to learn classical guitar, and Jorge is affordable, even if we are on opposite sides of the grant issue. He says I'm a quick study."

"Jorge, eh? Let me see your left hand."

Janice held it up, and Russ examined her fingertips.

"Looks good. You're developing a nice set of calluses, but you'll need to cut those nails on the left hand. I should know, I used to be in a band in the eighties. Toured the Midwest with my mullet and torn tee shirts."

"Spare me." Ernie Kakowski, the paper's distribution manager, stepped into the kitchen for the last stale donut on a plate in the middle of the kitchen table, making the kitchen wall-to-wall people. According to Janice, Ernie had gone to school with Russ and knew all his history. "I'm getting out of here before he starts on Bon Jovi's 'Living on a Prayer.'"

"Rumor is the camp is having a big fundraiser this spring. Hear things are tight, what with the economy," said Russ.

Well, this was awkward. "A bit. By the way, come visit us this this summer when we have a special tribute to local bands."

"Might be fun to have a reunion for the group. But say, we're overdue for a piece on camp," said Russ. "Let's try to do something to help get out the word on any fundraising."

"Okay." What was she supposed to say? Will had mentioned donations were down and they would have to figure a way to raise money, but she didn't know the details. He was careful not to dump a lot of worry on her, but she should be more aware of the camp finances. "Oh, things are fine. Will is good at juggling the budget."

"Well, if you need the band, give me a heads-up so we can practice." He glanced over at Ernie, who popped the last donut crumb into his mouth. "We were pretty good in our day, you'd have to admit, Ernie." Ernie rolled his eyes as Russ demonstrated his air guitar skills. "I could have made the big time."

"Yep, could have toured all the biker bars in the state," said Ernie.

❧

"Got a minute?"

Ally looked up from her computer screen to see her aunt standing next to her desk, cheeks flushed with excitement. "I've got a fifteen-minute window until I have to leave for my next interview. Shoot."

"I'm planning on entering this contest. Might be able to set aside some for Kylie's college fund." She pulled out a glossy brochure from her purse and plopped it in front of Ally:

Magnificent Maple Furniture Company is looking for a fresh new logo. We will pay $5,000 for a local artist who comes up with a design for one of our new products, a cutting board made of various strips of maple wood. The logo should be five inches by three inches. To enter, fill out the form below and mail it along with your design to our Traverse City office.

"That's perfect! You've been working on tree sketches all summer for the store."

"I've been drawing logo samples all morning and wanted to show you." She pulled out a sketchbook she'd been carrying under her arm and flipped it open. "How do you like this one?"

"Nice. I like the large leaf with the intricate veins. Only thing, it's detailed for a small design."

"True. How about these two?"

"I like the curvy silhouette better." A long red fingernail pointed to the picture.

Both women looked up. Janice peered at the design, teacup in hand. "I spent years in graphic design. This is my area of expertise."

"I'm sure it is." The excitement slipped out of Aunt Nettie's voice as she closed her pad and shoved it in her purse. She thrust her arms into her coat. "Better let you go back to work." The front doorbell jangled as she left.

"Why, I didn't know your aunt was an artist." Janice took a sip of her tea. "You said she dabbled in painting designs on old furniture, but I figured she'd picked up some hobby when she retired."

"My aunt's always been artistic. She can turn the ugliest stick of furniture into a work of beauty."

"You might be a wee bit prejudiced." The teacup clanked as she returned it to its saucer. Janice returned to her desk. "Say, what was the name of that furniture company?"

"Magnificent Maple, why?"

"Oh, no reason." She tapped a pen against her right temple as if she were in deep concentration. "I think we did a story on them last year. Is the owner Jack Lockard?"

"That name sounds familiar. Maybe."

"Sure, I met him at the chamber of commerce meeting last spring. Lovely gentleman."

Ally sighed. "I don't mean to be rude, but I need to hop on the phone for an interview."

"Not a problem. I'm about to run to the deli and grab a bite for lunch. Back in a flash."

Ally finished up her interview and decided she was hungry too. As she headed out to her car, she passed Janice leaning on the hood of her car, hunched over her cell phone. "Hey, Jack, it's been eons since we've talked. Love to hear more about that contest you're sponsoring."

CHAPTER SEVEN

Two more days till Thanksgiving vacation, and Kylie was ready for a break. She was sick of school and all the homework. The warning five-minute bell rang for second period. When she slammed shut her locker door, Emerald Goodman pointed her round face and lip-glossed smile directly at her. Kylie shuddered inside. That girl was the last person she wanted to see.

"Walk with me to Spanish," Emerald said.

"Are you kidding? I wouldn't hang with you if we were walking up the gangplank to a Disney cruise ship."

"Too bad, 'cause I would invite you to one. How did you know?"

"You turd. I love my brother. You posted that stupid picture all over Instagram. My brother may be autistic, but he doesn't run down the hall at school making racecar noises. Do you hate autistic kids?"

Emerald looked down at the ground. "Yeah, kinda stupid. I got sick of all the guys in homeroom talking about the new girl—how beautiful your hair was, so long you could almost sit on it, how you are so good at athletics, blah, blah, blah."

"People talk about me?"

"You're so pretty and you don't even know it. Hey ..." Emerald stuck out a stubby hand with three rings on her fingers. "Truce?"

"How do I know you aren't going nuclear on me again?" Kylie put her Spanish book into her backpack and slung one handle over her shoulder.

"Pinkie promise."

Kylie rolled her eyes. "So lame. That's third-grade stuff."

"I swear on a stack of Bibles."

"You don't even own one Bible."

"I can still swear on one. Come on, Ky, give me a break."

The second bell rang. Kylie sprinted to class. She looked back to see Emerald moving her short legs like a buzz saw.

Finally, huffing, she caught up with Kylie. "Sorry, really sorry."

"So, forget the whole picture thing. But leave my brother alone," said Kylie. She jerked open the door to the classroom. "I mean it."

At lunchtime, Kylie looked at her phone and saw a text message from Emerald. "Hey, it's not a Disney cruise, but I know about a party coming up with a bunch of kids. Major epic time. Want to come?"

Now what? Why didn't that girl quit pestering her? Sure, she was popular, but Em's girly personality irritated her. And so two-faced.

But the party intrigued her. Kylie felt a grin crawl across her face. Maybe she should give Em another chance. Maybe she'd meet majorly chill girls at the party. And that could be awesome.

"Maybe," she typed.

❧

Ally took the two corners on one end of the white damask tablecloth. Aunt Nettie held the other two ends. Together they lifted the material high, then let it flutter down, resting on the long walnut table in the dining room.

"Feels good to add extra leaves to the table and stretch it out for more company. My life is jam-packed again," Nettie said as she evened out the sides of the tablecloth. "For many years, Charlie and I spent Thanksgiving alone. Then I became involved at camp and invited the out-of-town staff to dinner." She stood back to admire her work. "Such a full table." She placed a ceramic turkey vase filled with orange and scarlet mums in the middle of the table. Next to the centerpiece, she positioned several Mason jars, the candles inside them held in place with colored stones.

"I miss Uncle Charlie. You two were so happy," said Ally as she rooted around in the china cabinet for the gravy boat. She pulled out the silver container and set it on the table, her fingers sliding over the smooth surface of the handle. Ally turned to her aunt. "I've felt so rattled since Will headed south to help his brother remodel his basement."

"I'm sure his brother appreciated his help."

"Yeah. He's struggling with issues in our relationship. I'm hoping he'll be here for dinner Thursday."

"I figured you two had had words. Too quiet around here, and Benjie's been moping. Not Kylie, though."

Thankfully, Nettie didn't glance up from arranging the silverware for each place setting. "Kylie's made it hard," Ally said. "Will feels like he's a replacement for her dad. I can't believe the change in her since last year."

"In what way?"

"She used to like Will, and now she hassles him whenever she can." Ally rearranged a drooping mum in the centerpiece and wished she could arrange her daughter so easily.

"You have a life too."

"But Kylie's been through so much—the fire, her dad dying, and now adjusting to a stepdad. So different from a year ago."

Her aunt examined a tall beverage glass for smudges before setting it on the table. "She needs more time to adjust."

"Not sure how long Will can wait. But I don't want to alienate my daughter either."

"Have you talked to her?"

"As best I can. She's certainly had the attitude lately."

"Can you say almost fourteen?"

"Tell me about it."

Nettie rummaged around in the china cabinet and found the tall silver salt and pepper shakers. "Let me talk to her."

"Talk to who?" Kylie stood in the dining room doorway, gripping a caffeinated energy drink.

"Kylie, you've had too many of those drinks today. They make your heart race," Ally said.

Kylie took another sip. "Talk to who?"

Nettie patted the seat of one of the dining room chairs. "Come, sit down a minute."

"Now what did I do?"

"Nothing that I know of. We were talking about the wedding," said Aunt Nettie.

"Mom's going to do whatever she wants. You know, get married. But I don't have to come."

"Kylie!" Ally put her hands on her hips.

"Whatever. I'm only the kid."

Nettie put her hand on Kylie's shoulder. "Your mother and Will care about your feelings too. And Will loves you."

"I don't need a stepfather. I had a perfect father, and he's gone. I don't need a substitute."

"Substitute?" Ally clenched her fists before uncurling them, trying to tame her anger. "Why would you say that?"

"He thinks he can boss me around."

Ally lifted the glass cake plate she'd pulled from the cabinet and slammed it onto the table. "You need a lot of bossing around right now, young lady."

Aunt Nettie turned to Ally. "Will you please go upstairs and grab those linen napkins I set on top of my bed? Take your time."

☙

Puzzled, Ally headed upstairs. Knowing she shouldn't, she stood in the stairwell and strained to hear the conversation. Oh, she was bad. So bad. One of those snoopy moms she vowed she'd never become. She leaned her head down and turned her ear toward the conversation.

"Dear sweet Kylie, what's going on here? Why don't you want your mother to get married again?"

"Will's okay, but the three of us are fine, perfectly fine. Benjie and I don't need another dad."

"I wouldn't be so sure about Benjie's feelings. But let's talk about you. What else is eating you, sweetie?"

Ally couldn't hear her daughter's answers, so she slithered back down the stairs on her rear, bump, bump, bump, until she hit the third step from the bottom. She was still hidden from sight. *It isn't technically eavesdropping if I need to figure out what is going on in my daughter's brain.* From where she sat she could see her daughter's head down on the table, Nettie rubbing Kylie's shoulder.

"I hate my life. I hate Michigan, I hate my school, and I hate kids mocking me because of my brother." Kylie's fist pounded the table.

"Hmm, lot of hate for a young girl."

Ally jerked her head up. There'd been taunting in the past, but she wasn't aware the teasing was still going on. Why had she been so clueless? Kids had always teased Kylie about her brother. She could kick herself for not being aware.

"I can't help it," said Kylie.

"Oh, honey, I'm sorry," said Nettie. "Kids can be so cruel, especially at your age. You should have told us." Nettie reached into her apron pocket, pulled out a clean tissue, and handed it to Kylie.

"It's not that bad except for this girl, Emerald, who thinks she owns the school. I came close to smacking her at the bus stop."

"Oh?"

"She thinks she's so cool because her father is the superintendent, and her cousin is captain of the football team. Emerald has a friend who has a sister at the elementary school, and her sister told Emerald about Benjie. Em says stuff like 'Too bad your brother won't make varsity. Oh, I forgot, he can't even hold a football 'cause he needs his hands to flap.' She and her friends giggle and whisper to each other. But then she turns around and tries to be my friend."

"Some girls your age are very fickle. Believe me, your friendships will grow stronger as you all mature. But I'm sure it's not much fun right now. Have you told anyone?"

"Are you kidding? I don't want to the entire school to think I'm a snitch."

"That I understand. Do you want your mother to talk to a counselor or to your teacher?"

"No way. I can handle this by myself."

"I do know karate."

"You rock, Aunt Nettie. It helps to talk about it. And actually, when I explained about Benjie to Em, she apologized and has treated me nicer lately."

"Well, the offer still stands."

Still on the stairs, Ally put her head down on her lap and ached for her daughter. Even after a year and a half, this move to Michigan had been hard on Kylie. *Oh, Lord, make a way for my girl. Let her find her place in Lake Surrender.*

❧

Ally sat on the front porch later that day, enveloped in a green down parka as she watched the thermometer on the porch railing fall. The sky had turned an ugly gray, choking out most of the light and suffocating any cheerfulness about the holiday. The temperature had dropped to the low thirties. She watched her breath appear like downy clouds in front of her. To prepare for Thanksgiving tomorrow, she, Kylie, and Nettie had hit the kitchen, preparing sweet potato casserole, bacon Brussels sprouts, three kinds of pie, and two dozen brownies. One more day until Will came home. She wondered what he'd sorted out. Ally's stomach did a figure eight. She had missed him terribly. And yet she didn't know what he'd concluded about them.

She checked her phone. No text.

Ally glanced up as a red Chevy truck pulled into the driveway. Don, the camp maintenance man and Will's best friend, jumped out of the cab and stomped up the porch stairs in his work boots. His solidly built frame, straight black hair, and smiley eyes had always been a welcome sight when she worked at camp.

"Hey, aren't you freezing out here?" He handed her a box of business cards. "Your cake cards came in today. I added them to Will's order."

"Thanks, I'll write you a check." She motioned to an empty place on the swing. "Have a seat."

Don lowered his sturdy body down next to her. She flipped opened the lid, then picked up one card to examine in the porch light. "Perfect. I love them. What do I owe you?"

"How about a turtle cheesecake?"

"Done. How's the fam?"

"Wilma is cooking up a storm. I told her I'd be right back." He stuffed both hands into his pockets. "I suppose you're waiting for boss man."

"You know he hates when you call him that."

"That's why I do it. Bet he's missed you."

"I don't know. He wanted to take a break to sort out things."

"Break? You're kidding."

"Guess he didn't tell you." Ally fingered the long chain that attached the swing to the porch ceiling, the cold metal sending an ache through her skin. "We've been having a tough time."

Don cracked the knuckles on his left hand. "Ah, shoot, all couples have tough times. Why, Wilma and I broke up about three times. But there's an old Native American proverb my father used to quote—'The soul would have no rainbow if the eye had no tears.' Ya have to expect some tears. Still, making a go of a relationship can be rough."

"Especially when a certain kid digs in her heels." Ally twirled an errant strand of hair around her finger and watched fresh snowflakes fall onto the street.

"Just because of a know-it-all thirteen-year-old? I've got a few teens piled up at home, and they think they're ready to rule the world." He pointed a finger at her. "Listen, don't be afraid to fight for him. I've known him for years. Few true blue like Will. He's worth it—even if he can't paint cabin walls worth a darn."

"Thanks, Don." Ally reached out and squeezed his arm. "You're the best. I miss seeing you."

He stood to go and hugged her goodbye. "Hope you have a fantastic holiday. And the other—it'll work out."

"Says you, the camp's biggest worrywart?"

"Hey, my constant vigilance as maintenance director has kept the camp from many a lawsuit."

Ally laughed. "Okay, safety monitor."

CHAPTER EIGHT

At lunchtime, Ally drove by Tapas Deliciosas Restaurante, a Spanish eatery where Jorge played guitar on weekends. As she entered, the aroma of roasted chicken made her mouth water. While the waitstaff clinked silverware and set out glasses for the evening crowd, Ally took photos of Jorge posing with his guitar on the restaurant's stage.

"Great, I got an excellent one of you, Jorge," she said, then handed him the camera so he could see the photo. "That will be great for your new guitar lessons business."

"You are so kind. Thank you."

"My pleasure. And don't forget I still want to interview you about donating your kidney to your brother. People need to know your story and all about the disease. What's it called again?"

"Polycystic kidney disease. It's a hereditary disease where one's kidney grows cysts. But I want to make sure all is well. Still much to do, medically." He smiled, but she saw a flash of suffering in his eyes.

"What a kind person you are. I'm not sure I could give up a kidney, even to a sibling. That's a tough decision."

"I love my brother. He taught me guitar and a love for music."

He laid the guitar on a table. "Might you be able to talk to me for a few minutes? I believe you can help." His jovial face creased with the beginning of a frown line, his eyes darting around the room. Jorge pushed aside a stack of music and gestured for her to take a seat on a chair.

"I want to ask you about Janice at your paper."

"Janice?"

"She is upset with me. Is student of mine. We talked about the town's grant program through the school. *Naturalmente*, the other music teachers and I want a music center. We applied together so we can all receive funding. The band program is small. Would be *perfecto* to have money for needy students to take private lessons and to take small trips for competitions."

"Sounds good," Ally said. Where was this going?

"*Pero* Janice has also applied for grant. Wants to start an art center. She has been planning it for years. I did not know."

"Yes, I believe she is a painter."

"She thinks the school does not need another music program. I wanted to explain the town might split the grant, but I don't think she likes that." He cleared his throat and hesitated. His eyes turned fiery. "She does not know me. I will fight for what I believe is right, and I want to back up Mr. Thomas."

"I thought you and Janice were special friends. Seeing each other. Dating."

"Oh, *Dios mio*, no. She came to see me last Saturday at the tapas restaurant, and we had lunch, but nothing more, although she has decided to take lessons from me." He leaned in and lowered his tone. "Between you and me, she has not much musical talent, but I believe she wants to be on my good side."

"How can I help you, Jorge?" Ally cocked her head to the side, flattered he'd sought her out.

"I need advice. In a fair competition, the best man or woman wins. I want to have happy feelings, but she doesn't understand. What can I say to her?"

Advice on Janice? I don't understand her myself. "You are a gentleman, and I'm sure she realizes it's a fair competition. The art center is important to her, but the town board will have to decide. I wouldn't worry about it. It will all work out."

"She called me last week, insisting the music department drop out of the running."

"Oh my."

"I tell her no. The last time we talked, she wasn't happy."

He lowered his voice and leaned toward her. "To tell you the truth, I don't understand American or English women."

"Sometimes we don't understand ourselves." Ally let out a laugh.

"You are a lovely lady. I'm sure your Will is lucky guy." He squeezed her hand. "And think about maybe you learning guitar?"

"Oh, maybe someday."

⤩

After stopping at the restaurant, Ally swung by Cherry County Coffee Shop to pick up Will's favorite Moose Roast coffee. The rustic establishment literally hummed with afternoon customers, from earnest businessmen closing a deal over a hot cup of java to a group of teens on Thanksgiving break blowing straw wrappers at each other. As Ally gave her debit card to the guy at the counter, a woman with a teenaged daughter waved at her from a far table. She picked up her drink and walked toward them.

"Are you Kylie's mom?" the woman with short blonde hair asked.

"Yes."

"I'm Sonja Goodman, Emerald's mom. Have you met Emerald?" She gave a nod to a short girl with a round face who looked up from her hot chocolate and waved. "Our girls are in class together."

"Kylie's talked about her."

"Have a seat," said Sonja. Ally slid into the chair next to her. "So glad to run into you. How is the wedding coming along?"

"Just fine, thanks."

"That's good. So glad the girls have become friends. Say, I wanted to run an idea by you that Stuart and I were considering." Sonja brushed her hand through her bobbed hair. "We're very proud of how well Emerald has been doing in her classes this year. When she brings home good grades, we reward her— sometimes with a trip."

"Usually an educational trip, like to an organic worm farm." Emerald crossed her arms over her chest. The thirteen-year-old didn't seem like she'd be excited about anything.

"Come on, Emerald, we've had several delightful trips. And I wanted to mention to Ms. Cervantes that we'd like to take Kylie with us this year."

Ally raised her eyebrows but bit the inside of her lip. Are they trying to get in good with me because I work for the paper? Or are they offering me charity?

"Anyway, we wanted to extend an invitation to Kylie. We're thinking of going skiing this winter."

Torn between appreciation for Sonja's offer and irritation with Emerald, Ally hesitated. "Why that's very generous, but …"

Sonja laid a hand on her arm. "It could be a nice break for the girls."

"Mom, you said we were going to fly to Cancún."

"Now Emerald." Sonja looked over at Ally and gave her a knowing look. "Teenagers. What I am trying to say is, we want to share our family life with Kylie. I'm sure being a single mom and with money probably short, it would be an opportunity for your daughter to have a rich cultural experience."

"With the perfect family," Emerald added, then smirked. "Our motto is 'we're small but mighty.'"

Ally stared at the woman. Was she kidding, a family motto? And, according to Kylie, she and Emerald were friends one moment and enemies the next. "That's very kind of you. I'll talk it over with Kylie."

CHAPTER NINE

"Come on in before you become any wetter. A certain young man has been waiting for you all day." Aunt Nettie wiped her hands on her brown-checked apron and gave Will, standing at the front door, an enormous hug. "Ally went to the gas station for a couple liters of pop."

"Turkey smells wonderful." Will handed Nettie a box of chocolates. He stepped over the front door's threshold, shaking off raindrops.

"Will!" Benjie came running down the stairs and plowed right into him.

"Hey, buddy, good to see you too." He put his finger under Benjie's chin and lifted his head to discover an infrequent smile. He loved this little guy. "I hear you set up the domino trail."

Benjie tugged on his hand. "Domono, domono."

"Hey, let me take off my coat first." Will hung the blue parka on the coat rack next to the front door and turned back to him. "Where's your sister?"

Benjie pointed upstairs, then started flapping his hands.

"Yes, I see you're excited. I missed you. Give me a hug?"

Instead, Benjie flapped his hands all the harder, turning in circles and spinning around.

"So let's go see what you have set up."

Will started up the stairs. A line of dominoes extended down the entire length of the upstairs hallway like soldiers and wound into Benjie's room. "Wow, this is amazing. Are you sure you want to do this right now?"

Benjie nodded.

"Sounds good, but first let me say hi to your sister." Will knocked on the door directly across from Benjie's. "Hey, Kylie, how about coming out a sec?"

A muffled voice came through the bedroom door. "I can't right now. Mom will be home soon."

Will sighed.

Squatting in front of the construction, he turned to Benjie. "Do you want to flick the first one?"

In answer, Benjie knelt next to Will and tapped the first domino. In thirty seconds, the entire trail lay flat. Benjie jumped up in glee, flapping his hands.

"Looks like Will's back," Ally's familiar voice drifted up from the kitchen. "Saw the Suburban out front."

"You fix them up again, and we'll do it again after Thanksgiving dinner," Will told Benjie. He pushed up from the floor and inhaled deeply. *Take it easy,* he told himself as he raced downstairs to see Ally.

Clad in a khaki raincoat and standing under the kitchen's overhanging light, Ally held plastic bags in both hands. The rain had curled her hair. Auburn wisps framed the edge of her face like delicate fragments of lace. She placed the bags onto the kitchen table and extracted a liter of pop, strawberry jam, and a pound of butter. She raised her head, and he saw deep circles under her eyes, contrasted against her pale skin—probably a sign she was working too much. If his income were larger, maybe then she wouldn't push herself so much.

"Here, let me help you." He grabbed the liter of pop and shoved it into the refrigerator. He ached to pull her in his arms but held back. "Tried to call you on the way home, but you must have had your phone off." Why did his voice sound so strained? *This is Al, for Pete's sake.*

She leaned over to kiss him on the cheek. "Hope you avoided the big storm."

"Not too bad until I reached Ludington."

"Sure missed you." She gave him a long piercing look.

"Missed you too." He looked down at the key chain she had dropped on the kitchen table and noticed the key was to an unfamiliar car. "What happened to your Audi?"

"Traded it in."

"Just like that?" His warm feelings gave way to surprise.

She went to the pantry and pulled out two cans of canned gravy. Then she found the can opener and opened them. "Aunt Nettie's in a tizzy because she burned the gravy and has to use canned gravy this year. Heaven forbid."

"When were you going to tell me about it?"

"The gravy?"

"The car."

"Let's talk later. Why don't you knock on Kylie's door and tell her to come out and visit with us?"

Uh no, already tried that. "Yeah, well, I'll see how Benjie's doing upstairs with his domino highway."

Why was she giving him that fisheye? She's the one who bought a new car.

"Sure," she said and gave the gravy a stir before it boiled over.

❧

At dinner, Kylie passed the butter to Will without looking up. Another grumpy mood. Great.

He turned to Ally, filling the silence with a few words. "So how's the paper going?"

Ally sighed. "Okay. I'm writing about fascinating things, like the new business, Mice Be Gone. Pulitzer Prize material."

"Workload better?"

"Yeah, although Russ has been on my case lately. I can't seem to please him. But let's not talk about me." Ally turned to Kylie. "Kylie, tell Will about being in the talent show."

"No big deal. I might lip sync with a girl in my math class. You know, Emerald. But we probably won't win. I never win anything."

Will laughed. "I don't know, there's nothing better than a great lip sync."

"Can you share any more school news, Kylie?" said Aunt Nettie. She peered down her nose through her reading glasses at the teen, who crinkled her nose in disgust.

"Uh, Christmas vacay is three weeks away. How's that for news?" Kylie forced an anemic grin and turned to Will, her eyes scrutinizing him. "So are you and mom going to get married or not?"

Ouch. Will cleared his throat and wiped his sweaty palms on his pants. He'd rather clean twenty camp toilets, paint the entire outside of the lodge, and build a six-foot retaining wall than shine the spotlight on his and Ally's relationship. He glanced out the window, but the vision of a sparkly new Ford Explorer taunted him.

"I see your new set of wheels." He nodded toward the driveway. "Didn't figure you'd buy a car while I was away."

"Found a good deal." Will thought she looked sheepish. She should.

"Cost much?"

"Enough."

"She surprised me," Nettie said. "Took the Audi in for a tune-up and drove the Explorer home."

She needed a better car for the winter, but why hadn't she waited for them to pick it out together? "I'm glad you have a safer vehicle going into the winter months. I'd like to test it out later." He swallowed his last piece of sweet potato casserole.

"How about now?" Nettie said. "I still have to make coffee. You two go." She made a shooing motion with her hands.

Outside, Ally handed Will the key and slid over as far as she could against the passenger's side. They drove in silence as he steered the vehicle down the water-splattered street that wrapped around Lake Surrender. The gray day put him in a bad mood.

He steered the car out of its lane and back again to miss a wild turkey crossing the street.

"Careful." Ally grabbed onto the door's armrest.

"Don't tell me how to drive."

"You were going to hit that turkey."

"Nowhere near."

They drove a few miles, the silence chilling the inside of the car.

"Probably should get back and help Aunt Nettie with the dishes." He glanced at her solemn, unsmiling silhouette.

This conversation is going nowhere. Will jerked the car off of the road and pulled into an empty parking space at Snowball Park.

He threw the car into park. "What's eating you?"

"You ought to know."

"Al, I haven't talked to you yet. Give me a break."

She turned and peered out the passenger window.

Trying to cross what seemed like the Grand Canyon of coolness, he reached out and touched the back of his hand to her cheek. "Can you hear me out?"

Her head turned slowly, her eyes full of uncertainty. The *whap-whap* of the windshield wipers punctuated the silence. Ally loosened the wool scarf around her neck. "I'm listening, Camp."

"I'm irritated you didn't wait till I came back to buy a car. Didn't you want us to make a decision together?"

"I needed a car and found a good deal." She crossed her arms in front of her. "Anyway, I can make up my own mind."

"You certainly can."

Ally sighed. "The truth is I was hurt that you took off. Maybe I did buy it out of spite. I wasn't sure what was going on with us, and I needed a good winter car."

Will pressed his palms together. "Babe, don't worry about the car. It's a done deal. But I've thought about other issues we have to work out. For one, Kylie isn't onboard with this marriage." Ally protested, but he held up his hand. "It's an enormous problem."

"So what's your solution?" Ally asked, intent on a thumbnail. *When did she start chewing her nails? Was she that stressed?*

"I mulled over a lot while I was gone."

"And ..." She glanced at him with that wide-eyed look that always gave him pause. He swallowed and turned his head to focus on the road as he gripped the steering wheel.

"This has to end. No teenage girl is going to sabotage our relationship." He realized he was yelling and softened his voice. "I'm going to be her stepfather. It's settled."

A loud sob erupted as Ally unleashed a torrent of tears—on her cheeks, in her eyes, dripping down her neck. How could one body produce that many tears? He started the car, ready to head back and call it a night. He hated feeling helpless.

"I'm sorry." Ally dabbed at her eyes and wiped her nose. "I'm sure Kylie loves you. She's being a typical tee-tee-teenager right now."

He turned off the motor and pulled out the key. "I didn't mean to come on so strong. My point is she can't come between us. She has to realize you and I are a couple."

"I know, but since Bryan has gone, she's put him up on a pedestal."

"So? You can't keep making excuses for her."

Ally blew her nose on a tissue, and Will handed her a fresh one. "And you can't take off when we have problems. We need to work things out, hard or not," she said.

"You have a point. Can you see I sometimes need space to work out my thoughts?"

Tears pooled in her eyes again, and Will braced himself for another onslaught. "But not right now. Get over here. You're way too far away from me." Will enfolded her in his arms before burying his head in a mound of curly hair. She smelled like a heavenly combination of orange blossoms and pumpkin pie spice. "I've missed you so."

Their lips met, and he relished her softness as Ally's entire body melted into his. "I want you so much."

"Me too," said Ally, her eyes shining. Their kisses grew deeper, and for a moment their problems dissolved into the warmth of their embrace. He drew her closer. The world became small—only large enough for the two of them.

Ally suddenly pulled away. "We'd better stop."

"I guess." He tucked her hair behind one ear, and whispered, "Let's call a truce."

Ally pulled out a new tissue from her purse and waved it in surrender. Then she chuckled. That did it. He was a goner now. He couldn't resist her laugh.

He leaned over to seal his promise with another kiss, this one stronger and more convincing, as his heartbeat drummed insistently in his ear. He wanted to enjoy that kind of kiss for a lifetime. *Whoa. Steady, guy.*

Reluctantly he broke it off, and Ally rested her head on his shoulder. They watched the raindrops splatter against the windshield, then slide down the window. He turned to her and wiped a tear off of her cheek.

"One more thing, and this is important." Will pulled back and looked Ally straight in the eye. "Could I have some leftover turkey to take home tonight?"

CHAPTER TEN

"Hey, your phone's ringing," Kylie called from her bedroom.

Ally trotted down the stairs toward the kitchen and stepped over Benjie, who had organized his rock collection into small groups in the middle of the downstairs hallway. She could hardly see anything in the late November dusk. She navigated around his piles with care, set down the laundry basket, and picked up the phone on the kitchen counter. The wedding caterer. Ally forgot she had planned to spend an hour nailing down the details for the wedding before heading out to cover a folk dancing festival for the paper.

"Yes, we're planning on simple foods," Ally said. "Limited budget." She scrunched her eyes when the caterer recited the prices, then glanced at Kylie who had raced in.

With long, dark hair framing her oval face, she wore the typical impatient expression of a teenager wanting her mother to end her phone call. Ally turned away so she could concentrate on writing the prices. Busy day ahead. Wedding gown fitting this afternoon, then shopping for the guest tables' centerpieces, with time set aside to work on the guest list. Right now eloping seemed like a better option.

She finished the call and turned around to talk to Kylie. The front door slammed. Ally intended to run after her, but Aunt Nettie showed up in the kitchen doorway, her face covered with the morning's newspaper. She lowered the paper and shook her head, her round face beaming. "Like it?"

She had colored her hair. The gray curls were gone, and in their place Nettie wore a short, light-brown bob that framed her face.

"It's so cute!"

Benjie raced into the room holding a piece of paper and tugged at the edge of Ally's workout shorts.

"Mama, see, see." He persisted until she squatted beside him to ooh and aah over his project, a paper scribbled with a red crayon. Hearing him say "Mama" still thrilled her. His verbal development had been slow in coming—he hadn't started talking until he was five.

"So proud of you, Benjie. Why don't we put it on the dining room table so everyone can see it?" said Aunt Nettie.

He stomped his feet.

"Stop that." She grasped one edge of the drawing, and Benjie grabbed the other and yanked hard. The paper ripped in two. Benjie shrieked, his pale blond hair flying this way and that like a human buzz saw as he reached out to scratch Ally. She grabbed his wrist and caught him before he could dig his nails into her. She would win this one.

"We're through with this scratching stuff, get it?"

He dropped his head.

"Now we'll walk to the family room, open the desk drawer, and find the Scotch Tape to fix your picture."

"Way to go," her aunt said. "Hang tough, Mom."

Ally escorted him into the next room, where she cut off a few inches of tape and put one end between Benjie's thumb and forefinger. He hesitated and then put the tape on the rip.

"Hope we learned a lesson," Ally said.

Benjie flapped his hands.

"Did we?" Her tone became sterner.

He looked up and stared at her. "No rips."

"Yes, no rips." She walked back into the kitchen. "Sorry for the interruption. The hairdo looks amazing." Nettie had also added a touch of mascara, pale pink blush, and smoky-gray eyeliner to her new look. "I like it."

"Thank you!"

Ally ran a ratty terrycloth dishtowel inside the skillet and put the cookware into the cupboard next to the stove. She should buy her aunt more towels. They'd been living with her for over a year—a debt she could never repay. "Makeover for a reason?"

"I've let myself go for too long."

"That's not true. You always look great."

"Tired of the gray. And over-permed hair is out."

"So is there anything else you'd like to tell me?"

Nettie turned away and busied herself with filling the sink with soapy water, scraping leftover bread crusts into the trash, and wiping off the counter.

"Nettie?" A few wet suds flew onto Ally's face as her aunt slid her hands back in the sink. Ally gave her aunt a half-hug before tweaking the top of her newly dyed do. "Wow, what a difference. You could pass for fifty."

"Oh, come on."

"And whoever he is, he'll love it." Ally smiled when her aunt's face turned bright pink. "I'm dying to know, and if you don't tell me, I'll nose around town."

"Well, I'll confess I ran into Detective Tom Whittaker. I've known him for years. We worked together last week at the soup kitchen."

"Sure, I interviewed him once. Seems like a lot of fun."

"He is. He dished up taco casserole while I spooned up canned peaches, and he kept me laughing the whole time."

"And ... I'm dying to know."

"I have a date tomorrow, that's all."

Ally gave her the okay sign and squealed. Benjie ran into the kitchen and mimicked her squeal.

"Now don't make a big deal of it. It's only for coffee."

"What are you going to wear?"

"Probably my new gray V-neck sweater with my silver necklace."

"I love that on you." Ally shook her head. "You sure have been sneaky."

"He's a great guy, but I don't want to get my hopes up. Anyway, I haven't had a lot of time to think about our date, I'm so busy trying to work on the logo design."

"That's right. Have you decided which to submit to the contest?"

"I think the more modern looking straight-lined tree with the single leaf on the ground might be my best work. Design has turned so contemporary. And a logo needs to be simple."

"True. I'm convinced your logo will win."

Ally heard her phone go off. When she saw Will's name pop up, she slipped into the long wool cardigan she hung from the front hall coat hook and stepped onto the porch for some privacy. She wrapped the thick sweater tightly around herself as an icy breeze assaulted her. "How's the weekend conference for EM physicians going?"

"Good. Come catch the campfire tonight after dinner? We'll have one if it doesn't rain. We can make out behind Girls' Cabin A while the docs roast marshmallows. And wear that Miracle Moose perfume."

"What? Oh, you mean Lyrical Muse."

"Yeah, that stuff."

"You saw me yesterday." Lately he seemed to miss her a lot, as she did him. "Honestly, I'd love to, but I have to cover one of the chamber of commerce events."

"So now you're offering me limited engagements?" Will asked. "Come on, take a break."

"Can't."

"We could put on a show for the board of directors president, Packey, and he could send you home for too much public display of affection."

"You're terrible."

"Please."

"I'd love to, I can't."

"Tell Russ to jump in the lake."

"No can do. It's frozen." But her joke fell flat, and an awkward silence followed.

"Well, you can't fault a guy for trying." Another pause at the other end, and then the line went dead. A flicker of guilt passed through her mind.

❦

His plans for the evening aborted, Will headed back early from the campfire to his office. Don was working late, painting a bookshelf he'd installed on the west wall of the dining room.

"Too much to do with only the two of us. It's an old camp, and the roof and bathrooms need major repairs," Will said. "You shouldn't have to work this hard on a Saturday night. Maybe I can track down someone in town to pitch in and help."

Don nodded. "So, if you're good, I'm heading for home for a late dinner. Beef stew waiting for me. Save any for you? You love Wilma's cooking."

"Nah." Will waved him off and headed back to his office off of the dining hall. He might as well check the internet for part-time workers on Craig's list and go over next year's budget. A lousy substitute for Al's company, but he needed to do a few hours of serious number crunching. Miraculously, he'd found six thousand dollars to fix the lodge's roof, but he still needed money to buy tiles to retile all the cabin showers. His to-do list never ended.

Deep into cutting next year's food budget, Will's phone rang. Was it Al, changing her mind? Number crunching would be more fun with her here. But when he picked up the phone, he noted Sarah, his ex-fiancée, had called. *Hmm, long time no hear. Why would she be calling?*

"Well, this is a surprise, Sarah."

"I was thinking about you and Michigan. Man, how I miss the autumn. Tell me, did the colors last long this year?"

"Yes, a great season. The maples especially."

"I loved the ones in the front of our high school parking lot. They always turned around homecoming. That seems ages ago. Anyway, I wish you could see the orphanage summer camp now. Remember what a mess we had with the construction when you came down last spring? Well, someone donated some extra funds, and we finished the girls' dorm. Oh, Will, you would be proud to see it."

Will smiled, glad he'd been able to get the project up and running. "That's great." He tried to ignore the catch in his voice. What was wrong with him? He and Sarah were history. Still, his palms were sweaty. He wiped them on the side of his jeans.

"I know we haven't talked for a while, but I have a huge favor to ask."

"Like what?"

"I don't suppose you have any time off soon when you could come down and take a look-see? We're remodeling the kitchen, and I could use your expertise. Might be nice for you to take a break before the snow really piles up."

Will sighed. "Sounds tempting." She would call tonight, of all nights. It shocked him to realize he enjoyed hearing Sarah's soft voice. She'd always had a calming effect on him, even when they dated in high school. "I'm sure the weather is great there about now."

"Fantastic. Don't even need a sweater yet. Daytime temps in the sixties. Is money an issue? If so, the mission could send you a plane ticket. We need more painting done, and the kitchen plumbing is still a mess. We've done everything possible to fix the kitchen sink, but it still leaks."

He puffed up his cheeks and blew out a breath. "Thanks for the invite, but I'm buried under with a big roof repair project right now."

"Will, if anyone needs a vacation, you do. You could work for a while and then take a few days off to sightsee. Think about it."

She asked about some of their high school buddies, and Will caught her up on their lives. He was about to sign off when Sarah lowered her voice.

"Will."

"Yes?" He could hardly hear her.

"This is kind of hard to say."

"What?"

"Did we make a mistake breaking up?"

He swallowed hard, as his mouth had suddenly gone dry. *Whoa, didn't see that coming.* He opened his mouth to answer, but the call had dropped. Only static on the line. He redialed the number, but the call didn't go through. Will pinched the bridge of his nose and jammed the phone back in his coat pocket before lowering his head onto the desktop. *Did* they make a mistake?

CHAPTER ELEVEN

The energy in the newsroom ran on full voltage, typical for a Monday morning. Ally looked up from her piece to see Clay leaning over his computer, typing madly. Janice, her head glued to the front desk's phone receiver, consoled a reader about his missing paper, and Russ, office door open, paced as he talked with their out-of-town publisher about advertisers. Nevertheless, Ally gritted her teeth and put her head down, determined to finish her article.

Russ hung up and yelled, "Cervantes, need to see you a minute."

Ally jerked her head up from her screen. Dang, she'd been in the zone, when words rushed out of her brain and onto the page. She hated to stop. What does he want?

"Coming." Ally hit the Save button and walked into her boss's office.

"Have a seat." He motioned to the molded plastic chair next to the desk. "I'll get right to the point. You need to submit your articles earlier—not ten minutes before deadline—so I have more time for editing. Problem with that?"

"No."

"Okay, now that we have that settled, I want you to step up and take more responsibility in the newsroom. We have a lot of things in the pipeline. For instance ..." He yanked open his middle desk drawer and pulled out a brochure. "I want you to enter this."

"The award has a few categories for smaller community papers. I think we have the best small paper in Michigan, and I'd like to showcase it statewide. I want you to hunt down the most provocative and compelling story you can find and really work it over."

Ally took the brochure from him, and her heart leaped when she saw an application for the Headliner Awards, a national journalism contest. She flipped through the pamphlet. Russ rubbed his hands together in anticipation. "I want our paper to have the recognition it deserves, and you might be the person to do it." He paused. "Deal?"

"Yes, deal." She clenched her fist and threw it up in the air. "Thank you."

"Cervantes, you nail an award, and you'll have a permanent spot on this paper—but watch those typos. Understand?"

"I do and I will."

Russ headed out of his office, followed by Ally. But before he could walk out the front door, Janice stopped him.

"Say, Russ, check out this editorial."

"Fine. Catch a burger with me, and we'll go over it."

"You should cut down on your red meat, Russ," she said as she threw on her coat. The two chattered as they left.

"So, you in trouble?" asked Clay as he looked up from his computer and eyed Ally. He never tuned into office politics, so it surprised her when he added, "He can be rough on the new guys."

She smiled at the gangly kid with a three-day beard growth and large ears that stuck out like Mr. Potato Head's. He wanted to clue her in, and she appreciated that gesture. "I'm not fired, can't get rid of me that easily."

He gave her a nod. "Good. You passed the three-month test. Few do."

❧

The next morning, Janice swooped by Ally's desk intent on delivering a message. She pursed her lips together. "Wanted to let you know, dearie, I always park in the spot right in front of the door. I work late, and I need that space so I don't slip on the ice in the parking lot after dark. Not to worry, no one told you." She crossed her arms and walked to her desk. Her skirt swayed in time to her clickety-clack high heels, a contrast to the other employees' rubber-soled shoes. Ally wondered if the woman still thought she worked in downtown London in the fashion district.

Sipping his cup of coffee, Clay looked up. "Hey, Janice, give her a break." When Janice sat down at her desk, ignoring the comment, he shook his head.

Ally hit Send right as her phone rang. "*Surrender Sentinel,* Ally speaking."

"I'm calling about that new teacher," said the caller.

"I'm sorry, sir, could you be more specific?"

"All I gots to say is that you reporters better earn your wage. I suggest you pay attention to that Spanish guitar player trying to pass for the high school band director. And another thing, the city doesn't hardly snowplow my road but once a month. I'm sick of being stuck inside or—"

"If you wouldn't mind giving me your name and phone number, I'm sure we can—"

Click. Guess he only wanted to vent. Obnoxious phone calls weren't what she had in mind when she took this job, but the paper sure had its share of them. Anyway, shouldn't Janice be taking them? *I have more important things to do than listen to customer gripes. I'd like to rake up some real graft and corruption in the community, or even better, write an inspiring story on someone helping his fellow man.*

The answer came a few minutes later when she talked to a mother whose sixteen-year-old son had been diagnosed with brain cancer. The family had asked the paper to write a piece about a silent auction to raise funds for medical expenses. She was calling to thank the paper for the article. When Ally hung up, she blinked back tears.

"That must have been quite a conversation. Some bad news?"

Ally glanced up from her laptop to see Janice. "Do you remember Julie Tenny, the woman whose son had brain cancer?"

"Yes."

"Well, they raised thirteen thousand dollars on the silent auction last month. Unfortunately, he died a week ago."

"Sorry. You did a suitable job on that piece," said Janice.

"Uh ... thanks." Wow, did Janice give her a compliment?

"I had to do a lot of editing on that piece, of course. Watch those last names. People are irritated when you misspell their name."

"Isn't that why you're here?"

Janice threw back her head and let out a strange strangled sort of laugh before narrowing her eyes into catlike slits. "You're the newest hire, and you want to keep your job, right?" Ally said nothing as the clickety-clack head walked back to her desk.

Ally told herself to ignore Janice's bossiness. Instead, she returned to her typing and clicked open a new Word document. The update on the auction article would be a joy to write. Working for a small-town paper gave her a front-row seat to the community's grief. No major heartache or success went unnoticed or unreported. Compared to Julie Tenny's situation, Ally had no problems.

She typed a few sentences before the front door flung open. Russ burst into the office, his long black trench coat trailing behind his solid frame, carrying a cardboard tray of coffee cups and a takeout container. "Meeting in the kitchen in five minutes." The staff stood and filed into the narrow kitchen.

Russ presided at the rectangular Formica table. The yellow-flecked top had seen its share of reporters gulping paper-bag lunches before heading out on a story. Now it held a plate of fresh Danish. Russ kept his employees well fed.

"Looks like we're running short on ad revenue this month. According to our occasional stringer who covers that part of town, Milton's Used Autos pulled their ad. And let me tell you, their weekly ad has been a staple for us. The owner is mad about the editorial we ran on scams at used car lots. Folks, you know we depend on their ads, especially now that it's three weeks 'til Christmas."

"So what's your plan?" said Ally.

"Don't tell me we need to hit the streets again, hunting down ads," said Clay. "We're as overworked as a lone snowplow in a January blizzard. Anyhow, I'm fixing to head south in an hour to see my girlfriend."

Janice mimicked his drawl. "Why, Clay, I didn't know you had a sweetheart hidden away. I think you're fooling us. You must show us a picture." The part in his hair turned as red as the Santa figurine sitting on the counter.

Russ rapped on the table. "People, I'm serious. I might have to cut salaries if we don't bring in more ad revenue." He'd transferred coffee from a takeout cup to his favorite mug, decorated with a picture of an old-fashioned newsboy waving a paper that said, "Get it while it's hot." According to Janice, Russ never finished more than half a cup of coffee before the phone interrupted him. Usually an irate reader had called or dropped in to debate an editorial, and it always happened on deadline day. "Monthly website stats are also in. Our sports coverage is the most read online—if you don't count The Complaint Department column." His eyes zoomed in on Ally, and her throat went dry. "Which reminds me—you screwed up the numbers on the estimated cost of the new wing being added onto the hospital. Each time you mess up, you make us look bad, Cervantes."

Ally picked at her thumb's cuticle. She didn't want to glance up, knowing several pairs of eyes would be staring at her. "I'm sorry."

"Hope you're also planning on interviewing the exchange teacher from Spain for an update on the music center plans. He called to confirm your appointment tomorrow," Russ said.

"Like he needs more publicity," murmured Janice.

"What did you say?" Russ flashed her a mischievous grin.

"Nothing," said Janice. "Just that he's charming and adds a touch of culture to our community."

Ally smiled. "Sounds like he's charmed you."

"Now girls," said Russ. "No time for gossip. We have a paper to get out."

"Always my chief concern," said Janice.

CHAPTER TWELVE

"Crackleberry Cake. Now that could be my signature," Ally announced as she flipped through a glossy-paged cookbook. Will grunted as he pored over the bills at his desk. "Really, Camp. A catering business wouldn't take much time. I even have my business cards." She studied his face. Black circles like half-moons hung below his cheekbones as he took off his reading glasses and rubbed his eyes. He had spent the last few hours juggling the budget to make it come out in the black. If she could bring in some extra money, it might relieve some of his burden.

"The economy is killing us. Early registrations are down thirty percent from last year." He ran his hand through his hair. "What did you say?"

"I'm telling you the cake business could cover some of the wedding expenses."

He looked up with a blank stare. "Did you say cake business?"

"You remember, I already have the cards."

"Like you have any free time. We hardly see each other as it is."

She drew her face closer to him and planted a kiss on his lips. "Come on, I promise it wouldn't be an enormous time commitment. And I already have a few customers."

"You're crazy."

"That's why you love me. I make life exciting."

"I don't need more excitement." He groaned as she left for the kitchen. She returned with a tray of three steaming mugs of coffee, a pitcher of cream, a sugar bowl, and a few slices of blueberry bread.

"What's this?" Will asked as he clicked off his computer and eyed her tray. "Company?"

"I told you. Jorge, the exchange teacher, is dropping off flyers for his guitar lessons. Russ said he could leave a pile at the office. I told him I'd be here Saturday morning and that he could bring them by and see the camp."

As if on cue, Jorge showed up in the doorway. "Thanks for meeting me here," said Ally.

"No problem. Here's my new ad. My English not very perfect." He handed a manila envelope to Ally, then turned to Will.

"Oh, excuse me. Jorge Esperanza, this is my fiancé, Will Grainger." Will and Jorge shook hands.

"So tell me more about this camp," said Jorge. "And yes, cream and sugar." He pointed to the tray.

As Ally distributed the mugs, Will talked about the summer programs and the camp's faith-based philosophy. Jorge probed for details about the programs, especially music.

"I'm afraid we have little in the way of music offerings," Will admitted. "Although a group of the older campers did jam together after campfires. I'd love to put together a worship band. All kinds of instruments, drums, guitars, mandolins, and even a flute or two. Why don't you stop by and visit this summer?"

"It would be wonderful, a privilege. I also help you with curriculum or shows for the camp?"

"Fantastic!" Ally said. "Music reaches so many kids."

"*Dios mio*, yes." Jorge threw up his hands in exclamation. "So many students—when they've learned to play an instrument and find a group where they belong, they—how you say?—'come alive.' They have a skill that is their own."

"Kylie seems to be enjoying the flute at school this year," said Ally.

"I like your thinking, Esperanza. Kids need to be a part of a vision larger than themselves," said Will. "Our board of directors has started a project to use the property next to the camp to grow wild rice. It's co-sponsored by the Native American Dad's Club. Don, one of my staff members, is heading it up. He has a vision to create a program for some of the at-risk kids in the community. He passed a map of the camp over to Jorge and pointed to the land he'd set aside for growing wild rice.

"Yes, I've heard about it. Don stopped by school to pick up a trumpet his son was borrowing, and he told me about the program. Very excellent idea." Jorge studied the map as he stirred a third teaspoon of sugar into his mug. Ally noticed his long, thin fingers, definitely those of a guitarist. He turned to Ally. "Say, my friend, I need a special cake for my landlord. His birthday is in a week, and I want to have a celebration for him and other neighbors. I want a cake that will be delicious. He has been very good to me."

"Crackleberry?" Ally said and looked at Will out of the corner of her eye. He was mock banging his head on his desk.

"What is this Crackleberry?"

"Sponge cake with caramel frosting between layers, iced with whipped cream, and covered with bits of butter brickle candy," Ally said. "I found this new recipe and was dying to test it out." She looked sideways at Will.

"What the heck. Go for it."

"If you, Miss Ally, say it is good, I believe. Please make enough for twenty-two people, and I invite you and Will."

"It's a deal. Does $35.00 work?"

Jorge pulled his wool fisherman's hat over his head. "Yes. You know I love Lake Surrender people. And if I didn't have *mi mama,* who is a widow back in my country, I might even stay."

"Even if you leave here, your heart will remain. The town grows on you," said Ally.

The door swung shut, and Ally turned to Will. "It's only one cake."

"One cake, two cakes, pretty soon a bakery."

"I won't overdo." She looked up at the wall clock and gasped. "Oops. I completely lost track of the time. I have an interview at the new deli … I promise it won't take long." His look told her he didn't believe her. "Really, I'll be back in two hours. Then we can catch a late lunch. Aunt Nettie said she'd babysit for me."

They both looked up when someone knocked on the door. Jorge popped his head through the opening. "Hey Ally, I meant to ask you if your aunt had heard anything more about the contest?"

"What contest?"

"The design contest—Janice told me when we had coffee last week. May the best *artista* win."

What was she doing, entering that contest? I had a hunch she was going to enter it. And why does Janice have to horn in on everything, just like the art grant she wanted to win. Did the woman have no shame?

✌

Ally waltzed into the camp office a few hours later. "Check out what I bought at Sandy's Deli." She unwrapped two large sandwiches stuffed full of warm pastrami and melted provolone cheese and two paper cups of pop and placed them in front of him. "Peace offering?" She kissed him on the cheek but noticed his mood was even more somber than when she'd left. He must be uber-mad at her.

"Thanks." He picked up the sandwich and took a bite, swallowing slowly. His mind seemed distant.

"Say, can you believe Janice decided she'd enter the contest?" Ally said. "You know, the contest to design a logo for that Maplewood business."

"It's a free country."

"I don't think she was aware of it until my aunt stopped by the office."

"Don't get involved." He put the paper cup up to his lips and sipped. They sat in silence for a few minutes, the furnace rumbling throughout the building. Ally chewed on her bottom lip. Something was eating him, but why wasn't he telling her? "So, spill. What's going on? It's more than the fact that I had to leave."

Will wrapped up the rest of his sandwich and put it back in the sack before pitching his empty cup into the trashcan. Then he picked up a pen and scribbled on a pad on his desk.

"Please tell me."

"Don called. Seems one of his kids saw Kylie behind Game World with Emerald Goodman."

"And?"

"Looked like they had purchased a bag of weed."

Ally tried to swallow but couldn't. She had talked to her daughter so many times about drugs. Must be someone else. "Kylie wouldn't be involved with that."

"Al, many teens experiment with drugs."

"But not Kylie. She loves cross-country, and she's always eating healthy."

Will stood, walked over to her chair, and took her hands in his. "Al, don't be naïve. Don wouldn't have called me if he wasn't worried. He cares about Kylie too."

Ally stood and jerked her hands away. "Whatever happened to thinking the best of a person? You sure didn't have a problem believing this could be true." Her face grew warm, and her words shot out like a sputtering geyser. "I suppose you think I'm a terrible mother."

Will raked his hand through his hair. "I never said that."

She took a deep breath. "Sorry. Maybe I've been gone too much. It's not only the weed. She's failing English too.

"You have to get to the bottom of this. Trust me. But you have my help and, better still, God's help."

❧

Early evening she drove back home, determined to talk to Kylie. "Where's my daughter?" she asked her aunt. "I need to talk to her."

"Oh, didn't she tell you? She had an extra band rehearsal, a fundraising meeting for new band uniforms, and then the annual party at school. I just dropped her off. I said I'd pick her up at ten."

"Really? Guess I missed the memo. I'll pick her up but first need a nap." Ally kissed Benjie, who was busy with his rock collection, and headed upstairs to crash. When she woke up, she looked at her phone and it read 9:46. She grabbed her purse and flew downstairs and into the car.

Kylie was waiting in front of the school. "Hey, over here," Ally waved.

She had a long talk with Kylie on the way home, and Kylie denied any involvement with the weed incident. "You're telling me the truth?"

"Yes."

"Well, what about your missing English assignments?"

"Call my teacher. I gave them to her on Friday. Or don't you believe me?"

"I'm starting not to."

❧

Monday morning, Ally passed Russ's office. His door was open, and his shoes pounded the floor in panic mode. He had that pinched look—like an invisible wrench had gripped his face and was trying to tighten it. She'd often seen that expression when things weren't going well and the paper's deadline loomed a few hours away.

"In my office, please." He gestured toward his desk.

Ally dropped her purse and lunch onto her desktop and scurried into his office. Russ closed the door, and her heart dropped. A closed door signaled trouble. What had she done?

"Stuart Goodman called. He said he had one of the student photographers take a picture for the Teacher of the Month feature, and you were a no-show this morning." His eyes crunched down on her. She squeezed her hands till her knuckles turned white. How could she have forgotten that appointment? Had she had written it down or put it in her phone's calendar?

"I don't know what to say except I'm sorry."

"Sorry doesn't work. If there's one thing I count on from you reporters, it's reliability." He slammed a manila file he was holding onto his desktop. "Get your act together, Cervantes. What's going on? If you have problems at home, don't bring them to work."

"I'll be more conscientious."

Russ perched on the edge of his desk. His two days' worth of beard gave him a haggard look. Must be the stress of deadlines and ad sales—especially a week before Christmas. "You bet you will. I'm putting you on probation. If I don't see some changes, you're out the door."

Ally left his office and raced to the bathroom. She choked back the tears until she was inside and had locked the door. Then the flood came. She couldn't lose this job, and she didn't dare cry in front of anyone. So unprofessional. One of her high school teachers had always quoted a line from his favorite movie, "There's no crying in baseball." Except he changed it to journalism. After five minutes, she dried her eyes with a paper towel and studied her face in the mirror. Dang, she wasn't a dainty crier. Her puffy eyes, smeared mascara, and red nose stared back at her. She looked like a woman who'd been on a three-day drinking binge.

As she examined her blotchy face, she gave herself a pep talk. "You can do this, Ally. You're smart and capable." She sighed. "You have to." But a voice inside her head whispered, "You can't do this on your own." Oh, that thought stung. But she *was* in over her head. She closed her eyes. "Please, Lord, I need your help. I can't lose this job. Too much is riding on it."

She opened her eyes and wiped her raccoon mascara circles. Then she marched to her desk to figure out a good subject for the Headliner article, determined to win the contest and prove herself to Russ.

৵

After work, Ally headed over to camp to meet Will. She followed the footsteps he'd made in the snow. They led to a picnic shelter behind the camp's dining room, where twin white pine trees hid the table there. Campers had etched connections to each other on the table with a carving knife to immortalize their summer romance. Kylie once counted twenty years of campers' love.

A figure in a dark green parka slumped over the table. On time as usual, Will waited, tracing circles with a stick on the snow-covered table.

When he heard her footsteps, he scooped up a handful of soggy leaves off the ground and stuffed them down her neck.

"I'm not in the mood for games," Ally picked the wet mass out of her coat. "Yuck."

"You're sure grouchy."

"Russ put me on probation."

Will's jaw dropped. "Oh, babe, nooo way. You're a brilliant writer."

"And you're not prejudiced?"

He flung his arm around her shoulder and squeezed it. The warmth of his body comforted her. "Well, he's nuts."

Ally bit her lip. She would not cry. "I doubt I'll be canned, but he hurt my feelings. Anyway, I don't want to talk about it right now. Cheer me up."

"Did you say 'throw me up'?" He grasped her by the waist and lifted her several feet off the ground. "Tell me I'm the best-looking man in Michigan, or I'll plant that pretty face of yours in that leaf pile over there." Will headed toward the mound.

Ally screamed, and he twirled her around before dumping her in the heap.

"Why, you—"

But he took off running.

"You're paying for this!" She picked herself up but had no traction on the icy ground. Will had a ten-foot head start, but she picked up speed and caught the edge of his muffler and held on tight. Will stopped short, and her body slammed into his.

"Ouch!"

One bulky arm reached over and pulled her closer. "Hey, California girl, you need to learn how to navigate our icy terrain."

"Didn't do so bad last winter."

"Warmest winter in twenty years. That didn't count."

"Are you calling me a weather wimp?" Ally made a face at him."

"Yep."

She studied his face. His eyes, the color of polished brown agate, were set in a squared face. It still amazed her he'd become more than her boss. Two summers ago, out of desperation, she'd taken a camp cook job she wasn't qualified for. But between Will's kindness and camp life, God had healed her soul.

"What's going on in that overworked mind of yours?"

"I was wondering how we ever ended up together."

"God has a sense of humor, sending a West Coast city girl to the wilds of northern Michigan to work in a camp." He wiped a snowflake off of her forehead.

"And to give your life more culture and sophistication," said Ally, raising her pinkie.

"How's this for culture?" Will leaned into her, and her mouth met his. Oh, how he could kiss. The sweetness took her breath away. She craved more and more.

He pulled back for a moment; her eyes locked together with his. "I love this face," he said as he studied her every feature, a nostalgic look in his eye. "We survived a lot that summer. A revengeful attack of an ex-employee, an arson incident, and then taking care of Bryan."

"I'd rather go through those trials with you than sail along trouble-free with someone else. I'm a lucky woman. No, a blessed one. I love you so much." She reached up and rumpled up his hair.

"You're my Always Girl." He pressed his lips to hers again, and heat spread to her frigid cheeks as his embrace warmed her. Her personal campfire in the middle of winter. "Can't wait until we share the same name," said Will. "And bed."

"Me too. So hard to wait. I need you."

"I know." His mouth twisted into a wicked grin.

Ally landed a mischievous hit on his arm. "You're sort of needy too. You couldn't survive without my cooking."

Will chuckled. "Ha! You've come a long way, girl, on that one." His expression turned serious again. "It's too cold here. Let's head inside the lodge. I need to talk to you." His playful smile dropped, and he put his hand on the small of her back and steered her toward the lodge.

Will threw open the door to his office and flipped on the overhead light, the fluorescent bulb humming. Piles of leadership manuals filled one corner of the room, with more stacks sitting on the floor. On his desk, two Bible commentaries, three boxes of craft kits, a plastic Ziploc bag of broken candles, and a Bible had found a permanent residence.

She leaned over and picked up a manual. "Let me organize your office."

He shook his head. "Not now." His mood had cooled considerably. He ran a hand through thick hair that begged for a haircut he often neglected, then pulled up a chair for her. "What's going on with Kylie?"

"What do you mean what's going on? She's a normal thirteen-year-old girl." Ally pulled off her stocking cap and added it to the heap of papers on his desk.

Will picked up a pen, doodling on a yellow legal pad. He paused, planning his words carefully. She knew that look. "Did you talk to Kylie about us?"

Ally put her hands on her hips, trying not to have her words bristle. *Lord, help me not lose it.* "Sort of. She has a report due, so I plan on spending more time with her this weekend. We'll talk more then."

Will stood and put a hand in his pockets, the clinking of loose change irritating her. He paced behind his desk.

"What's going on?" Ally tried to keep the panic out of her voice, but it still betrayed her.

"Running a camp, you … hear things."

"Just say it."

"Someone saw Kylie and another couple of girls riding around with two high school guys."

"Probably her friend Emerald. Her cousin gave the girls a ride home from school the other day."

"You sure?"

"Why are you so suspicious?" Ugh. Her voice ratcheted up to a screech, reminding her of her peevish old-maid high school English teacher, Miss Borden, who squawked at the class when they didn't understand a finer point of grammar. *Calm down.* She took a breath.

"We need to face family problems head on."

"I'm trying. Jeez, Camp." Was he right? She couldn't imagine Kylie hanging out with high school guys. "I'll talk to her. I'm sure she's not doing anything wrong."

She kissed him on the cheek and left. She had her work cut out for her at home, but she would wait for the right time.

CHAPTER THIRTEEN

Tuesday morning, four staff members gathered around the oval table in the conference room right off of Russ's office. In the middle of the table stood a tiny Christmas tree lit with a string of battery lights, but it didn't elicit much holiday cheer for Ally, Clay, and Janice, or the two ad saleswomen who showed up once a month. Only the sound of the water sputtering through the coffee maker broke the heavy silence.

"Because the pre-Christmas edition goes out soon, we're ordering in—Liu Ling's takeout—so we can work through lunch hour." He waved toward the kitchen with a grin. "And if anyone finds a positive report in their fortune cookie, I'm laying claim to it. We'll take any good news."

His jolly eyes belied the fact that the paper now operated on a slim profit margin. She'd caught enough scraps of a phone conversation coming from his office to know he had been talking to the bank about another loan. He looked over at the coffee maker. "Coffee's done, so grab a cup, and let's start." He flipped over a page in his yellow legal pad.

"We need to plan out the big holiday issue. Any suggestions to jazz it up? We're looking at a stand-alone photo for the front page, featuring Boy Scout Pack 192's holiday food drive with Miss Winter Snow Queen standing behind the cans of food."

"Isn't that somewhat cheesy?" Ally asked as she craned her neck to view the photo on his laptop. She looked around the table, and the expressions on the other staff's faces told her she'd said too much. *Why can't I keep my big mouth shut?*

"This is what community journalism is all about," said Russ. "Christa Conner lives one town over, and Wolverine Hill is proud of her winning the title. Hometown heroes belong on the front page."

Humiliation heated her face. Would she ever adjust to the cultural differences between the fast-paced Bay Area and sleepy Lake Surrender?

Janice's neckline had slid dangerously low over her ample chest, causing Ally to wonder who her lunch date was today. Janice leaned across the table and patted her hand. "We're not quite Mayberry, dearie." Ally wanted to reach over and rip off one of her false eyelashes.

Ally closed her eyes. *I need patience, God.* "Um, I didn't mean—"

"No offense taken," Russ said. "Any other suggestions?"

"The high school's winter one-on-one basketball tournament takes place the week before Christmas. I'm planning on behind-the-scenes action pics, kind of photo journal story. Probably a half page," Clay said.

"Take several close-ups of the athletes, especially the kid who won a full ride to Michigan." Russ clapped Clay on the shoulder. "And make sure you shoot a few images of the pep band led by that Spanish teacher in charge of the music program this year."

Janice said. "He's an amazing flamenco guitarist. Why—"

"Not my style." Russ ripped a page off his pad. "Ally, here's a good lead for you. Cover this human-interest story for the Faith section. Amazing story on how a local teacher gave up her baby decades ago and found out years later that he was in her kindergarten class. Turns out she was his favorite teacher. Since you worked at Camp Lake Surrender last year, I figured you'd appreciate its religious overtones—she prayed for years to find him."

Oh yes. A rush of adrenaline shot through Ally. "I'd love to highlight this woman's faith. I'd be a mess without my faith."

Clay said, "No comment."

Ally swatted him on the arm with her notepad. "Ha ha."

"Fine. Make sure you tell her story. No preaching," said Russ.

"I will tell her story honestly." A *bing* from her phone interrupted her. Will.

"That's the signal we're through. I like short meetings. Now let's hit it." Russ clapped his hands together.

Ally headed out to the parking lot and crawled into her freezing car. She shivered as she pulled her phone out of her coat pocket and bent down to read Will's words.

"Can never take Kylie's dad's place. You know that. But I'll try my best to help you raise her. That you can count on."

All the stress of the last couple of days evaporated faster than the snow melting off a Michigan car window in April. Her fingers flew across the keyboard. "I don't deserve you."

"Yep."

His teasing always made her smile.

"Lunch tomorrow?" she texted back.

"Meet ya at your office, 12:30."

❧

Will parked in front of the *Sentinel's* office, opened Ally's door on the passenger side of his Suburban, and took her hand to help her out of the cab. Back from lunch at Arby's, she faced an afternoon of editing two articles and conducting a phone interview with the mayor. Instead, she lingered outside the vehicle, draped her arms around Will's canvas Carhartt coat, and leaned her head against his chest, his body warm and secure against the icy wind. With his gloved hand, he brushed the snowflakes off the top of her hair.

"Let's not fight," he said. "We'll figure it out, the parenting thing."

"I'm sorry I overreacted."

Will pressed his lips to hers, and she marveled what a perfect fit they made. His grip around her grew tighter and tighter. Darn, the last thing she wanted to do was go back to work.

"I want you so much," he murmured.

"May seems far away."

"Don't look, but Russ is flashing the outside porch light at us."

"What!" She jerked her head toward the office's door. Russ wasn't there, but Clay stood on the doorstop waving frantically.

"Sorry. It's the mayor on the phone, and he said he has a max of ten minutes to talk."

Ally untangled her arms from Will's. "Benjie misses you. Stop by tonight?"

He nodded. "Tell him it's dominoes night."

❧

"Let's finish up our route," Ally said to Kylie as they jogged side by side around the indoor track at Beautiful Bodies Gym. She scrunched up her nose to avoid the smell of rubber coming from the track and sweat coming from high school jocks passing her. The overheated gym amplified the already strong odors.

"Beating you, Mom," said Kylie, calling back over her shoulder as she pushed ahead.

Ally cupped her hands together and shouted, "You'll definitely make the cross-country team this spring." She jogged around the track two more times and then collapsed on a nearby bench in the lobby, panting heavily as she joined her daughter. She didn't realize how out of shape she was. *I need to run more.* Finally catching her breath, Ally turned to her. "Hey, let me ask you something."

"Do I like the paint color of my soon-to-be bedroom at Will's?"

106

"Be serious. Word has it you've been riding in a car with a high school boy."

"So?"

"What do you mean, so? Why is a high school junior taking you and a bunch of other eighth-graders to hang out at the donut shop?"

"It's Em's cousin and he took us once. And, yeah, he hung with us. No big deal."

"Yes, big deal. Just because I'm at work doesn't mean you have free rein to do whatever you want."

Kylie took the towel around her neck and wiped off her forehead before stuffing it back in her gym bag. "We stopped for donut holes. He takes us home after school." She zipped up her bag. "Is that a crime?"

"From now on you take the bus home."

"No way."

"Yes way. And while we're talking, have you've been hanging out with kids doing weed?"

"You already asked me that."

"Are you telling me the truth?"

"Do you think I'm that dumb?"

"I don't know, you've been acting pretty apathetic this year, and someone told Will they saw you."

"Mom! I can't believe you're taking Will's side. He always thinks the worst of me."

"He doesn't."

"He hates me."

"End of discussion. You will take the bus home."

"Nobody takes the bus."

Ally's phone dinged. A text from Russ. He wanted her to cover an emergency town board meeting this evening. Why, of all nights, when she had planned a relaxing evening with Will?

She turned to her scowling daughter. "So that means you'll have the whole bus to yourself after school." Ally slung her gym bag over her shoulder and fished for her car keys in her jacket. "I hope I've made myself clear."

"Crystal clear," said Kylie and chucked an empty water bottle at the lobby wall, barely missing a middle-aged woman walking by. "Oops, sorry," Kylie said.

"You are in such trouble," said Ally.

The woman passed them, shooting Ally a dirty glance that said, "Take control of your teenager, Mom." Then she stopped, pivoted, and walked over to the bench. She studied Ally's face for a minute. "You look familiar. Didn't you work at Camp Lake Surrender last summer?"

The blood rushed to Ally's cheeks, and she wanted to find a hole and crawl into it.

CHAPTER FOURTEEN

"Whoop, whoop. Get ready, Benjie! Looks like it's boys' night, and we have the entire family room to ourselves!"

They worked side by side for an hour setting up the path. There must have been five hundred dominoes. Then Will snatched Benjie's right hand and raised it high. "Ready?"

"I first."

With a light touch, Benjie flicked the beginning domino. The first ones fell. They started from the leg of the couch in the family room, then swirled back and forth in an *S* shape as the black tiles moved out of the family room and into the back hall that led to the garage.

Will looked at his stopwatch. "Seventy-two seconds! That's a record."

He lifted Benjie up and spun him around. Benjie screamed in glee. When Will put him down, he ran around in a circle in front of the television. "Again, again, again, again."

After two more rounds, Will announced it was bedtime.

"More."

"No, not tonight. Bedtime." Will put a firm hand on Benjie's shoulder as the child's foot stomped. "Benjie, I want to see your eyes."

Instead, the boy crashed his body onto the carpet and threw a handful of dominoes against the wall to the left of the fireplace. *Clink, clink, clink.* Each one left an indentation, creating a pattern of black marks. Darn him. Will saw a painting job in his future.

"Your mom and aunt aren't going to be happy."

The dominoes flew faster and harder, one barely missing a photo of Aunt Nettie and her husband on the table next to the sofa.

"That's it for now." Will seized the boy around his waist—arms and legs flying in a full-blown tantrum—and bounded upstairs to Benjie's room, two steps at a time. He deposited him on the rug in front of the bed. "When you act like a big boy, you can come out and pick up the dominoes with me."

Will snapped the door closed and held it shut, anticipating a protest. He felt the force of what seemed like two mules straining against him on the other side. Where did this kid get his strength? For several minutes, the door inched open and slammed shut in a power struggle. He was sure the doorknob would break. Finally, Benjie let go of the door handle, and it stayed shut. Will waited a minute before heading downstairs.

The front door swung open, and Ally swooped in. "How did it go?"

"Not so good. Benjie's in his bedroom, and there's a domino mess he needs to clean up." Will rose to brush his lips against her cheek. "Up for pie at Cherry Country Coffee when Nettie gets back?"

Ally plunked down on the sofa and flipped open her laptop. "Sorry, babe, I have to submit this article tonight, and I haven't even started. Thanks for watching Benjie."

"Sure." He rummaged in his pocket for his car keys. "Let me know if you ever have free time." He loved being with Benjie, but lately he felt more like a glorified babysitter.

"I promise I can hang with you tomorrow night."

He reached for the doorknob, its smooth steel cold in his palm. "Your schedule, your life."

"I'm sorry. I know I keep saying that, but, really, things will start to settle down." He saw that tiny frown line between her eyes he used to find endearing. Now that frown irritated him.

He kissed her on the cheek and closed the front door behind him, the arctic air blasting him in the face.

A mile before the turnoff for his house, his phone rang.

"Sarah! Didn't expect to hear from you."

"I ... I ... I ..."

"What's wrong?"

"It's Dad." A loud wail followed. "He's had a heart attack. Oh, Will, please pray, please pray." After a bit of static, she said, "Gotta go, it's Mom."

❧

"It's a bit tight." Sharon, the owner of Bridal Gowns and More in Traverse City—the closest sizable town to Lake Surrender—assessed Ally in an ivory strapless dress. "I can let it out a half an inch on either side. You know ... room for holiday weight gain." She looked up and saw a woman waiting at the counter. "Oh, excuse me, I have another customer. I'll be right back." She headed to the front of the store.

Ally spun around and looked at Kylie. "What do you think?"

"It's pretty, but sort of weird."

"Weird? What's weird about it?" Ally stepped down from the platform that faced a three-sided mirror and stared at her daughter. *Please, Lord, not another argument.*

"Seeing my mom in a wedding dress."

"Rather normal when one gets married." Sharon laughed as she walked back to the dressing room.

Ally placed her hands on her hips and lowered her head, her eyes fixed on her daughter. "What's looping around in that mind of yours?" She picked up the long, lace-covered train and walked to where Kylie sat watching Benjie color an entire fifteen-page coloring book in orange crayon. When Benjie chose a color, no one could change his mind. This week he insisted on orange.

"I guess that means when you and Will get married for real, and … you know, I mean, uh, we'll live with him in the stone house. And we won't see Aunt Nettie much."

"So …"

"So that means I got to take that crappy bus and live next to the creepy guy who has a locker next to me and always wipes his nose on his sleeve, and …"

"And?"

She paused and looked down at the floor. "And Will and you will sleep in the same bed."

Ally puffed out her cheeks and let out a burst of air before sitting down on the customer bench. "Is *that* what's bugging you?"

Her eyes brimmed as tears poured down her daughter's cheeks. Ally patted the bench. "Come sit here, sweetie." Reluctantly, face averted, she plunked down next to her mother.

"I thought you liked Will."

"I do, but he's so strict. Dad wasn't like him."

"So this is more about Dad." Ally closed her eyes, agonizing over how to answer, aware Sharon's assistant caught their entire conversation as she walked past them to hang up another dress. *Why do we have to have this discussion in the middle of a store?* She searched for words to comfort her daughter. In a hushed tone she said, "Your father loved you, and he will always be your father. I was proud of how you helped take care of him at the end."

"You didn't want him to come stay with us when he first told us he was sick. You probably hoped he'd die alone in California."

If Kylie had balled up her fist, pulled back her arm, and slugged her in the stomach, the pain wouldn't have hurt as much as those words. She sucked in air and closed her eyes to control her voice. What was that thing everyone was saying now—"Keep calm and carry on"? Are they kidding, calm with a teenager? *I don't know if I'm more hurt or angry.*

"But he didn't." She grabbed her daughter's hand.

Kylie yanked it away. "And now Will and you will always be together, and you won't ever have any time for me and Benjie, because—"

"I will always have time for you, sweetie, but ..." Ally leaned over and whispered, "Can we talk about this at home?"

"You'll probably forget. Sometimes I wish that instead of Dad dying ..."

"That's it," she told her daughter. She sped back to the dressing room, frantically tugging at the dress's zipper. Her body shook with anger as she pulled on her jeans and threw on her turtleneck sweater. She knew Kylie was only a teenager, but her comments pierced Ally's heart. She and Kylie seemed a million miles apart. *What happened to my daughter?*

❧

Ally pushed her cart down the baking aisle at Oleson's Farm Fresh Market. Where was the baking powder? Now that payday had finally come, she needed staples to fulfill her holiday visions of cookie-making. She had planned for her and Kylie to spend some mother-daughter time baking cookies together. Ever since their conversation at the bridal shop, she'd prayed even harder for her daughter and looked for ways they could connect. She studied the variety of chocolate chips, looking for the dark chocolate ones for her mother's English Toffee candy. Making the confectionery had become a Christmas tradition. As she tossed a package into her cart, she spied a familiar figure across the aisle, looking at tubes of cake-decorating icing. The clickety-clack of high heels confirmed the presence of her co-worker Janice.

"Funny running into you." When the woman glanced up, Ally waved.

"Early jump on Christmas?" Janice peered at Ally through her reader glasses.

"Yes, my daughter and I plan on having a baking marathon."

"I'm baking a lot too. Say, I read your article on Jorge Esperanza and the teacher exchange program."

"Hope you liked it."

"Adequate." She lowered her voice. "Just a warning about Esperanza. Watch out for these Spanish men."

"What?"

"You know, they think they invented romance and sex."

Seriously? "I doubt that, and, anyway, I'm happily in love. But Jorge's an affable guy."

"When you're older, you'll understand." Perfectly penciled eyebrows rose on her forehead. "Dearie, things aren't always what they seem on the surface. And while we're talking, keep your eye on that handsome man of yours. Other women notice him."

"Is that so?"

"You should know that. *Be observant.*" She emphasized the words as if Ally were incapable of understanding English.

"Whatever."

Ally chewed on her lower lip. Was Janice implying that Ally was naïve about people? Jorge was a nice man and nothing else.

Janice pushed her cart closer to Ally, studying her face. "You know, if you layer your hair a bit, it might frame your face nicely." She tugged on a strand of her own hair. "If I were younger, I'd grow mine."

"My hair's fine, thanks. But I wanted to talk to you about something." She pushed the cart closer to Janice. "I understand you entered the design contest."

"I can't imagine how that would be any of your business, but yes."

"I think you entered when you found out about it from my aunt the day she stopped in."

"And what if I did?"

"Winning this contest would mean a lot to her."

"It's a free country."

"Well, the owner, Jack, called my aunt the other day. He said she had entered a design similar to the one you had submitted, and you entered yours after she did."

Janice's eyes narrowed into catlike slits, her nostrils flaring. "You don't say."

Ally moved the cart even closer to the woman. "You know exactly what I'm implying."

Janice's steamy stare could have defrosted the entire frozen food section in the store. This woman was now officially her enemy.

Back home, she stopped her aunt in the hallway before she flew out the front door for a meeting at church.

"I just talked to Janice."

"Ally." Her aunt's tone told her she didn't appreciate her help.

"I let her know that Jack had contacted you and mentioned how similar both your designs were."

Her aunt's face showed no emotion.

"But I'm sure she copied yours."

"You don't know that. I appreciate your loyalty, but I'm a big girl and I can handle the situation. Let it go." She grabbed her purse and left.

CHAPTER FIFTEEN

The next day, Ally rushed into work with Benjie in tow. She explained as soon as she saw Russ.

"I'm sorry I had to bring Benjie this morning, but my aunt is displaying the old wood furniture she decorates today at The Painted House and couldn't babysit, and Benjie was off because the school had scheduled Teacher's Work Day, and ..."

"Not a problem. How 'bout you set him up in the conference room?" Russ tilted his head toward the meeting room to the left of the kitchen. "Benjie, so glad you could come help your mom with the paper."

"Hand out," Ally directed him to shake hands with Russ. "What are your words?" She watched her son—busy studying a pile of last week's editions stacked on the floor—slowly raise his head.

"Eyes," she reminded him.

Painfully, his gaze lifted to Russ. "Nice seeing you." He pried out each word slowly.

"You too, son." Russ handed Ally a sucker from a jar he always kept for visiting kids. Ally took off the wrapper before passing it to her son. "He'll be fine in the back room."

Janice swooshed by Ally's desk, reeking of the latest Dolce and Gabbana cologne. "Hello, little man, aren't you a cutie?"

The high pitch of her voice prompted Benjie to put his hands over his ears. *Don't, Benjie.*

"What's his problem?" Janice frowned at Ally.

"He occasionally reacts to certain sounds." *Or irritating voices.*

"Sounds? Like my talking?" Janice asked. "Honestly, I never."

"Janice, autistic children have sensory discrimination problems. Sounds sort of ..."

"Upset them? I'll try to keep a lid on it this morning." She shook her head and returned to her desk.

Ally turned her attention to Benjie. With his hands on his ears, he watched Janice as she pulled a bottle of red nail polish out of her top desk drawer. Ally had never seen any other woman fuss so much with her nails. Any chip or break, and Janice was filing and polishing, filing and polishing.

"Come with me." She led Benjie to the conference room and settled him in a chair at the round table. She rummaged around in his backpack and pulled out his favorite coloring book and a box of crayons. "Now stay here and play nicely. I'll be in the next room."

At her desk, Ally delved into her article about a birth mother and her son reuniting, after finding out she'd been his kindergarten teacher. She pictured readers wrapped up in the details of the serendipitous meeting. What a privilege to peek into other people's life stories and give them a voice to share with readers. She pounded her computer keys with passion, absorbed in the story. Then, feeling guilty, she checked on Benjie, who colored contentedly in the next room.

She looked up to see Russ standing in the middle of the office. He announced, "Pizza today for all you hard-working staffers. Or should I say, impromptu lunch meeting?"

She gasped. It was almost noon.

Ally checked again with Benjie, who was happy playing with his button collection and didn't want pizza. She drifted into the kitchen. Clay was out interviewing the middle school basketball coach, so that left Janice, Russ, and Ally to attend the meeting.

"How's the story working out?" Russ looked at Ally and swallowed a slice of pepperoni with green pepper. He followed it up with a napkin swipe to catch a greasy drip on his white shirt. The napkin smeared the spot even more, but Russ seemed oblivious to the stain.

"Great," she answered.

"Good." Russ gathered up the empty pizza boxes and took them to the trashcan behind the building. When he walked back into the office, he let out a shout. "Hey Cervantes, check this out."

Ally's motherly instincts kicked in faster than a waxed sled speeding down an icy hill in January. She rushed from the kitchen into the newsroom to find that her son had tipped the entire contents of a bottle of nail polish labeled Lethal Crimson onto Janice's desk. The bottle now lay horizontal, with the nail lacquer dripping onto the wooden floor. Worse still, Benjie was using the brush to slather it on his arms, jeans, tennis shoes, and what seemed to be an advertising contract on Janice's desk. It looked like he'd had a fight with a carving knife and the knife won.

Janice followed right behind Ally, recoiling when she saw the mess. "I can't believe this. Why would he meddle with my stuff? Have you not taught this child any manners?" Janice glared at Benjie, who turned in circles. The louder she yelled at Benjie, the faster he twirled, around and around at a dizzying pace, screaming, "Eech, eech!"

Ally took Benjie by the arm, pulled him to her, and threw both her arms around him, squeezing him tight to calm him down. She looked at Janice, whose mouth hung agape.

"This is a horrendous mess. You have no idea how to control your child, do you?"

Ally bit her tongue, knowing she'd never be able to explain Benjie to her co-worker. And why bother? He didn't act up because she didn't discipline him. Life was a lot more complicated with an autistic child than simple disobedience.

"I'm so sorry." She leaned over to Benjie and whispered in his ear that he needed to head to the kitchen. Thankfully, he did.

"So am I. I'll have to retype this entire contract and have it resigned. Don't know why you had to bring him."

"I didn't have anyone else to watch him."

"He's an awfully wonky kid to bring to work. If you ask me, he needs a good spanking." Janice pulled tissues from her desk drawer and tried to wipe up the mess, but all she did was smear the nail polish around, leaving a bright scarlet stain on her desktop. She looked at her coat and gasped. "Good Lord, he's ruined it."

"Oh, I'm so sorry, Janice. Here, the least I can do is take your coat to the cleaners." Ally released her hold on Benjie and picked up Janice's off-white wool coat, bright red spots all over the collar.

Janice took the arm of the coat and wrestled it away from her. "Children don't belong in our office. I'll get it cleaned myself, thank you."

"Ally, take the afternoon off. I'm sure you have plenty of Christmas shopping to do." Russ, standing behind Janice, flashed Ally a big wink. "Go. You've submitted all your pieces for the week."

⁊

Ally poured two cups of coffee, one for her and one for Will, and settled back into the shabby upholstered chair in her aunt's kitchen. She glanced at the black-cat wall clock hanging above the stove. Its pendulum tail swung back and forth. Five o'clock. J Bean's head moved in time with the cat's tail as he growled intermittently, ready to pounce.

Will slapped his leg. "Benjie did what to that old battleax?"

"Will." She tried to put on her sternest face.

"She is. The entire town knows it."

"I'd be mad, too, if I were her. It's the way she talked about Benjie that angered me."

"Who said something mean to Benjie? I'll tell them where to ..." Kylie threw open the door from the garage to the kitchen, ushering a pile of fluffy snow onto the beige tile floor. She dropped her backpack and threw her black parka on the kitchen table.

"You're late." Ally put her hands on her hips.

"You're never here to notice." Kylie helped herself to a bag of Doritos, then slammed the cabinet door shut.

"Please, don't start snacking. Dinner's close to being ready."

"You mean you didn't make Aunt Nettie cook tonight? Wow, that's amazing."

"What's amazing is your horrible attitude, young lady." Ally pointed to the backpack on the floor to remind Kylie to hang it up on the hallway hook. "And you're cooking dinner next week."

Will walked over to Kylie and put his hand on her shoulder. "Guess you had a terrible day."

"Every day in this dumb house is a terrible day." She pushed Will's hand off. "And don't think you can fix it, Will, by praying it all away."

Hitching the backpack strap onto her arm, Kylie slipped around Will and raced upstairs. The entire house thundered with her footsteps as she sped upstairs, and windows vibrated when she slammed her bedroom door.

Ally put her fingers to her lips. "Why don't you let me handle this?"

Will put both hands over his head and drew his hands down over his face, attempting to pull an answer from his brain. He turned to Ally. "You can't let her—"

"Let her what?"

"The way she talks to you."

"How do you expect me to fix it? Like magic? You think I don't correct her? That I don't try?" Ally jerked open the cutlery drawer and rattled the knives and forks. "I feel you're judging me."

"I'm not. But if you let me—"

She started to set the table but instead slammed all the silverware down in a pile.

"You're telling me you have the answer? You think it's easy to raise a teenager?" She glared at Will, whose bewildered expression showed her outburst shocked him. She went to the pantry, picked up a pile of paper napkins, and dumped them in the middle of the table. "You have them for two weeks at camp, and they are angels, but try living with a teenaged girl. It's a lot different."

Will picked up his coat and car keys before glancing over at her. "Sounds like you don't think I'll be much of a father to your kids."

Ally didn't move. *Come on, Ally, say anything. Don't let him leave.* But anger froze her mouth shut. She couldn't answer.

❧

Later that night after putting Benjie in bed, Ally tapped on Kylie's bedroom door. No answer. Well, she wasn't going to talk to her daughter through a locked door, and she didn't have the energy for another fight.

Discouraged, she headed downstairs for a dish of ice cream. Moose Tracks, rich with chocolate chunks and fudge ripple ribbon, would improve her mood. The calendar on the wall next to the refrigerator reminded her ten days remained 'til December twenty-fourth. What a mess she'd made with Will, and, worse still, at Christmas. She dipped into the carton and scooped up a larger serving than she'd intended.

But even the ripples of fudge swirling throughout the ice cream couldn't soothe Ally. "Why can't I communicate with my daughter? And why am I so hard on Will?" she asked J Bean, who snoozed underneath the kitchen table. "He'd be a

122

great dad. And he's different from Bryan. Well, can't figure it out tonight. Come to bed, J Bean." His feet pitter-pattered behind her. Upstairs, Ally threw herself down on her bed and wrapped herself in one of her aunt's quilts, a colorful tapestry of soft grays and blues. She picked up the framed picture of Will on her night table. Her aunt took it on the night they became engaged. She thought back to the effort he'd put into making the moment a surprise, even involving some downtown local merchants. The evening was magical. She studied Will's picture. Even in the photo, his eyes connected to her. She put the frame back on the table. An achy feeling tunneled through to her heart when she remembered the sound of Will throwing his truck into reverse tonight as he backed out of the driveway, the wheels crunching through the frozen snow.

On impulse, she called her sister, Georgia.

"I'm bummed, Sis."

"What's going on?"

"Will and I had a big fight."

"What happened?"

"He told me Kylie was too disrespectful, and I jumped all over him. I realize I've not been the mother I should with her but …"

"But you don't trust his instincts? Why not? He's worked with a lot of teens."

Ally fingered the dust on the top of her bureau and wrote the word *Will*. "It's more than that. I really yelled at him. Like a crazy woman. Georgia, sometimes I feel like I'm a rotten person and start to doubt my ability to love again."

"I'm listening."

"I suppose it goes back to Bryan and me. I still nurse scars from the divorce. The last date we had, he leaned over a plate of coconut prawns and muttered, 'You have gaps in your love for people. That's your fatal flaw.'" She cleared her throat. "Maybe I can't really love anyone."

"For crying out loud, of course you can love another guy. Bryan flung out that insult because that's the stuff people say when they divorce. They blame the other person."

"I know. I'm overreacting."

"You said you had some kind of spiritual epiphany, whatever that means, when you moved to Michigan. Isn't that helping you learn to love him?"

"You're right. I am a different person."

"Don't be so hard on yourself. Anyway, Will differs a lot from Bryan. From what you've told me, he cares about you, and I know he wants the best for Kylie. And the best for Kylie is for her to learn to respect her mother."

"That stings."

"Truth stings."

They talked a few more minutes, and then Ally hung up. She stuck her head under the bed.

"Think I'll make it, J Bean?"

The Jack Russell groaned.

"You're no help."

Ally pulled out her hair tie and picked up a hairbrush. As she brushed her hair, she thought about a song she had learned at camp last year. The song "His Eye Is on the Sparrow" haunted her all summer. She hummed the tune softly to herself. She needed to feel His eye on her right now. *This sparrow needs to know there is a plan I can trust.*

"Lord, are you listening? What am I doing wrong? Somehow I seem to mess things up all the time." She hugged the pillow and walked to the window. How quiet—how otherworldly—a winter night could be. She watched a few cars chug past the cottages, the engine noises muffled, as if swathed in white cotton, putting the whole world on mute.

She peeked out the window again, wanting her life soft and peaceful like the road below. Instead, she wondered if she was headed straight toward a blizzard.

CHAPTER SIXTEEN

When Will jingled his car keys, Kylie looked up, a cheese fry dangling from her mouth. Her face instantly hardened. "What are you doing here?"

"Your mom had to cover a school board meeting and asked me to pick you up at Burger Hut. Mind if I—?" He reached for a fry dripping in yellow sauce. Kylie snatched the carton away, her face turning into a tornadic scowl, lips down, eyes squinting. *Is this the sweet girl I knew at camp?*

She crossed her arms. "I'm not leaving. Mom said I could hang out till nine. Besides, I'm on Christmas break."

She turned to the group of her sketchy-looking friends. Derrick, who Will knew from around town, had the beginnings of a beard and sported a large sword tattoo on his arm. He sat next to two girls who, despite the weather, wore tight jeans that would make a streetwalker blush.

"I'm sorry, your mom instructed me to give you a ride home. Six inches of snow predicted."

"I don't believe you."

"The snow or what your mom said?"

"Both."

He pulled out his phone and showed her the text. Then he leaned over and whispered in her ear, "I don't want to make a scene. Please come."

"Way to ruin my social life." Tossing the rest of the fries in the trash, Kylie turned to look at her friends, who shot her knowing looks. With Will on her heels, she dashed out the glass front door.

He found Kylie waiting for him at his Suburban, hands on her hips, foot tapping. Her expression said, "Don't mess with me." He closed his eyes. *Lord, do I want to take on raising a teenaged girl who seems headed toward a minefield? I'm really tired of this.*

The atmosphere in the restaurant was toasty compared to the frosty silence in the Suburban. Kylie slammed her door as Will put the key in the ignition.

"You're not my father, so quit treating me like I'm your daughter. You don't have any right to spy on me."

"You needed a ride home, and I'm your driver. Complain all you want, but your curfew is nine. And for the record, I have better things to do than spy on a bunch of teenagers. I'm here because I care about you and your mom."

"Yeah, right."

"What do you mean, 'yeah, right'?"

"You know."

"Know what?"

"You don't care about Mom. I think you still like your old girlfriend, Sarah."

"What?"

"I think so. I saw you still call her."

"And how would you know that?"

"I checked your phone."

Will slammed his hands down on the steering wheel. "You don't have any right to snoop on my phone. And besides it was an innocent call. Oh, why am I telling you all this?"

Kylie crossed her arms and stared out the window as they passed barren woods with spindly trees. He shook his head. *I can't win.*

After he dropped off Kylie at Nettie's, he headed east on Highway 37 to cool off. Even with all the experience he'd had working with kids at camp, he didn't have the words. He couldn't reach this girl. Will exhaled a lengthy breath and focused on the scenery. The evening, achingly cold, shone with quiet beauty. The brightest pinpoint of light, Sirius, rose in a field of shimmering stars. He loved winter nights, when he could see the sky more clearly. Out loud, he offered a prayer. "Lord, You created Kylie, and You know best how to handle her. Please give me the wisdom of a father. I can't do this parenting thing without You." Will thought of his mother, who'd died several years ago at Christmas. She would have known what to say to Kylie.

Al's right—parenting's a lot different from running a camp where you see kids a few weeks a year. But I will be a father figure in Kylie's life, so I worry about how she will turn out. Why can't Al see that? Why can't Kylie see that what she thinks is meddling is really caring?

The questions tumbled around in his brain, but no answers came. The longer he thought about it, the more he wondered why he wanted to take on the challenge. Life was so much simpler as a bachelor. He craved peace, but the last few months had been a continual upheaval of emotions, and he was tired of the turmoil.

❧

Kylie, stretched out on the family room couch with the remote in hand, flipped through the television channels. Nothing but old movies and infomercials. Aunt Nettie didn't believe in spending money on cable channels. She and Benjie had gone to bed an hour earlier. Kylie leaned over and petted the sleeping J Bean in his doggy bed, who yipped at imaginary cats in his dream. *Dogs have it made. They eat when they want, and they don't have a zillion people bossing them around. "Don't wear this, don't drink this, and don't go here."* Kylie sucked down a Red Bull energy drink and ripped open a bag of tortilla chips, determined to stay awake until her mom came in.

I'm still mad at Will. Why did I have to come home so early? I'll be on a short leash when Mom gets married. She jumped up when her mother raced through the door and headed for the recliner.

"I see Will picked you up."

"He was real late. I almost had to go home with Derrick." She knew that would bug her mom.

"That's not happening, Kylie." Her mother kicked off both shoes and stretched out in the recliner. "Wonder why he was late? He's always on time."

"That's what you think."

Her mother frowned and waved away her comment. "Honestly, Kylie, sometimes you don't make sense." She yawned. "Be sweet and grab me a diet soda out of the fridge."

"Sure." She came back and handed her mom the can. "Mom, I love you."

"I love you too."

"So that's why I need to tell you something about Will. When he picked me up, he stayed in the car and honked the horn. And when I got in, he was on the phone, talking real quietly."

"So?"

"So guess who he was talking to?"

"I don't know or care …"

"Just guess."

Ally yawned and picked up her shoes. "I'm tired and going to bed."

"Guess!"

"Taylor Swift?"

"His old fiancée."

"Yeah, right."

"Mom, he hardly said anything to me when I got in the car 'cause he was so into the conversation. He even stepped out of the car for a minute and walked around so I couldn't hear what he was saying."

"I'm sure it was nothing."

"Mom, get real. He's still crushing on her."

❧

Ally snapped her boots into the cross-country skis and pushed off with her poles. "Hey, wait up."

Will slowed down until she pulled up alongside him. Their skis glided back and forth in tandem, a gentle dance for two. Snowball Park was all theirs. They passed a chickadee bouncing in the lower branch of a pine tree as a red fox passed in front of their path. Other than the fox, the entire world had turned white.

Will turned to her, his cheeks red with windburn. "You seem rattled," he said as they sashayed together, the skis making a gentle shushing sound. "Everything okay?"

She wanted to ask him about what Kylie had said to her. Instead she said, "Had a near miss on the road. My car slid toward oncoming traffic. I guess I hit a patch of black ice."

"Al, be careful. You're still learning to drive in winter weather." They turned left where the plowed path took a bend and passed by a frozen creek. The path then dipped, and they sailed down the hill before stopping for a break.

Ally took a few deep breaths, as her heart raced. "This is a workout. I love it!"

"Yep, and it's free."

"Free works."

"Yep."

"Speaking of spending and not spending money, there's something I want to splurge on for Christmas," said Ally. She backed away as he positioned his poles in the snow.

"Oh?"

"Growing up, we always had prime rib at Christmas."

"But isn't it pricey?"

"It's a family tradition." Ally closed her eyes. Here goes. "Less than twelve dollars a pound and it's grass-fed."

"Grass-fed. Hmm." He formed a "wow" with his mouth, then pulled his knit cap lower down on his head. "The wedding's only a few months away. We need to slow down on our spending, babe."

Ally clamped her lips together. *Here he goes again. Mr. Tightwad.* "So do you want hot dogs and beans?" She threw her face into a grimace.

"Maybe we can find something in between. Like meatballs."

"Meatballs?"

"Camp directors have a limited salary."

"I wanted our first Christmas together to be fun."

Will said nothing as he ground his pole into a snowdrift.

"Will, I'm serious." Ally put one pole in the air to punctuate her speech. "Hey, there's nothing wrong with having fun."

"I agree, but when you run out and buy an expensive SUV, there's not much left for fun."

"Oh, that was low, Camp. Do you want me to pawn my engagement ring?"

He bowed his head, pinched the bridge of his nose, and then looked up. "Sorry. Maybe you want a guy who is rolling in dough."

"No. But maybe you want someone different?"

"What's that supposed to mean?"

"Nothing."

Will took a sharp turn, maneuvering his skis back toward the head of the trail. "Weather's turning icy. Let's call it a day. Besides, the sun has almost set."

They skied back to the car with slow, deliberate movements. Ally didn't want to slip on any icy patches. When the sun went down, the cooler temperature hardened the soft snow that had fallen earlier that day. Ally unlatched her skis, opened the back of the Suburban, and slid them in. She walked around to Will, who was scraping ice off of the windshield.

"Sure collects fast," he said, chipping away at a half inch of the solid stuff.

"Hey, can you stop a minute?"

"What?" He turned to her, and she saw he had already chiseled a patch of three inches, enough space to start the rest of the windshield melting when the car heated.

"I'm sorry. I shouldn't have made the comment about hot dogs and beans."

"That wasn't fair, Al."

"You're right."

He jumped into the driver's seat and turned on the windshield wipers to help speed up the melting snow. Then he hopped out and leaned his body against the open door, staring at her. "I think this fight is about more than money. I think something else is troubling you."

❧

At home Ally slipped into the kitchen. She pulled a mug out of the cabinet, filled it with tap water, and slid it into the microwave for a cup of ginger peach tea. The beverage always calmed her down. *Such a silly argument and I overreacted. And I hurt him.*

Aunt Nettie flipped on the overhead light.

"Hey, you're home early." She positioned herself in one chair and selected a banana from the fruit bowl in the middle of the table. "Mind if I join you for a late afternoon snack? Kids are watching a movie upstairs."

Not trusting herself to answer, Ally stood with hunched shoulders, watching the mug spin on the microwave's turntable.

Nettie took a bite of the banana and swallowed. "What's wrong, honey? Did you and Will have another fight?"

Ally turned around and faced her aunt. "I think I hurt his feelings. I said I wanted to buy prime rib for Christmas, and he took it to mean I thought he couldn't afford the luxury. I asked him if he wanted me to pawn my engagement ring."

Nettie shook her head and laughed. "Tell me you *didn't* say that?"

Ally looked up and scrunched her eyes. "Uh, yes."

"Well, I can't say that I blame him. How much did you pay for the meat?"

"Twelve-ninety-nine a pound." Ally pulled the cream pitcher from the refrigerator and poured a glug into her mug before heading over to the pantry for one of her aunt's chocolate crinkle cookies. "But it's grass-fed beef."

Her aunt peeled back the skin of the banana farther and took a bite. "Good grief. Didn't you two set a limit on how much you'd spend for Christmas dinner?"

"Yes, but ..."

"You both have to make some rules and then play by them. He doesn't earn a lot, and neither do reporters. He's thinking about what it will be like when you two marry. And, anyway, he may think you're too extravagant."

"That's ridiculous."

"I know you're not a snob, but I have to take his side. It's more than money. It's about not showing off to our Christmas guests."

"What? I didn't think I was."

Ally hadn't thought about that. How dense could she be?

"You're in a small town. Maybe in the Bay Area families spend big bucks on Christmas dinner but not here. Think about it, Lake Surrender isn't a place where women buy high-end cosmetics at a department store. And you don't see many guys wearing designer labels."

Ally laughed. "Will is far removed from the Ralph Lauren crowd."

Aunt Nettie took her last bite of banana and held up a finger while she swallowed. "And isn't that one of the things you love about him? He's the real deal—doesn't do fancy or pretentious." She folded the banana peel and dumped it into the trashcan under the sink. "I want to ask you something."

"Sure, what?"

"Why do you work so hard? What drives you?"

Ally stared into her mug, the steam wafting over her face. She took a sip, then put the mug down and looked at Nettie. "I don't want to be in the situation I was two years ago after the divorce. The kids and I need security."

"Life has been especially hard for you these last few years. And then, this fall when you almost drowned …"

"It still haunts me. Some nights I still wake up in a sweat."

Her aunt reached over and squeezed her arm. "I'm so sorry about that. What a horrible experience. But here's the deal. You had no control over your fate when you nearly drowned. You had to give up control. Well, it's the same with all of life. We aren't promised anything. Not jobs, marriages, or well-behaved children. The only security we have is our relationship with Jesus."

Ally propped her elbows on the table and rested her chin in her hands. "I've been thinking about that a lot recently. I mean, what is important in life. You're right."

"Only after doing it wrong for many years," said her aunt.

Ally wanted to say more, but she couldn't tell her the genuine reason her stomach churned. Kylie's comments about phone calls from Sarah had stirred up her fears.

Aunt Nettie seemed to read her mind. "You don't have to tell me everything about your fight. Some things we have to wrestle through by ourselves. But I will say this, you need to release control of your life. When you fight the deep end, you drown. But when you release yourself to the water, you will be able to swim." She reached for her arm and squeezed it. "And honey, when you're at the deep end of the lake, you'd better know how to swim."

᳘

"See if you can find seats in the back." Will pulled the Sub-urban into the overhang to drop off the family in front of the Lake Surrender Community Church's covered walkway.

Ally pointed her finger above Benjie's head. "FYI, I had a brief talk with Mr. B., and it will not happen again. No hiding under the pew. He will sit with us."

"Good. I'll park the truck and meet you," said Will.

Ally clutched her son's arm and helped him step down out of the Suburban. She hoped the worship band's drummer wouldn't be too loud and set off Benjie again. She looked heav-enward. "Oh, Lord, we're trying real hard to get it together. We even made it on time."

"Who are you talking to?" asked Kylie.

"The only one who can help this stressed-out mom." As they walked through the main double-door entrance, Ally pressed her lips together to even out the lipstick she'd applied in the car. Kylie chose an empty pew in the back and motioned for Benjie to sit beside her. Out of the corner of her eye, Ally saw him stomp his foot. Evidently, that pew wasn't to his liking.

"No foot stomping."

He turned and glared at her, his icy blue eyes conveying his determination.

"Now, Benjie, we can't always have the same pew. Someone else is sitting there." Jeez, maybe we need "Save" markers so no one will sit in Benjie's seat. How ridiculous is that? He needed to learn how to adjust to change.

She centered her gaze on her son, whose boot thuds became louder and louder on the tile entryway. *Oh, please don't anyone turn around. And why is that stomping so loud? It echoes through the entire building.* She felt her face burn. The church members would understand, but for one Sunday she'd like to slip in with no fanfare.

In a loud whisper, she said, "You have two choices. You can sit by your sister, or I can drive you home, and you will sit in your room with nothing to play with."

"Sit by Ky."

Ally pursed her lips and exhaled. One battle over. Now if she could last the rest of the service, she'd be a contented woman. Maybe she could even concentrate on the sermon. The congregation sang one of her favorite praise songs and then recited the Lord's Prayer together. When they came to the part, "Forgive us our trespasses as we forgive those who trespass against us," she glanced at her aunt next to her. In her mind, an image arose of Janice holding her aunt's logo design in one hand and a check for $5,000 in the other. Her heart hurt, thinking Janice had submitted a fraudulent entry and might win. Could she forgive that woman for cheating her aunt?

All went well until the middle of the service when the usher passed the offering basket to their row. Ally held her breath as Benjie took the basket from his sister and plopped it in his lap.

Here we go again.

Kylie hissed, "You're supposed to pass it to Will." She elbowed her brother and tried to grab the edge of the basket. But Benjie wouldn't let go.

"He's fascinated by the coins in the bottom." Will shrugged his shoulders.

"Like he's never seen money?" Ally watched him finger the nickels, dimes, and quarters, then start to put them into piles. "Not now," she said. But he continued to stack the coins.

"Come on," said Kylie as Benjie examined the one-dollar bills and gathered them together. "You're embarrassing me."

"Please tell your son to pass the basket," said the elderly usher, politely.

"That's God's money, and you need to give it to the man," said Will, his tone gruff.

Benjie put down the five-dollar bill he'd been admiring and looked at Will. The boy's face was a study in pleasure versus obedience as he looked from the basket to Will and back again. It struck Ally that her son had struggles like anyone, even if his temptations were different. He let out a yelp and threw the basket up in the air. The bills floated down to the padded pew cushions, and the coins made a clinking sound when they hit the floor, rolling and spinning and dancing under the pew.

Before Ally could utter a word, Will lunged toward Benjie, grabbed him around his waist, and hoisted him over his shoulder like a sack of potatoes. "Excuse us, excuse us," he said as he passed in front of those sitting in the pew. Benjie let out a high-pitched screech. Heads turned as the two exited and headed toward the parking lot.

Will shut the out-of-control child in his room and headed to the kitchen where he found a leftover donut and some luke-warm coffee to tide him over till lunch. J Bean sat nearby.

"You've got it easy, dog. Try doing what I had to do, carrying sixty pounds of wriggling flesh down the aisle at church." He tossed the dog the last remnant of his pastry. "Sometimes I wonder if I'm cut out for this." He stood and put his plate in the sink.

It would be a half an hour until church was over. Might as well stretch out on the sofa and see when the Detroit Lions game would be on. He pulled up their website and saw they would play at one that afternoon. Satisfied, he closed his eyes for a quick nap.

His eyes popped open as a loud clanging woke him up. What on earth? Benjie stood above him, shaking a Mason jar half full of coins. A label on the jar read, "Benjie's Bank."

"I sorry."

Will took the jar. "What's this?"

"Money for Jesus."

"What?"

"Money for Jesus."

Will put his hand on the boy's shoulder. "You don't have to give all your money to Jesus. He's happy that you said you're sorry. I'm proud of you, and so is He."

Benjie smiled. "Yep, proud of Jesus."

"No, not proud of Jesus. Oh forget it," He threw Benjie his jacket. "Put your coat on. We have to go back and pick everyone up."

"Proud of you," said Benjie as he zipped up his coat.

CHAPTER SEVENTEEN

In the kitchen, Ally finished up a Yule log she'd iced for Christmas dinner. Exhausted from writing for the paper, planning a wedding, and making a few cakes for her new business, she perched on a stool for a bite of lunch. Midway through her dry ham sandwich, she put her head down and almost nodded off to sleep. She jerked herself awake. Last thing she wanted was for Will to see her napping. He'd say she was working too hard. And she supposed she was. After the wedding, she'd cut back.

When Will walked into her aunt's kitchen, Ally gave him a progress report on her spending cuts. "Hey, our Christmas Day dessert for tomorrow cost under five dollars. Help yourself to the lunch meat. I bought *it* for two dollars off the original price."

He stuck his head in the refrigerator and rummaged around for ham slices. "I'm proud of you. And I'm sorry about hassling you about the prime rib. I'm sure the beef will be delicious." He came up behind her and nuzzled her neck.

"And I have burned nothing since—"

"Those sugar cookies last week, when you had to throw away the pan and—"

Ally narrowed her eyes. "You're asking for it." The bowl that had contained the whipped-cream frosting sat at her right elbow. Oh, this could be fun. She scraped up the last glob onto a rubber spatula. "You need a shave. Let me lather you up …" She lunged at him and smeared frosting all over his chin.

"Why, you—" Will grabbed a wet dishrag sitting on the counter and threw it at her. It hit her right in the chest and made a big wet spot. "Oops!"

She yelped. "Thanks a lot. Now I have to take this blouse to the cleaners. This means war, Camp."

Ally backed toward the sprayer connected to the sink, grabbed the handle, and turned it on full-force. Will ran toward her with the obvious intention of wrenching the sprayer from her hand. Instead, he slid on a puddle, skidded to a stop, and fell on his backside. As he went down, he clutched at the edge of the towel underneath the Yule log she'd used to roll up the cake.

The cake rolled to the edge of the counter, and—*splat*—fell on the floor. An ax might as well have split it straight down the middle.

Ally groaned.

"I'm sorry!" said Will half serious and half in jest.

Her temper rose, but when she saw the astonished look on his face, she couldn't help but giggle. "Way to go, Camp." She held her sides and laughed. "Maybe we can use it for firewood."

Will joined in.

"You should see your face," she said.

"You should see yours." Will bent over to help pick up the mess.

"Pepperidge Farm frozen cake, anyone?"

"Works for me," said Will.

❧

Christmas morning, Ally crept downstairs and slipped into the kitchen. She punched the button for the coffee maker and watched the first drips of welcoming Kona brew. Before the cycle finished, she jerked the decanter off the warming element and filled her mug.

Back in the family room, she flung herself onto the sturdy upholstered chair and watched through the window as the snow meandered from the sky, in no hurry to add to the white stuff already on the ground. The sun peeked through the clouds in a radiant wedge of light that lit up the frozen cove to the east of the cottage.

"Mind if I join you?" Her aunt settled into the recliner next to her.

"I was thinking of past Christmases. Growing up, Christmas was a blowout celebration of presents and over-the-top meals. Our family raced through the holidays."

"That happens to a lot of people."

"Finding faith changed that. Christmas became a completely different day when I understood what Jesus' birth meant to me."

"That it is. But don't set your bar too high for the perfect holiday. Instead, treasure the joy in your heart. That's the greatest gift from God." Her aunt stood and opened the curtain further to view the rays of sun growing brighter as they glanced off the water to fan out their brilliance. The message wasn't lost on Ally. The world in all its glory celebrated the day Jesus was born.

"Sany here?" Ally turned and saw Benjie shuffle toward her in his Paw Patrol pajamas. He held out his hands, palms up, giving her a questioning look.

"But Santa said you have to give me a hug first." He scooted closer, and she placed both his thin arms around her neck. He hesitated as Ally pulled him close. "Okay, turn around and check out the fireplace." She gently rotated his shoulders.

He cried, "Yippee, yippee," at the sight of the two stuffed stockings on the fireplace.

"Are you going to spin or go check out your stocking?"

As he raced to the fireplace, a knock sounded at the front door. Ally jumped up and ran to yank it open.

"Merry Christmas, dollface." Will stood, wearing a red plaid scarf. His lips pressed against hers, chilly from the outside air.

"Let me warm you up." Ally closed the door behind him and wound her bathrobe-clad arms around Will's waist, as they stood in the entrance.

"Never a problem to warm up when you're around. Do you know what you do to me?"

"Real creepy, guys." Kylie walked into the family room and made gagging noises as she headed toward the fireplace to look at her stocking.

"Get used to it, Kylie," Will said. "You'll be seeing more of this pretty soon."

Kylie rolled her eyes and sat down on the rug to survey the goodies in her stocking. Ally scurried to the kitchen and poured two more mugs of coffee for Will and her aunt, who were waiting to see the contents of the kids' stockings.

Aunt Nettie inserted an old CD into the player. "Crank up the music." Ally waltzed around the room, singing, "God rest ye merry, gentlemen, let nothing you dismay. Remember Christ your Savior was born on Christmas Day."

She froze while waving her arms in mid-air when J Bean started barking to announce visitors: Don, the maintenance director from camp; Wilma, his wife; Betty, his administrative assistant; and her husband. After a loud knock, they strolled through the front door. "Merry Christmas," they shouted, arms full of wrapped gifts and casserole dishes.

"Oh my, it's eight already." She flew upstairs, threw on her favorite maroon sweater, and a pair of dressy black slacks. Ally added a sparkling snowflake necklace and silver hoop earrings for a finishing touch before heading back downstairs. She pulled two extra dining room chairs into the family room for the guests.

"Rest gentle, rest gentle," sang Benjie, spinning in a happy motion, holding the metal spring coil toy he found in his stocking.

Faster and faster he spun, with the Slinky flying in a centrifugal path around him. The toy's orbit grew wider and wider until it smacked his sister, who was sitting on the rug. Her grumpy mood escalated into a hostile one.

"Knock it off, brat." She stood and rubbed her cheek where the giant spring had hit her. Kylie gave her brother a shove. "Do you have to always do that dumb spinning thing? Make him stop, Mom."

Ally pried the toy out of her son's hand, thankful she got a good grip. When Benjie became obsessed with a particular object, it could take the strength of the entire cast of *The Avengers* to extract it from his grasp. She prayed he wouldn't erupt. *Please, God, not today.*

To Ally's astonishment, he looked at his sister. "Sorry."

"You should be. I've got a big red mark—"

"It shows progress that he apologized, Kylie," Ally pointed out.

"Whoopee."

Not now, Kylie. "Both of you cut it out, or else." Ally's dream Christmas was quickly dissolving into mush, and with an audience to boot.

"Or else what?"

The guests looked on as one thirteen-year-old girl determined to make trouble sucked the Christmas spirit from the room, like water draining from a bathtub.

"Do you want to find out?" Ally stood and headed toward Kylie.

Will stepped in front of her. "Let's take a minute to calm down."

"Fine." Ally stepped around him. "Kylie, we're going to have a peaceful day."

"Anyone for sweet rolls? Made them yesterday," called Nettie cheerily from the kitchen.

The four visitors hightailed it to the kitchen.

Benjie walked up to his sister and hugged her leg. Her mouth turning down in disgust, she shook her leg. "Go away." He started flapping his hands. "And stop that hands stuff." She slapped his hand.

He screamed and ran to Will. "Mean, mean."

"I'm not mean. I'm sick of you." Kylie wagged her finger at him.

"Cut it out, Kylie," said Ally. She dug her fingers into her daughter's shoulder.

The guests returned to the family room with plates of cinnamon rolls in hand.

"That's enough," Will said and rushed over to break up the argument. "Can't we be happy today? It's Christmas."

Kylie flopped down on the sofa, tears filling her eyes. "Why should I be happy? Nobody misses Dad but me."

Ally put her head down, her stomach a dull ache. Part of her wanted to cry, and part of her wanted to reach out for her daughter. She glanced at Will, who was chewing on his lower lip—a bad sign. He always did that when he was upset. So much for a warm and fuzzy holiday where everyone sat around the fire sipping cocoa and trading cheerful sentiments. Instead, her daughter had ripped open their family issues in front of an audience—blood, guts, and all. She went to the kitchen and fished around in the cabinet for some antacids before coming back to the family room.

"Let me try," Will whispered to Ally.

Not trusting herself to speak, Ally nodded.

He walked over to Kylie, who had slumped down against the wall. He held out his hand. She ignored it. Instead, she wiped her tears off with her bathrobe belt and slipped her hands into her pockets. Will's hand hung in mid-air, asking for a connection.

The roomful of people held their collective breath as the house's old furnace hissed and groaned. Ally peered out the window. Outside, cars sloshed by as the roadways turned to mush. One car, two cars, and then a big pickup truck. She counted them as her aunt's old CD player pumped out more Christmas music. The moment stretched out for an eternity. Somehow she didn't envision the day like this. She swallowed a lump in her throat the size of Lake Michigan as she watched her daughter's meltdown. How could this be happening?

"Come with me." Ally stood and took Kylie's hand and pulled her into the garage, where they could have some privacy. "That was very rude. What's going on?"

"You know."

Ally leaned against a bike. "Actually, I do. You miss Dad."

Kylie took the tissue she had in her hand and wiped her nose. "So much, Mom."

Ally wrapped her arms around her daughter and pulled her hair away from her face. She rocked her daughter like she did when Kylie was a toddler. "Sometimes there are no words for sorrow. Just cry, baby." They clung to each other. Then she pulled away from her daughter so she could look her in the eye. "But remember, your father will always be in your heart." She held her, listening as the sobs became fewer and fewer.

❧

It was early afternoon when Ally and Will waved goodbye to their guests. "Let's see if we can help Aunt Nettie put the food on the table," said Ally. She and Will walked into the kitchen. "What can we do to help?" she asked her aunt, who was stirring gravy.

"Nothing. Kylie and I have it all under control. Just go relax."

After a dinner of prime rib, cheese potatoes, spoon bread, green beans almandine, candied carrots, and Caesar salad, Will and Benjie marched upstairs to complete the domino trail in the upstairs hallway. Kylie sat on a kitchen stool, talking on Ally's phone. She was busy telling Emerald what she'd gotten for Christmas as the adults finished putting the extra food in the refrigerator and doing dishes.

Ally breathed a sigh of relief. She slipped into the family room. Will had already crashed into the tan recliner and tipped back the chair, unbuckling his belt one notch to accommodate the large meal he'd eaten.

"Best Christmas dinner I've ever had." He raised his head to look at Nettie, who sat by the tree, using the glow of the lights to work on her knitting. She peered over her readers and smiled. Will then turned to Ally. "And that log cake thing—that was, uh …" Ally threw a pillow at him, and it ricocheted off his head.

"I know it didn't look that great, but you must admit, I nailed the whipped cream frosting. Anyway, I scraped off the part that hit the floor …"

"Tell me you're kidding," said Will.

"What do you think?" She grinned.

Her phone rang. "It's Mom. She finally called back." Ally had been unable to talk her parents into joining them for Christmas. "I'd freeze there, and, anyway, all our friends are here," her mom had said.

"Hey, Mom, I was going to call you again. I miss you guys."

"Me too. But I'm staying busy. I sure hope you're able to come here next Christmas. Do you think Will is going to work at that camp very long?"

"Mom."

After a lengthy pause, her mother finally spoke. "I was hoping you four would move back here. I've talked to a friend, and she told me of an exceptional opportunity at one of the local publishing companies, lots of opportunities for you to further your career. And I'm sure Will could also find work to suit him. Surely a talented guy like him won't want to work in a backwoods camp the rest of his life."

Ally started to comment but closed her mouth. What was the use? "Mom, I'm hoping you guys can fly here soon. Like for the wedding. I'll call later this week. The kids loved their presents."

"Glad to hear that. I miss them." She paused a minute. "Are you sure about marrying Will? It's not too late to back ..."

"Oh Mom, I think Aunt Nettie wants to talk to you." She handed the phone to her, avoiding Will's look. Instead, Ally walked over to the Christmas tree and pulled off a dented metal bell hanging near the top—one of her father's childhood ornaments. She shook it. The tingling sound took her back to her childhood on the West Coast. On her ninth Christmas, her dad had bought her a new purple bike. She had admired the bike for months in the bike shop, but the week before Christmas he came home and told her the owner of the shop had sold it. When she walked into their living room on Christmas morning, she screamed with delight to see her new wheels sitting under the tree. She took it out for a ride up and down the street in seventy-degree weather. Perfect weather. She had ridden that bike everywhere. It gave her freedom. Ally sighed. She would always miss California. And if she were honest, part of her wanted to hear about the job that had opened up.

❧

Later that evening, Ally's phone rang again, and she picked it up. "Kylie, you have a call." It seemed like she was fielding a lot of her daughter's calls since she'd dropped her phone in a snowdrift and ruined the battery. Kylie rushed into the room and grabbed the phone.

"Oh, hi ... Ski trip?" Kylie plopped down on the sofa next to her mother. "I don't know how to ski." She slid her sock-clad feet onto the coffee table. "No, you don't have to pay for me. Anyway, I think we're going out of town over the break. Mom likes to visit her family, and we'll probably spend time on the beach—Daytona. My grandmother has a beach house." Another pause. "Sure, see you at school, I guess." She hung up.

"Who was that, and what's this about a beach house? Your grandmother doesn't live in Florida."

"It was Em. I had to think of a good excuse not to go."

"I was meaning to talk to you about the Goodmans' offer. Why don't you want to go?"

"Costs a lot of money."

"So you lied? Anyway, I thought you and Emerald weren't friends anymore."

Kylie curled her lower lip into a sheepish grin. "Well, not exactly, but sort of." She headed for the stairs.

Ally groaned. "Here we go again with that Emerald. Are you friends or not?"

"Mom!"

Will slipped on his coat. "Great Christmas, but I'm heading home. Big day tomorrow."

CHAPTER EIGHTEEN

Ally scurried to the office's kitchen, threw her brown-bag lunch in the refrigerator, and returned to her desk. *I have to finish three articles by 5:00 p.m. Yikes.* As she edited the first one, Ally looked up to see Janice stroll through the door in a stylish black trench coat. She walked over to Ally. "By the way, there are three u's in curriculum. Thankfully, I caught that when I was proofreading your article."

Ally pressed her lips together and squeaked a "thank you." Oh, how she hated it when Janice had to proof her pieces.

"And you forgot to close the mayor's remarks with ending quotation marks."

She loves to find my mistakes. Why was this woman so annoying, so critical, so …

But another idea interrupted her train of thought. *I wonder if she has many friends. She never talks about doing anything on weekends.* She forced a smile. "Any plans for New Year's Eve?"

A flicker of sadness crossed Janice's face, then disappeared. She drew up her lips into a sedate smile. "I was planning on meeting a couple of girlfriends at the Tapas Deliciosas Restaurante in Traverse City."

"Isn't that where Jorge plays on weekends?"

"Oh, is it?"

"Sounds like fun."

Janice's gaze turned toward the window, then back to Ally. "Fun? I guess if you don't mind a bunch of unattached women sitting around whining about the lack of men in town. Michigan winters can turn quite dreary."

Unexpected compassion filled Ally. *Lord, let me be a friend.* She remembered how it felt to be single when the rest of the world paired off, especially on New Year's Eve. On impulse Ally said, "Maybe I can join you someday. I love guitar music."

Janice stared at her for a moment, looking surprised. Then she smiled. "Maybe so."

Was that the sound of cracking ice? But then Janice looked down at the floor by her desk where red stains of fingernail lacquer discolored the floor. Ally had tried to scrub the area, but the stains stood as a reminder of that awful day.

Janice looked up, and Ally felt her face flush. "So sorry about your coat and the mess Benjie made with your nail polish," Ally said.

Janice nodded. "Not a good day, but it's in the past."

❧

The next morning, Will parked his ancient Suburban in front of the lodge. He rolled down his window and called to Don, who was guiding the snow blower down the path leading to the entrance. Sprays of snow flew out of the machine.

"Did you say something?" said Don, trying to talk over the loud motor.

"Hey, give me a hand." Will yanked open the back of his Suburban. He reached inside, slid out a fifty-pound bag of salt, and hiked it into his arms.

Don turned off the snow blower and followed suit. They piled the four bags against the farthest corner of the front porch, in preparation to salt the steps the next time the weather turned icy. He found a seat on the newly cleared steps to the lodge. "So how's Ally's baking business going?"

Will sat next to him and punched his friend in the arm. "I know what you're thinking. But she's come a long way since two summers ago. Have you tasted her Black Forest torte?" Even now he could taste the moist chocolate cake with cherry topping. Heaven. "And I know you ate half of that turtle cheesecake she brought over to camp."

"I'm pulling your chain. I know she's a good cook." He rubbed his gloves together to warm his hands. "Say, how are things going between you two?"

"Rough. Relationships are hard."

"No kidding." Don stretched out his hands to crack his knuckles. "So here's the drill."

"Great, more free advice." Will groaned and put his hands over his ears.

Don continued. "You start off exchanging sweet nothings inside an old Chevy truck. After you marry, you're forced to tackle tough topics like how to budget the money and how her mother annoys you. Then you have a bunch of kids, and you pass each other in the driveway at five o'clock, arguing about who was supposed to pick up kid number three from band practice."

Will stood. He picked up a snow shovel and tapped the slender icicles that hung down from the edge of the roof. They'd grown a good batch of them this year. Several were eight to ten feet in length, like the ones he and his brother used for weapons when he was a kid. "You make it sound so, uh—"

"Ordinary? Yep, for Wilma and me, ordinary works. I'd rather do ordinary with her than extraordinary with someone else. She's the one I want to spend time with. She says she's no runway model, but she sure hits my hot button."

"Guess you didn't end up with a pack of kids by osmosis," said Will as he chipped away at a thick icicle that hung over the porch stairs. He whacked it again, and it crashed onto the porch floor. "Say, how did you and Wilma meet anyway?"

"Native American Heritage Day's parade, twenty-five years ago. She wore a traditional long red jingle dress—you know, the kind with those metal cones tied all over. I watched her perform, and a small voice inside said, 'That's the girl for you.' I was only eighteen, but it didn't matter. I didn't want any other girl."

"Hey, you did well to catch her." Will winked at his friend. If anyone had a solid marriage, it was Don and Wilma. "But, come on, don't you guys have disagreements?"

"Are you kidding? It's called in-laws. The minute I started dating their precious daughter, I became an outlaw. And then there's disciplining children. Me, I let things slide, but Wilma's a stickler for rules."

"So how do you agree on what to do?"

"Still ironing things out. But we're committed to each other, and any guy who messes with her will have matching black eyes and a broken collarbone. How's that for Christian love?"

"Works for me." Will cupped his hands together and breathed into them for warmth. "Have I mentioned Kylie's giving us fits?"

"Not surprised. Kylie's headstrong. All I have to say is Ally's talented but sort of clueless. You'd better help her pay attention to what her daughter is doing." Don walked up the stairs onto the porch and dipped a scooper into the salt bag. "Think we'd better spread some of this now." He sprinkled several scoops of salt onto the porch floor. "So what do you expect from Ally being your wife?"

Will paused for a minute. "Nothing complicated. A woman who will hang with me through thick or thin and be a part of this camp. A lover, companion, and a good mother. Ally has those qualities, but it's been hard with Kylie. We've been squabbling a lot lately. I hate that kind of stuff." He stood and knocked a couple more icicles down with his shovel before leaning his tool against the front porch railing.

"More often than not, raising kids means going to war," said Don. "You two against them, and you'd better be united. I've seen kids tear couples apart."

CHAPTER NINETEEN

Mid-January, the town of Lake Surrender dug out from an overnight dumping of fresh snow. Ally woke to the scraping of the snowplow, followed by its backup beeper—shrill enough to wake anyone still asleep. She groaned. The early start of the work crews made sleeping in impossible even with Aunt Nettie volunteering for breakfast duty. Someone tapped on her door. Benjie pushed it open and entered, his Spiderman slippers shuffling against the wood floor, stuffed squirrel in his hand.

"Stay Home Saturday!"

She clapped her hands, and Benjie responded with a single clap. "Come here." She patted the side of the bed next to her.

He looked down at the ground.

"Can I see your eyes, please?"

He looked down, but his lips turned upward in a sly smile.

"Hey, I know you heard me. I want to see those blue eyes."

Benjie jerked his head up. "See!"

Ally wrapped him in a hug. She stroked his silky hair and treasured the moment. He rarely allowed her to fuss with it.

"Where's your sister? It's eight o'clock, and we have a lot to do." Even as Ally spoke, she caught a glimpse of Kylie streaking past her half-opened door. "Hey, come back!"

No response.

Ally jumped off her bed and rushed into the hallway. "You and I had a date to talk some more."

"Later, Mom." Kylie looked up at Ally before continuing. "I've got plans."

"Whoa." Ally raced down the stairs after her daughter. "You're not going anywhere."

"I won't be gone long," said Kylie. She pulled her parka off the hook next to the front door and slipped into her snow boots. With one quick twist of the wrist, she flipped open the door and disappeared.

Ally's stomach churned. Still in pajamas, she threw on her peacoat and trailed her daughter out the door. She'd win this skirmish. "Hey, come back here. I need to—"

But Kylie tromped through the front yard and ducked into an older model sedan waiting for her in the driveway, its motor running. A teen boy shoved the vehicle into reverse and backed into the street, black exhaust coming out of the tailpipe.

Feeling ridiculous, Ally plowed down the unshoveled sidewalk, waving her arms. The mushy snow seeped into the top of her boots, chilling her toes. About a block down the road, she gave up and trudged back to her driveway.

She didn't count on Janice driving by and pulling up alongside her in a Lexus SUV. Janice rolled down her window and pointed toward the getaway car. "Doubt they're within listening distance, dear. Why don't you call her on your phone?" She waved an envelope out the window that Ally recognized as her paycheck. *Why is she bringing my check? Oh, yeah, we changed payroll companies, and no automatic deposit for another week.*

Of all people, why did Janice have to see that spectacle? Benjie's tantrum in the office, and now this? *Okay, look nonchalant.* She pulled her coat tighter around her bathrobe and nodded to Janice. "She forgot her gloves, and I was trying to get her attention."

"Uh-huh." Janice handed her the envelope. "I'll tell her to scoot home if I see her." She rolled up the window before driving down the street.

Back inside the house, Ally flopped on the couch, every atom in her body ready to explode in anger. She had no idea where her daughter had gone.

Aunt Nettie walked in from the kitchen and set a steaming mug on the coffee table. "Sit down and drink this. Can't talk without coffee first."

Grateful, Ally sipped the smooth brew as Nettie settled on the piano bench. "Did she tell you where she was going?" Ally asked.

"No."

"I'd like to smack her upside the head. It looked like Derrick was driving the car!"

Nettie handed her a cell phone. "Here, call her. She used my phone a few minutes ago before she found hers. Had I known she was taking off with some hoodlum boy I'd have stopped her."

Ally hit the number and got a voice mail. She left a message and hung up.

When she finished, Ally scurried to the kitchen, unplugged her phone, and texted Will: *Kylie's gone. I'm terrified. You are right. She is in trouble.*

He called immediately. "Hey. I'm filling out an annual report, but come on by, and we'll use the Suburban to look for her. We'll figure it out."

The phrase "We'll figure it out" was a warm, fleecy cyber-hug. "Thank you, Camp."

After throwing on a pair of jeans and a sweatshirt, Ally raced to her car.

Fifteen minutes later, Ally pulled her Explorer into the camp parking lot. She grabbed the black metal handle of the mammoth wood-stained door and hurried through the camp's lounge, past the empty dining room, and down the hall to the camp office. She stood in the doorway, out of breath, as she focused on the back of Will's head in the dimly lit room. Feet propped up on his credenza, he scribbled notes by the light of a small table lamp.

"Hey," said Ally.

He swiveled around in his chair and glanced up. "Good timing, I just finished."

Ally couldn't keep the despair out of her voice. "She hasn't called."

"Come here, babe."

Ally walked over to him. Perched on his lap, she turned her head sideways against his chest and listened to his heart as it beat a gentle *padump-padump* through his worn gray staff sweatshirt. Steady like him. *Thank You, God, that I don't have to search for Kylie alone.*

"I'm scared I'm losing her."

Will shook his head, the back-and-forth movement of his chin gentle on the top of her head. Then he broke away from the embrace and gripped her shoulders. "She's hitched a ride on the wrong train if she's hanging out with Derrick and that group."

"I think that's the name I saw last night on her phone."

"He's sixteen, and he's had a few brushes with the law. Don't mean to scare you, but they know him down at LSPD."

"I've been so busy at the paper, I let things slip."

"Can't do that at her age."

Ally. "I feel like an idiot."

"And I'm sorry for sounding like I was pointing a finger at you."

"Yeah, we have to do things better. Focus on Kylie," said Ally. They stood and Ally grasped both sides of Will's shirt and stared into his eyes. "I need your help, Will. I don't have a clue where to start looking for her."

"Let's think about where she could be." He scratched the side of his head. "Do you know any of her friends' phone numbers?"

"No." She rummaged around in her purse. "Wait, she used my phone to call Kristen yesterday."

Ally scrolled down the contact list and hit the selected number. She texted a few sentences, sent the message, then placed her phone on top of a pile of bills on Will's desk.

She stared at her smartphone with the designer cover, which reminded her she'd changed. Her values had been so shallow back in California. Now nothing mattered but finding her daughter and working things out. She'd changed her priorities, but she had a long way to go. *Okay, God, I'm paying attention.*

"I want to be a good mom."

"You are. And you're learning. Don't be so hard on yourself. It's difficult to raise any teen in this culture." Will picked up a key ring from his desk. "Look, we're not making any headway sitting here. I'll lock up. You hop in the truck. We'll hit all the teen hot spots in town. Knowing all the hangouts is one thing I've learned from being a camp director."

"Okay." Ally stood.

Hands on her shoulders, Will turned her one-hundred-eighty degrees toward the door, placed his hand in the small of her back, and gave her a gentle nudge. Kylie could be in all kinds of trouble, and they had a lot of territory to cover.

๛

The ancient Suburban slipped and slid on yet another road that had been covered by mushy snow before it refroze last night. The digital clock read four, and they'd been searching what seemed like every country lane in the county since nine. Finally, they stopped at a kiddy park, which faced the lake.

Will pulled out his phone and texted Aunt Nettie. "Any sign of her?"

Will tilted the screen of his phone toward Ally so she could see Nettie's answer: "No."

Fear swelled and erupted into a panic. She let out a muffled cry.

"Now hold on," said Will. "Let's sit here and think. We're missing something."

"I don't know what."

Will stared at the roof of the Suburban and then closed his eyes. "Lord, we're at a dead end, and we need Your help here."

Ally wasn't holding her breath. God *could* have helped them all day. Even still, she closed her eyes and prayed with all her might. "God, please show us where my daughter is. I'm frightened, but I know You can take care of her if she's in danger. I'm trusting You."

She held her side, her gnawing anxiety had turned to hunger. They hadn't eaten for hours. Ally had had some coffee but no breakfast or lunch. She fished inside her purse and found a bag of peanuts.

"Have a few." Ally offered the bag to Will before taking a handful. She munched in misery as she watched snow pile up on the kiddy slide. At least another half-inch had accumulated while they'd been sitting in the parking lot.

The wind caught the new snow on top of the vehicle's hood and whisked it away. Will pointed to something on the lake. An object appeared on the ice, headed for the middle of the lake.

"What's that brown thing? Surely that's not a car," said Ally as she shaded her eyes with her hand to look straight out onto the horizon.

He responded by leaning over Ally, opening the glove compartment, and extracting a pair of binoculars. "Looks like a Ford Escort. Not sure why anyone would be out on the ice now. Needs to be at least eight inches thick before you can take a car out there. I know kids like to drive on the lake, but that car is in danger. He dropped his binoculars on the floor and picked up his phone. "I'm calling 911."

As Will dug in his coat pocket for his phone, the car performed figure eights before zig-zagging in the middle of the lake. The *padump-padump* from cranked-up car speakers carried all the way to their side of the lake. Something was familiar about the car. "Quick, the binoculars." Her mouth went dry as doors flung open and passengers burst out of the car. Two boys and one girl with long dark-brown hair.

Will froze, staring straight ahead too.

Before Ally could say anything, a second *crack* rang in the air. The sound caused a sickening sensation in her heart.

Ally dropped the binoculars into her lap as a strangled scream escaped from her tightened throat. She pointed as the front of the car slowly descended into the opening in the ice, first the headlights, then the front bumper, and finally the entire hood of the car—heading into a cold, wet grave. The three teens slipped on the ice, running toward the shore.

"That's Kylie." Ally let out a sob.

CHAPTER TWENTY

Will punched a few buttons on his phone and yelled into the phone to the dispatcher at the Lake Surrender Police Department. "We have an emergency. A car has fallen through the ice." He provided a few more details, then threw the Suburban into gear and drove like a demon.

Gripping the armrest, Ally kept watch on the teens as Will navigated the curves of the road around the lake. Ally pointed out an all-weather dock that stretched into the lake near the kids. Normally people took their docks in after Labor Day, but a few homeowners left them out and used bubblers to keep the water from freezing around the structure. "I wonder if we can reach them from that."

In response, Will pressed harder on the accelerator.

"Faster, faster, we don't have much time," Ally said.

The Suburban fishtailed a few times as he corrected his course, whizzing by pine trees burdened with snow. The all-weather tires gripped the icy road, and Ally clung to the dash.

She peered through the openings in the woods. Yes, three figures still skated flat-footed on the lake, trying to reach shore. The entire windshield of the car now dipped into the widening crack.

"What were they thinking?" Will pounded the steering wheel for the second time that day, as they pulled up to the dock. "And where is that fire department?" He backed up the truck, aligning the rear of the vehicle with the front of the dock, then yanked open the back door and pulled out a long yellow nylon towing rope. Hooking it onto his Suburban's towing hitch, he unwound the rope over the length of the dock and then threw the rest of the line out as far beyond the dock as he could. "It's not much but might buy a few feet."

Back inside the car, he leaned on the horn until one of the group waved in response. The kids headed toward the Suburban, slipping and sliding, their figures becoming more distinct. Ally and Will rushed to the end of the dock.

With a groan, the brown sedan slid into the water. The hole widened. The teenagers screamed and scrambled. The car was no longer visible.

Ally covered her mouth with her hands. "This is a nightmare."

"No kidding." Will ran his hands up and down the sides of his jeans, always a sign that he was stressed.

Finally, the kids came within shouting distance. Will cupped his hands to make his voice carry. "You can make it!"

To Ally's horror, Kylie twirled around a couple of times on the ice and waved.

"Is she smiling?" Ally squeaked, her voice failing. *Am I trapped inside of a Stephen King novel?*

"At least they got out in time." Ally took his hand and felt it shake. "They don't know how close they came to falling in." Will shook his head as the taller boy with a shaved head tripped over a mound of ice and pulled himself up.

The wrench that tightened the knot in Ally's stomach turned another revolution. *Was one of those idiots laughing?*

Face grim, Will broadcasted his voice by cupping his hands. "Take it easy, you're almost there. Come on, sweetheart, you can make it."

The three reached the dock.

"Kylie!" Ally ran to her daughter. She wanted nothing more than to wrap her arms around her daughter and hug her. *Then* she'd strangle her. But Kylie put her hands out in front of Ally to stop her from getting closer as the wail of sirens punctured the icy air.

"Jeez, Mom, think you overreacted?" She pointed to the fire and police vehicles pulling into the parking lot. "Way to embarrass me."

"We knew we'd make it." The boy with the shaved head waved her off.

Ally turned to look at Will, whose mouth had also dropped open. Fury burned inside of her.

Another boy who Ally recognized came up behind Kylie. "Derrick, you destroyed a perfectly good car and about fell into the ice." Will gripped the teen's arm so hard he yelped. "You're lucky to be alive, dude."

"Hey, chill, bro," said Derrick, yanking his arm away. His bloodshot eyes peered out from beneath a stocking hat. "It's all good."

"Depends on your perspective—and I'm not your 'bro.'" Will took the teen's shoulder and steered him toward the back seat of the Suburban. He jerked open the door so hard that Ally wondered if he had ripped it off of its hinges. "Sit."

The other boy ambled over, giggling at some secret joke, and slid in beside his buddy.

Kylie stayed outside the vehicle, hands stuffed into her coat. "We're safe. What's the big deal?"

Could this out-of-control teen be any more stubborn? The ire of the last few months gathered in Ally's stomach, then exploded through her lips.

"Why, you ungrateful brat. We've been driving around looking for you all day."

A short, solidly built policeman walked up to Will. "If you don't mind, I'd like to talk to these teens in my squad car."

"They're all yours." Will tossed up his hands. The boys scooted out of the vehicle, and he and Ally crawled back in. They waited in silence as the teens spent fifteen minutes with the officer. Kylie then exited the car accompanied by the policeman. Ally got out of the Suburban as they approached.

"Are you Kylie's mother?" a burly officer asked.

"Yes."

"I had a good talking-to with the kids. Looks like it's Nathan's brother's car. Nathan's the one with the shaved head. I'll have to write him up for driving without a license. Also going to do a drug test on the two of them. Kylie seems to be a nice girl and way too young for these bozos. She doesn't need to be mixed up with a couple of potheads."

"Yes, I understand."

He asked Kylie to come over to the police car. After a few minutes, Kylie got out of the car, and the officer drove off with the two boys.

Kylie slipped into the back of the Suburban. "It isn't like you think."

"Save it," Will said as he started the car.

Ally glanced over her shoulder at her daughter's sulky face. "You and I will have a talk when we get home."

"No way." Kylie unbuckled her seat belt and tried to open the door.

"If you'd like to walk, it's all right by me. Only two miles to the house," Ally said.

❦

As soon as Will pulled into their driveway, Kylie flung open the Suburban's door, leaped out, and raced into the house.

"I'd be happy to come in," Will offered as Ally climbed out of the Suburban.

She paused, her hand on the car door. "I've got this, but thanks so much for helping me."

"I'd like to—"

"It's okay. I can handle talking to her." Ally tugged at her muffler, wrapping the cloth tighter around her neck to ward off the wind, which whipped off the frozen lake across the street.

Will jutted out his chin. "You need me right now." He lowered his voice and in a gentler tone said, "She needs a firm hand."

Ally studied his face. Why was it so hard to trust him and give up control? Will had a good head on his shoulders.

"Okay."

He smiled at her as he got out of the car. On impulse he grabbed her hand and squeezed it. Inside, they brushed past Nettie and Benjie in the family room and found Kylie locked in her room. Ally pounded on the door but didn't get a reaction. She tried again.

"I don't want to break the door down, Ally," said Will. "Let's call it a day."

Ally agreed. They had taken a step in the right direction, and they were working together. Somehow they'd work this out. She loved being able to count on him.

～

Next morning, Ally jerked awake with a splitting headache. After dressing, she headed downstairs to fortify herself with coffee before tackling Kylie. The tantalizing fragrance of fresh cinnamon rolls told her Aunt Nettie had been up a while. Lowering herself onto a stool at the kitchen bar, she watched as Nettie slid the pan out of the oven and set it on the counter.

"Thought you needed carb reinforcement today." Nettie winked as she measured powdered sugar, milk, and vanilla into a small glass bowl and whisked them together for the glaze.

"Thanks." Ally took a sip from her mug, thankful for the hot, brown liquid.

Aunt Nettie dribbled the thin icing in delicate swirls on top of the pastry. "Glad things didn't get any worse yesterday." She wiped excess glaze off of the edge of the blue stoneware plate.

Thank you for not giving me any advice or pat Bible verses. Ally loved that Nettie offered her wisdom when only when solicited.

She snatched a roll from the plate and took a bite. If heaven were a food, this would qualify. She savored each flaky bite until only a few crumbs remained on her napkin.

"Thanks, Aunt Nettie." Ally paused, then heaved a sigh. "Suppose I'd better face the lion's den."

Nettie smiled. "God will give you the words."

Upstairs, Ally knocked on Kylie's door and listened. Kylie was talking.

"Now that's the way you fasten your shoes. Take the strap." There was a pause. "Okay, now pull it over the top. That's right. Now do the other one. Yes! You did great."

Allie couldn't believe what she was hearing. Kylie was helping her brother, and that hadn't happened in a long time.

"Hang on." Kylie opened the door. "Teaching Benjie how to do the Velcro straps on his shoes. Show Mom."

Benjie, who sat on the side of the bed, pumped his legs up and down to show his accomplishment.

"Nice job!" Ally nodded at Benjie.

Her enthusiasm diminished when Ally looked around the room, which had been completely cleaned a few days ago. A sheet straggled half-on, half-off the hand-painted wooden bed. A pair of skinny jeans lay next to the bed beside a pair of socks, a muffler, and Kylie's winter coat. Ally suppressed a gag. The room smelled like a month's collection of dirty clothes, trendy perfume, old French fries, and Tahitian Vanilla body lotion. Kylie was stretched out on her bed while Benjie struggled on the floor with his shoes.

"Benjie, there's a cinnamon roll for you in the kitchen." Ally waited until her son darted down the stairs, then she approached the bed, tossing aside a pillow to make room. "I appreciate you taking the time to help your brother. But we have business to talk about."

"Ah, what happened yesterday wasn't that bad." Kylie pulled a second throw pillow over her face.

Ally nabbed the pillow and flung it onto the floor. "Look at me."

"Okay." Kylie jerked up and rubbed her eyes. "Thanks for picking us up yesterday."

Is that what we did all day? Track her down and offer her taxi service?

Ally took a deep breath. "I'm furious with you. For starters, you know I've said you can't hang around older guys."

"They used to come to youth group."

"That's not the point."

"Well, anyway, I was bored yesterday, so I asked if I could hang with them. No big deal. We drove around, stopped at Nathan's house, watched a movie, and then they thought we could try car skating. Don't get so bent out of shape. It's usually safe."

"You're telling me you have a name for this idiotic activity? You think this is some sort of a new Winter Olympics event?" Ally took two deep breaths. "I was worried sick about you. We were supposed to talk over breakfast and then do some Christmas shopping. If you didn't want to go shopping, fine, but to pull that trick—"

"I needed space. Jeez, Mom, you're always hassling me."

"And with two boys sixteen—"

"Nathan is fifteen." Kylie stood, put her hands on her hips, and tossed her hair.

Ally leaned close and cupped Kylie's chin in her hands. "Let me make this clear. You're grounded until ... well ... at least a month." She straightened up. "And hand over the weed."

"What?"

"Now."

"I told you I'm not smoking anything. You don't believe me."

"Kylie!"

"You need to trust me."

"Why?"

An odd look on Kylie's face made her suspicious. Ally dug under her mattress and pulled out a plastic bag of dried green leaves.

"The only reason I had the stash was so my friends wouldn't get in trouble," Kylie said. "I didn't smoke it. Honest."

"That's the oldest excuse in the world. You've also lost cell phone privileges while you're grounded. Don't you dare leave the house while I'm gone. I have to cover a special church service, Aunt Nettie's visiting a sick friend, and Will had to call AAA because his battery died, so we'll have to skip church this morning. And when I come home, I'd better find you in your room—with it cleaned."

"Okay, okay. Jeez."

Ally took a deep breath when she stepped into the hallway. She had a pounding headache and wondered how Kylie had gotten so off the beam. Weed, older boys, a near miss on the ice. What next? From now on, she was tightening the rules and keeping a close eye on her daughter. Will might be questioning if he was ready to stepparent a teenaged girl. Ally shuddered and blinked back the thought, but she didn't blame him. Parenting teens isn't for the faint-hearted.

CHAPTER TWENTY-ONE

Ally looked at the Christmas tree. It had been devoid of packages for weeks and dropping dead needles onto the tree skirt. She needed to put away the decorations but instead decided to camp out on the family room sofa. *Oh, that lovely, saggy sofa is calling to me.*

She still had to write another article before this week's deadline. Ugh. The last thing she wanted to do was to boot up her laptop. But before she started it, she'd check upstairs to see if her daughter had cleaned her room.

Kylie was curled up in a ball, sleeping. Her clothes had been put up and and her schoolbooks organized on top of her desk. Even her stuffed animal collection was neatly lined up against the wall. Glory, hallelujah. One battle won.

She slipped downstairs again and settled into writing. Reluctantly, she pressed the power button and clicked on her email. There was a request for her to do a piece on the Newcomers Club. She typed, "Sure, send me the contact person's info." She figured she could whip up the story while Will watched the Lions game on television.

Ally checked her phone. Three o'clock. She stretched out on the couch in the family room.

❧

She opened her eyes and looked at her phone. Five o'clock. Yikes! She checked outside and saw the sun had dimmed in the late afternoon. Where did the afternoon go? A light sprinkling of snow had settled on her car out in the driveway, enough to remind her she'd overslept. Realizing they were out of milk, she jumped in the car to buy milk for breakfast the next day.

When she returned, she found Will lounging on the couch in the family room. A recent trim had his hair cropped close to his head, a look she loved. He also had doused himself with her favorite lime shaving lotion. Wow! In his navy blue shirt with his beard filled in, he looked amazing.

He stood and took both ends of her scarf, slowly drawing her toward him until they stood inches apart. He drew her into a tight embrace before planting a long, slow kiss on her lips. They were the only ones in the world right now, in their own private moment. Then she pulled back.

"Will!"

"They went to order pizza. No one is around." He swept back her bangs with a gentle caress and gave her another kiss, a short, soft one, before running his hands up and down the side of her arms.

Ally breathed in deeply as she stroked his beard. "You're looking good. Give me time to jump out of my sweats. Back in a flash."

Ten minutes later, they drove toward Traverse City. The downtown area glistened with newly fallen snow. "People seem happy to be out shopping," said Ally.

"Probably have cabin fever and want to shop before a big snowstorm hits."

"Ready for a surprise?"

Ally clapped her hands together. "Of course."

"Okay, first I'm taking you to *Chez Louise*, and then we're going to check out a nineties tribute band. You'll love it."

Ally squealed. "No way. Wait, I thought we were supposed to be saving money. That restaurant costs big bucks."

"Ah-ha, that's the cool part. I know the owner at *Chez*, and he begged me to bring you by. I think he's hoping you might feature his place in an article. Meal's on the house."

"You know we aren't allowed freebies over ten dollars. I could be in a lot of ..."

"I'm kidding. But the concert—I won the tickets on a radio giveaway."

"Now that I will accept. You're amazing."

"All I know is tonight we're on a real date. No kids, no camp problems. Only you and me."

His phone buzzed. A few seconds later, his voice mail alert sounded.

"Go ahead and listen."

"No, later." He shut off his phone and pulled into a gas station to fill up. While he was paying for the gas, Ally flipped over the phone and checked the last call. Sarah. How odd. He always told her about calls he had. She swatted away the uneasy sensation in her stomach. Maybe Kylie was right? *No, that's ridiculous. Quit being insecure, Ally.*

When he hopped back in the car, Ally toyed with admitting to him that she'd checked his phone but decided he'd think she was being insecure, which she was.

CHAPTER TWENTY-TWO

"Killer game of Zelda," said Emerald as she scooted off of Kylie's bed. They had been playing the video game on the iPad all afternoon, and she was winning. Emerald tossed a throw pillow at Kylie, who was lying on the floor messing with her controller. "Got to go. I promised I'd be home for dinner. Keeping on my dad's good side. You still coming tonight?"

"I'm not sure. Kind of tired."

"You're going to back out? It's Saturday night, and you said you wanted to meet my friends. Don't let me down."

"I don't know."

"No maybe. You said you were up for it." Emerald grabbed Kylie's wrists, pulled her up, and started jumping up and down with her.

Kylie yanked her wrists away. "Back off." Boy, Em could irritate her. She was so pushy.

"Don't be mad. I'm trying to get you a life and out of this dump."

"This place isn't a dump. And, anyway, my aunt is the nicest person in the world."

"Sorry, didn't mean that." Emerald shot her an apologetic glance. "But you have to admit you're stuck here with the fam. You need more social in your life." She did a little dance. "Looking out for my bestie."

Kylie squeezed her eyes shut, then opened them. "Arghhhh. You sure don't give up." She lowered her voice. "And, anyway, Mom's on Secret Service duty right now."

"She'd let you go to a little birthday party, right? Logan is only the most popular girl in school." Emerald walked over to the mirror, looked at her reflection, and shook her head like an old-school metal band musician. "Be ready to paaaar-ty."

Kylie threw a running shoe at her, and Emerald caught it. "So who's going to be there?"

"Tons of people that matter." Emerald shoved her feet into her shoes and tied the shoelaces. "I'll text you at eight, Ky. Later."

Kylie slipped into her mother's room. She crossed her fingers that her mother would be in a good mood. She found her lying on her bed reading a novel. How boring was that?

"Good book?"

"Yes, you ought to try reading once in a while," her mom answered.

She sat on the edge of the bed. "I've tried to be good lately."

"Yes."

"I was invited to Logan's birthday party tonight."

"Do you think you deserve it?"

"Probably not. But if you let me go, you can add two more weeks onto my grounding. Don't you want me to make some friends? There'll be lots of girls, and I can make more friends."

"True. Will her parents be there to supervise?"

"Of course."

Her mother studied her face. "I don't know."

"Please, just this once."

"You have been a big help lately, and your attitude has changed. But only for one night. You are still grounded after that."

"Thanks!" Kylie leaned over and hugged her mother. "I'll be ready in five minutes. "Mrs. Goodman will take us. She said to just drop me off at the curb. Everything's so icy, and she doesn't want you to slip on her walkway."

❧

Kylie leaped out of her mother's car and slammed the door before jumping into the Goodmans' waiting SUV.

Twenty minutes later, Kylie opened the door as subzero air blasted her face. "Thanks for the ride to the party, Dr. Goodman." She put a tentative foot onto the ground to test for ice. Confident she was touching snow, she jumped out of the car, followed by Emerald. Dr. Goodman rolled down the window and gestured to his daughter.

"You gave me the parents' cell number, right?"

"Sure, Dad, remember? On the kitchen table." She giggled and leaned over to give him a kiss. "I'll call you when it's over."

"Well, I trust you, sweetheart. Have fun with your girl-friends."

He wasn't gone a minute when Emerald clinched her fist in a victory gesture. "Yes! He has no clue."

"Clue about what?" Em wasn't making sense.

"If I'm sweet to him, he asks fewer questions. My mom's the suspicious one."

"It's only a birthday party. What's the big deal?" Kylie followed Emerald up the hill on the newly plowed driveway to the house above. It shone like a bedazzled jewel among the surrounding cottages on the water. On the front porch, they both stopped and turned around. Kylie gasped at the panoramic view of the lake, a long wooly finger of snow stretched out below. She could hardly see where the water began and the shore ended. "Wow! Logan's parents must be loaded."

"No kidding. Now don't ask a bunch of questions. Follow me and I'll show you how it's done." She pushed the doorbell next to the massive wooden double doors. Kylie peered into one of the side windows to see if anyone was coming. A guy with a bottle of beer in his hand sauntered down the long entryway and jerked open the door.

"Hey," he said. "I'm Aiden, Logan's brother."

"Hey yourself, Aiden," said Emerald, as a giggle escaped her lips.

Kylie's eyes widened. This didn't look like any middle-school birthday party. Oh well. This guy was probably Logan's brother's friend.

He reached out his hand and gave both of them a fist bump. "Welcome to the shack." He turned behind him and yelled, "A couple of hotties." The response sounded like a pack of hyenas looking for dinner. "Sorry, they're kinda lit. Judgment-free zone here."

Kylie noticed her friend's confident look faded. She herself was trying to calm a jumpy stomach as they followed Aiden into the family room.

"Holy Guacamole," said Kylie. The girls both gasped at the two-story floor-to-ceiling window with a view of the lake. In front of the window, a large sectional sofa filled the spacious room with kids playing video games. A couple of girls leaned up against the fireplace, taking selfies—future bragging rights to be posted on their social media accounts. She looked around for Logan's parents. Mom had always taught her to greet her friend's parents. She really wanted to make a good impression. Right now she wanted to turn over a new leaf. Maybe they had gone to the store for a minute.

"Pretty chill," said Emerald. Her tone sounded too casual, like she was trying to act like a veteran partygoer. "Reminds me of our summer house on Lake Charlevoix."

Kylie turned to Emerald and hissed in her ear. "You big liar, you don't have a cottage." She elbowed her friend. "Where's Logan? Isn't this her house?"

Emerald gave her the evil eye and put her finger up to her mouth to warn her to keep quiet. She leaned into Kylie's ear. "Hey, just play the game, girlfriend." She took Aiden's arm and gestured to Kylie. "Aiden's going to give us the tour."

Kylie started upstairs and then decided not to. "It's okay. I'll stay here." Kids at school talked about what went on upstairs at parties. *Wonder where Logan's parents are? I've been in trouble enough this year. Still, it's pretty grown up to be at this cool place.*

As she thought about the evening ahead, her heart raced, and she wished Em would hang with her.

Emerald disappeared up the open spiral staircase, her chatter floating back down to Kylie. "Back in a flash," she said over her shoulder.

Kylie walked over to the family room and stood frozen in the doorway. She looked around but didn't recognize anyone. This wasn't how she pictured the night. Self-assurance seeped out of her like a leaking balloon. *Should I call Mom?* She dug around in her jeans pocket. *Shoot, forgot my phone.* As she was reaching into her coat pocket for a piece of gum, a tall boy about six feet three inches approached her. A tingle of excitement rushed through her body. *Bet he's on the varsity basketball team.*

"Who's this?" The tall guy with a cleft in his chin looked Kylie up and down and paused in the middle. "Don't remember seeing you at school." Kylie stared at him, not knowing what to say.

"Hey, my friend isn't a very good host. I'll take your coat." Kylie slid out of her jacket and handed it to him. He disappeared around the corner and was back in a minute.

"So, you didn't tell me who you are. You're sorta cute." said the guy.

"One of the chill ones." She closed the three middle fingers on her hand, held her hand high, and rotated her wrist back and forth. *If you only knew how not chilled I feel.*

He threw back his head and laughed, a loud horsey laugh. "Says who?"

"If you hafta ask, you aren't cool," she retorted. *Hey, I'm doing pretty well faking this being a high schooler.*

"Okay, I'll ask again. Name? Oh, let me guess. Reagan? Jennifer? Kate?"

"Kylie." His brushed-back hair caught the light. He was pretty cute.

"Well, Kylie, my girl, let me introduce you." He grabbed her wrist and pulled her into the middle of the room. "Hey, meet Kylie, guys." One girl looked up, nodded, and went back to fiddling with the remote controller. The rest ignored her.

"What's your pleasure, my little Kylie?" He steered her over to a bar on the side of the room, crammed with miscellaneous bottles with bright labels. Cocktail glasses of every size flanked the assortment of beverages.

"Oh, a Coke."

"Nothing else?"

"Well I usually take a shot of"—she looked over the labels to pick a name—"Grey Goose, but not tonight." *Hmm, what is Grey Goose?*

He opened up the lid to the acrylic ice bucket and dropped a couple of ice cubes in a cup. "Do you like Cherry Coke?"

"Uh, yep." That probably wouldn't be too bad.

He turned a tall bottle around, but she couldn't see the label. "A bit of cherry flavoring." He handed the drink to her. "Try it."

She took the cup from him. "Thanks. Hey, I think I know you. Saw your picture in the paper. You're a forward on the varsity team." She raised her voice a few decibels, as the crowd in the other room was growing rowdy.

"Smart girl."

"Mom works for the paper, and I read all the articles. I also go to all the home games, but I can't remember your name."

"Malone." His large hand picked up a bowl of chips. He grabbed some and handed the container to her. Her growling stomach was grateful. They munched in silence, still standing by the bar. Malone poured himself some from the bottle with the gray goose on the front, took a swallow, then another one. He refilled her glass with more Coke from the can and added more of the cherry flavoring. Wow, this beats hanging around with Mom and Benjie on a weekend night. A haze of blue smoke surrounded the three playing a video game on the sofa as one tall girl inhaled a joint. *Tried that once. No thanks.*

Malone smiled and Kylie noticed a dimple in his right cheek. *Wow, he's the cutest guy I've seen in Lake Surrender.* "Let's go hang out with the kids in the living room," Malone said. He steered her through the family room to a smaller room where the lights had dimmed. Two couples—one on the sofa, one on the floor—were making out, their bodies tangled together with legs and arms going every which way. It was quiet except for the sound of someone playing a song on their phone. Kylie felt her whole body stiffen and surveyed the room for someone she knew.

"Um, I'm still hungry." She looked around for Emerald, wondering when she'd come back from her "tour." She needed a new bestie.

Malone looked at her. "Sure you don't want to hang out here?"

"I'm sorta hungry."

"Well, okay, I think someone ordered some pizza." She followed him to the kitchen where a short boy wearing a Michigan sweatshirt and a toboggan hat was throwing up in the sink. She turned to Malone. "Aren't Aiden and Logan's parents here?"

Malone's eyes studied her, an amused look on his face. The way his eyes looked, all crinkled up, made her think he'd burst out laughing any minute. Wow, what did she say? He raised an eyebrow. "Yeah, sure, they're upstairs. Don't you get it? Tonight's Open Crib—you know, no helicopter parents around …"

"Does that mean?"

"Yep, parent-free." He put two thumbs up before turning on his heels to leave. Kylie picked up a piece of pizza off of a cardboard box and took a bite. Malone returned with a red Solo cup full of Coke in his hand. "Thought you might need some of this with your pizza."

"Thanks." She was thirsty. She slipped two pieces of pizza onto a plate and handed it to him. "It stinks in here." Between one guy barfing into the sink and another lurking around the kitchen doorjamb, green around the gills, the walls seemed to be closing in on her.

"Maybe we can sit on the stairs?" That might be the best way to catch Emerald when she came down. She had plenty of questions to ask her—like why she had abandoned her. She bit into the slice of pizza and gulped down some Coke. Pizza always made her thirsty.

"Sure." They found a place on the bottom step and sat. Malone clicked his plastic cup against hers. "Cheers." He leaned over and kissed her on the cheek. "You're pretty hot. How did I miss seeing you at school?"

Kylie closed her eyes. Her stomach was doing backflips. *Please, God, don't let him find out I'm an eighth-grader.*

CHAPTER TWENTY-THREE

Ally sat with Aunt Nettie on the sofa as the two worked on projects in the family room. On the coffee table sat two sundaes smothered with hot fudge, ready to be devoured. "Great we could have some time together," said Aunt Nettie, as she dipped into the ice cream. "Pretty rare we are able to squeeze in time to visit." She savored a few spoonfuls of the dessert before putting down her bowl and picking up her art pad.

"Yep, worked out with Kylie gone, Will at a meeting, and Benjie in bed." She gestured at the sketch her aunt was drawing. "What's that?"

"I'm working on a design for a table I purchased at the Goodwill store. The piece will look darling after a new coat of paint and adding these morning glories around the legs."

"You're so creative. You amaze me." Ally pushed a needle through denim material. "Well, I'm being industrious too. Any money I can save, like letting down the hem on Kylie's jeans, can be put toward the wedding. She's grown so much this year, her pants are turning into capris."

"Good. Will is proud of you."

"He started calling me Stretch. I went from Miss Starbucks to Miss Stretchy Bucks." She suppressed a giggle. "We're working on our budget together now, and it's a relief to have our living expenses line up with our income."

"Good for you."

She and Nettie worked in silence until the grandfather clock in the hallway chimed ten. The familiar tune always took her back to summers in her childhood when her family stayed with Aunt Nettie. "Kylie said she was staying with Emerald."

"You know that."

"Hmm."

"Hmm, what? Are you worried about something?"

Ally tied a knot on the end of the thread and tossed the jeans down on the coffee table. "I don't know. Call it mother's intuition, but I'm uneasy." Biting her lower lip, she picked up her phone to see if she had a missed call. No.

"She asked you to trust her. I'm sure the Goodmans will be responsible. He *is* the school superintendent." Nettie reached over and pulled out a robin-egg-blue pencil from the box on the table.

"Kylie seemed pretty excited, and I do hope she will be able to make some new friends," said Ally.

"That surprises me because they have had some fights at school. Guess she and Emerald have made up. Emerald was trying hard to be her friend," said Aunt Nettie.

"Who can figure out teenage girls?"

Ally headed upstairs to put the hemmed jeans in Kylie's closet and then checked on Benjie. He slept, tucked under a heavy quilt, the nightlight casting a soft glow on his pale blond hair and ruddy cheeks. What a sweet boy. She kissed him and pulled the covers securely under his chin, thankful to have only *one* teenager. Another one might put her in an early grave.

Back in the family room, she plopped on the sofa and clicked on Netflix. Comedy, suspense, family drama—nothing piqued her interest. What was wrong? Again she picked up her phone, and again there was no missed call.

She sent Sonja Goodman a text but didn't receive a response. She finished up her ice cream sundae and tidied up the room. Then she decided to take her ice cream bowl to the kitchen sink, cell phone still in her hand. As she slid her bowl into the soapy water, she dropped her phone into the sink.

Ally let out a yelp as she pulled it out. She tried to turn the phone on again, but the battery was dead. "Well, that's it for my phone for a while."

❧

The minutes dragged as Kylie and Malone sipped their drinks. *This is real boring, and I don't know what to say to this guy.* She'd rather be playing a video game, making cookies, or even cleaning her room. That dumb Em. Some bestie she is.

"You look so familiar," said Malone, breaking the silence.

Wow, he did have amazing eyes and such long eyelashes.

"Did you go to that paddleboard party out on the lake last summer at Harrison's?"

Kylie took another sip of her pop. "Probably not. I spent a lot of the summer at camp.

"Camp?" He looked puzzled as if that was the last place he'd expected her to be. "What kind of camp? The only one I know about is that Christian camp at the other end of the lake. I hear they learn how to tie knots and collect berries for dinner. Not my kind of fun."

Kylie's jaw dropped open. Suddenly Malone didn't look so cute. "It's chill. Not so bad. I learned a lot of really good stuff there. She glanced at the basketball star whose gaze had wandered to a long-haired blonde girl sashaying by.

Malone looked back at Kylie. He tipped his head back and put up his hands in an apology. "Good stuff? Like Bible stuff?"

Kylie nodded.

"Looks like I picked the wrong girl to hit on. You're too perfect for me." Then he bowed and put his hands together. "But say a little prayer for me." He stood, turned, and headed to the family room.

Embarrassment spread through her body. *So what if I'm an eighth-grader? I know when I'm being dissed.* She clenched her fists. Her whole body shook. Still seated on the bottom stair, she watched Malone flirt with a girl wearing a white tee shirt. Hair piled on top of her head in a top-knot bun, she leaned in as they exchanged whispered comments.

Kylie bounded upstairs and saw a long hallway with closed doors on either side. She stood in the middle and hollered, "Em, got to talk to you." But no one answered. Kylie took a deep breath and started rapping on each door. "Hey Em, are you up here?"

"Go away." The sound came from the last bedroom on the right.

"Come on, please."

She heard a guy's voice say something, and Em responded with her annoying laugh.

Kylie pushed open the door and stared at a king-sized bed. Em was lying on top of the bed in her underwear. Aiden hovered over her, drawing pictures on her bare stomach with a colored marker.

"What are you doing?" shrieked Emerald. She threw a marker at her.

Kylie's eyes grew wider as she took in the scene.

"Haven't you ever played the Roadmap game?" said Aiden, squinting at her. "A guy takes a marker and the girl tells him where he can draw ..."

"Get out of here." Emerald bolted straight up in bed.

"I'm trying. Can you call your parents?"

"You're not serious."

"I want to go home."

"Well, I'm not going."

"I don't have a phone, remember?"

Emerald threw her phone at Kylie. It clattered onto the wooden floor and Kylie picked it up. "Go ahead. Call your mommy to rescue you. What a baby."

Kylie tore out the door and sprinted downstairs into the powder room, her stomach ready to launch its contents. Oh no, the flu. Funny, she didn't have any symptoms earlier. She lowered her body to lie on the tile, cooling her forehead. She was not going to throw up, no she wasn't.

She pulled out the phone and dialed her mom's number, but it went to voice mail. "Jeez, Mom, why don't you ever recharge your phone?" She pitched the phone down on the floor and pulled herself up onto the toilet seat. Her head rested in her hands, warm and sweaty. How could she have gotten into this mess? Right now she needed a ride home, and Mom wasn't answering. Who could she call?

Maybe Will would come. Actually, he was the last person she wanted to talk to, but she was desperate. *He'll probably give me a big lecture about what a bad person I am.* She looked at the phone, trying to remember the number Mom insisted she memorize in case of emergencies. Oh, what was it? She didn't want to do this. Fighting a wave of nausea, she finally pulled it from her memory and punched it in."

"Hi, who is this?"

"Uh, it's Kylie. Sorry to bother you, I had to use a friend's phone, and Mom isn't picking up."

"Do you need something?"

"A ride, please. I'm sort of stuck at this person's house."

"What person's house? You're slurring your words."

"This guy's house."

"A party?"

She paused. "I guess." She held her stomach.

"I'll be right there. What's the address?"

She told him as tears roll down her cheeks in salty rivulets. The bathroom seemed like the only safe place right now.

Please be quick, Will.

The nausea crept up her throat, bringing up her dinner. She tried to hold the eruption back, but it was too late as she up-chucked pizza, chips, and Cherry Coke all over her jeans and the toilet seat. She looked at the contents of her stomach as some guy pounded on the door. "I'll be out in a minute." Kylie looked around, grabbed a handful of tissues to sop up the mess and then stuffed the tissues in the wastepaper basket. The stench made her gag. She lowered her body until she lay on her back on the hard floor and waited for the next eruption. She wouldn't mind sleeping there all night. As she fought back more nausea, she wondered if maybe she had food poisoning.

Someone pounded on the door. "I'm in here." The pounding continued. "Okay," Kylie said and dragged her body up off the floor. She turned the doorknob and a large, burly guy with a beard pushed the door open. He looked like one of the tackles on the football team.

"Hey, cutie. Why you hiding in here?" He staggered toward her until he was inches from her face, every pore of his body reeking of beer. He reached for her hand and brought it to his face. "Like my beard? Kind of sexy, eh?"

Kylie froze. He was blocking the door, and she was trapped. On top of that, he probably outweighed her by at least 150 pounds. Her heart pounded, every beat warning her of danger. Slowly, she pulled her hand away from his.

"Heeey, what's yourrrr problem?" He leered at her and her body shook.

If she had a guardian angel, he'd better show up right now.

⁂

No music ever sounded as sweet as the doorbell chime. Kylie shoved past the bathroom intruder. She bolted down the hallway, leaving Emerald's phone on a table before she surveyed the living room for her coat. She finally found it on the back of one of the sofas. Then she yanked open the heavy wooden door and saw Will standing on the welcome mat. She threw her arms around him, almost knocking him down.

"Whoa there." Will grabbed her by the arm to support her as they stepped gently down the front stairs and shuffled to the Suburban. He opened the car door and snapped her seatbelt. "You're in over your head tonight."

"I know. I thought I was going to a girl's birthday party." Her head was spinning, and she had difficulty forming her words. "I ... I ... didn't know what to do and then this guy ..."

"This guy what?"

"Don't know. Think he kept giving me Cherry Coke ..."

Will shook his head. "That old trick." He started the engine, then reached over and put his arm around her shoulders. "I believe you. You did the right thing, and I'm proud of you. We'll explain it to your mom, and we'll have to call the Goodmans. But right now, close your eyes and rest."

They drove for a while, and then Kylie opened her eyes. "I was really scared tonight."

"I can imagine. Did I ever tell you what I do when I'm afraid?" said Will as he pulled the truck through the McDonald's drive-thru.

"No."

"Want a plain Coke? No cherry flavoring?"

"No cherry. I'll hate that flavor for the rest of my life."

He ordered two Cokes through the outside speaker.

"I feel so stupid." Kylie started to sob.

"It's okay." Will put his arm around her shoulder. "So, believe it or not, I was a kid once. I used to whistle when I was scared. My father taught me how to be a good whistler. I used to go out into the woods, and if it had turned dark and I was lost, I always whistled. Summer evenings I'd explore the woods behind our house and almost forget to come home until the sun started setting."

"Uh huh," said Kylie.

"I'd whistle to myself until I calmed down. Then I always found my way back home."

"Really?"

"Yep. Tell you what. I'll teach you the best way to whistle this summer. Oh, and speaking of summer, you've been chosen for the counselor-in-training program."

"I am? I didn't think you'd let me. I mean, especially after tonight."

"Ever heard of a do-over?"

"Really?"

"Yep."

"Wow, thanks!"

"Okay, but don't start crying again."

Will paid for the drinks and pulled out of the drive-thru lane. "You'll be great. You're good with the younger kids. I watched you the last two summers at camp when you volunteered to help out. And you've had a lot of practice with your brother." He studied her face. "Is that drink helping?"

"Not so sick to my stomach."

"We'll drive around a little more until you sober up, and then you'll have to talk to your mom."

"Can you pull over for a minute?" Will turned onto the shoulder of the road. Kylie threw open the door and emptied her stomach again. "Thanks."

He took the drive the long way around the lake and then headed to Ally's. When they pulled up, Ally rushed up to the passenger's side. Her mom's eyes squinted as she yanked open the door, and it looked like she'd chewed off the lipstick from her bottom lip. That signaled big trouble.

Kylie rolled down the window. Will leaned over the seat and held up his hand. "This isn't what it looks like."

"It looks like you're drunk, Kylie," said Ally.

"I'm sorry, Mom. I know I screwed up. I'm really sorry. I didn't mean to, though." She didn't care how long her mother grounded her or how much allowance she'd lose. She was home and safe.

෴

"Thanks for rescuing Kylie last night." Ally set a steaming mocha down on Will's desk at camp. "I'm so disappointed in her."

"Thanks," Will took a sip. "I believe she honestly thought she was going to some girl's party, and Emerald talked her into staying. Don't be too hard on her. She's had a bad enough year already, and she's so naïve she may not have realized that the cherry flavoring was cherry liqueur."

"She and I had a long talk last night. I am glad she called you. My phone was out of commission, but she should have dialed someone the minute she realized what kind of party it was."

"I agree."

"She's grounded for several weeks, but the weird thing is she seemed relieved."

"I'm sure she is. She's learning about not being so reckless."

"She's become such a handful this year."

"A lot of teens are."

With two hands propped up on his desk, Ally leaned toward him. "Not feeling like Mother of the Year." She swallowed hard. "I have to be stricter. I guess I've babied her and trusted her too much. It's my fault."

"You know the famous saying of Ronald Reagan ... 'Trust but verify.' Goes for teenagers as well as politicians."

"Yeah, the verifying part is exhausting." She picked up a card on top of his desk. The front had a St. Bernard dog with a placard around his neck that said, "Thanks!" "Hey what's this?"

Will, who had returned to his huge pile of paperwork on his desk, grunted but didn't look up.

"Hmm, looks like it's from Sarah." She flipped it open.

He glanced up. "Oh yeah. She called me a while back to let me know her father has had some serious health issues. And she asked for plumbing advice. It's a thank-you note."

"Oh, that's nice. I have to be honest, though. I was sort of worried about you and ..."

"Darn, I thought I brought the file with me this morning."
Will rifled through a pile of manila file folders. "I'm crunched
for time, have a meeting at ten. Could you …"

"I have to drive past the cottage for an interview. If you tell
me where you left the file, I'll bring it to you in time for the
meeting tonight," Ally offered.

"Thanks." Will sat back in his chair surveying his desk's flat
terrain heaped with unpaid bills, receipts, camp counselor ap-
plications, and a first-aid handbook. He turned first to the pile
of bills and started flipping through them.

"Bye."

He looked up. "Huh? Yeah, see ya."

❧

Ally swung by her aunt's house to pick up Benjie and then
headed toward Will's cottage. Located about ten minutes from
camp, the house offered the solitude of country living. Ally
passed a couple of pastures, a grove of pine trees, and a dairy
farm before she turned onto the gravel road. She'd first seen the
stone cottage when Will asked her to preview his purchase—
said he needed a woman's opinion. He had bought the cottage
for his former fiancée as a surprise, only to be surprised by
Sarah's disinterested reaction.

Ally, however, loved the hundred-year-old cottage built out
of flat gray stones collected from the area. What the house
lacked in space, it made up for in charm. The curvy front path
lined with boxwoods, the brown-shake roof, and hollyhocks
against the west wall in summer resembled an English cottage.

The family room, dining room, and kitchen were all in one
room with the kitchen window offering a panoramic view of
a pasture that backed up to a thick forest of deciduous trees.
About once a week, either the resident fox or a doe and her
fawn stepped into the yard to eat from the pile of field corn
Will bought weekly at the local farmers' market.

She handed her son a coloring book and markers, then settled him at the kitchen table. "Sit here. I'll be right back."

Back in the bedroom, on top of Will's old walnut desk, she found the file she was looking for. Ally went back to the kitchen. "Let's head on." She motioned for Benjie to follow her. But, as usual, once he started a project, he showed no interest in changing gears.

Ally drummed her fingers against the painted kitchen table. Was it worth fighting over, or should she wait a few more minutes until he finished? No matter. She didn't have to do the interview for another hour. She took off her coat and relaxed.

While she waited, Ally surveyed the décor. She'd dubbed it the "Woodsy Will" look. She itched to put her touches on it and make this into *their* home. She hoped she could talk Will out of those deer antlers over the fireplace and that garish modern-art painting over the sofa. And then there was that brown corduroy sofa with material that sagged around the furniture's form and probably had for several years. Still, the couch was comfy and an object Benjie couldn't destroy, unlike—

Ally leaped to her feet as Benjie veered off of his coloring book and onto what looked like an opened book with handwriting covering the pages. "Hey, slow down. You need to color only in the coloring book." She put her hands around his and with gentle pressure guided him back to the book.

Curious, she picked up the book and discovered a journal in Will's handwriting. Unlike his desk at work, his handwriting was neat and readable. *I had no idea he kept a journal.* Her eyes fell on the open page, and a jolt like a crack of thunder went through her body.

Is she the right one for me?

CHAPTER TWENTY-FOUR

How could she stop reading now? She fought a voice inside that warned her to back off. But she *had* to know. He had been acting distant lately. Looks like he'd been keeping secrets from her too.

She took a deep breath as her eyes poured over the page.

"Pros—Pretty and what a figure. We also have a lot in common. We both love the outdoors." Ally paused. She'd learned to love the outdoors, but that wasn't a natural. She continued to read. *"She is committed to her faith and would probably make a good mother."*

"What do you mean 'probably would'?" Ally murmured out loud. "I'm already one." *Probably meant future children.* She turned the page.

"Cons—she's used to doing things on her own and might find it hard to adjust to being a spouse. Also, she's not very flexible."

"He thinks I'm not 'flexible'? I moved across country to a new town, moved in with my aunt, and started a new job as a cook. How flexible is that?"

"I'm still not sure if my life vocation will always be running a camp. Would she come with me if I'm led to another career? She seems to be married to her job."

What? That really hurt. Ally's mouth grew dry as she read to the bottom of the page.

"I want to find Your will. Please direct me. You know I'm having doubts."

"He has doubts?" She said it out loud.

Her hand shook as the journal slipped out of her hand and hit the wooden floor with a thud. He wasn't sure, was he? And when was he going to tell her his concerns? Well, she had a few fears of her own. Was she failing again? Worse still, was he backing out? What a fool she'd been to miss seeing his struggle. She choked back bitter tears.

"Mama?" Benjie put down his markers and tilted his head sideways. Her head throbbed, as if it had been smacked with a cast-iron frying pan, but she held out her hand, and he took it. "It's okay, sweetie."

"No crying." His menthol-blue eyes relayed the message that he meant what he said as he nodded his head for emphasis.

She looked out the kitchen window and then back at her son. "Mama is sad right now."

He stroked the top of her head. "Sad, sad."

Ally found a tissue in her purse and wiped her eyes. "You're a wonderful son."

"Yep." Benjie nodded.

❧

After leaving the cottage, Ally zipped through McDonald's and headed toward Traverse City for her 1:00 p.m. appointment. Luckily, Benjie sat quietly while she interviewed the director of the senior center about their upcoming event, Silver Slippers Dance. But her mind drifted during the interview. Nothing was making sense. What were Will's intentions? Did he have cold feet again after they'd worked through so much? Or had they? And if things fell apart, what would she do? Live with her aunt forever? She loved Aunt Nettie, but she was a grown women. Her thoughts came fast and frantic.

Back in the car, Ally steered her vehicle onto the snow-packed highway past Grand Traverse Bay. All she wanted to do right now was to drive endlessly. The sun shone on the lake, outlining the rugged waves on the shore, frozen mid-motion, and depositing piles of jagged blocks of ice and mountains of snow. A heap of frigid confusion and turmoil. After a second winter in Lake Surrender, she was beginning to hate the season, really hate it.

Pressing down the gas pedal, Ally picked up speed, tires whirring like her mind. If she drove long enough, she might make sense of what she'd read at Will's. Random phrases looped over and over in her brain like a stone rattling inside an empty tin can. "Would be a good mother? Not flexible?" *Why didn't you tell me, Will?*

She'd go to the grocery store. Shopping always calmed her. She steered her car into a parking space at Oleson's, loaded Benjie into a cart, and headed for the baking aisle.

Ally tossed a box of powdered sugar and two five-pound bags of flour behind Benjie. Then she accidently pushed the cart past the candy aisle. She grabbed Benjie's hand, which had found a bag of red licorice—his weakness. Too late. He clenched his treat in a death-grip and let out piercing squeal.

Ally took his face in her hands. "Not today." She locked her eyes with his. *Please, not another meltdown. I don't need this right now.* His boot banged against the cart, rattling the metal seat. "I said no."

The kicking grew more insistent. Benjie's eyes blazed with anger. "Mine," he screamed.

His flailing leg smacked Ally in the midriff. The hit took her breath away for a moment, but she caught herself before she started to yell. She didn't want to make a scene. "Those are special treats, and you've just lost your privilege. You are so in trouble." Although she kept her gaze on her son, she sensed the stares of other customers as they steered their carts around the two of them.

Ally pushed the cart toward the freezer section. An elderly, plump woman pulled her cart alongside of her and patted her on the arm. "Hang in there, dear."

A tightness closed around her throat, an invisible hand choking the breath out of her. She could barely breathe, and her head spun. She thought she'd conquered the panic attacks, but they were back. *My old enemy is back and I'm in deep.* She hated that she had these attacks.

Will's journal entry had unleased memories her of her final years with Bryan. She remembered all of her ex's accusations, mainly when he blamed her of neglecting him. Am I doing that to Will?

Ally closed her eyes and took several deep breaths. But her heart still raced. How could she drive her son home in this condition?

This is not a heart attack, this is anxiety, she told herself as she yanked Benjie out of his seat. She pushed the cart to the far back of the store and parked it by the bin of clearance items. *Lord, help me.* She grasped the smooth metal handle, trying to stop the dizziness by counting to thirty and then forty.

"I can count too," Benjie joined in.

"Yes, you can." Finally her head stopped spinning, and her heartbeat slowed. She let out a long breath, her body drained of any energy as doubts still circled her brain.

CHAPTER TWENTY-FIVE

She lifted her son out of the cart and grasped his hand before stumbling to the shelter of the greeting card display. "Please be home," Ally muttered as she texted her aunt. Nothing. She leaned against the store's early exhibit of Valentine's Day cards, not missing the irony. *Wonder if they sell condolence cards for a busted engagement?*

"Okay?" Benjie tilted his head sideways. Somehow he always could read her mind when she was upset. Although he didn't communicate well with words, he could sense human suffering, especially hers.

"Mama will be fine. Give me a minute, son." She slid her phone back in her coat pocket and used the cart handle to steady her shaky legs.

"Ma'am, are you all right?" A large man, one of the store managers, touched her on the shoulder.

"Just slipped. Very clumsy." She forced a smile. "I'll be fine. Come on, Benjie. Need to run you home." She grabbed her son's arm, and steered him toward the front door, leaving behind her cart of groceries.

Back in the car, she pulled out her phone again, hands still shaking. *Where are you, Aunt Nettie?* Panic pushed the air out of her chest. Ally grabbed the steering wheel for stability before she reached into the back seat and snapped her son into his car seat.

Her phone dinged.

"Yes, I'll be around the house this afternoon. Drop him off."

"Thank you," she typed. "And please pray for me."

Ally looked into the rearview mirror and shoved the car into reverse. After dropping Benjie off, she pointed her car toward camp, her body shaking.

She turned the windshield wipers to high and cranked up the car's heater. The snowstorm the news had predicted was beginning, and flakes came down in mass. What a day for her windshield defroster to quit working. She took her gloved hand and wiped the inside of the window so she could navigate the road. So much for buying a new car.

When she pulled into the camp parking lot, Will's Suburban was nowhere in sight, so she dug in her purse for the key to the lodge's front door and let herself in. Once inside the lodge, she walked through the drafty dining room to the back hallway where his office was.

Ally stood in the doorway of his office. The light was off, and he had cleaned off his desk. She probably just missed him. Ally flipped on the light and saw his phone on the edge of the desk.

Now what? She walked over to the desk and laid down the file, then picked up Will's phone. It was plugged into the wall socket. He must have stepped out for a minute. She settled into his chair, drumming her fingers against the arm. The snow outside was piling up, and the sun was setting. She should go. But she sat glued to the chair, eyeing his phone. She picked it up. She punched the lower button on the phone and the home page came up. Then Ally pushed the Phone icon and an electronic message popped up. Two missed phone calls from Sarah.

What! The only Sarah he knew was his ex. Why would she be calling him so much? Had he been contacting *her*? How long had this been going on? But then again there was no law saying he couldn't phone her. *Will, where are you?*

Calm down, Ally. Will was the most loyal person she'd ever met. But evidence against him was mounting faster than the snowdrift outside the office window. He was trying to get back with Sarah.

She clutched the edge of the desk and took several deep breaths. She had no one to blame but herself. Stupid woman. Stupid, stupid. She'd been neglecting him. She thought of the proverb that talked about the foolish woman tearing her house down with her own hands. Well, she was that woman. She'd neglected him, and now she was paying for it. She'd found an awesome guy, and she didn't appreciate him like she should. And if she were honest, in the back of her mind, she'd always had a plan B in case Will bailed on her. Her drive to succeed at work, her plan to open a catering business, they all pointed to one thing—fear of their relationship failing. Deep down she didn't trust God that this second marriage would work out.

That reality stabbed her in her gut. She dropped her head onto the desk and pounded it with her fist. "I'm sorry. My faith is weak. I've been trying to live this life on my own, not believing You, Lord, would take care of my needs.

Feeling like a trapped rabbit, Ally stood, buttoned her coat, and headed for the parking lot. The wind had picked up, and the oncoming flakes stung her eyes like tiny needles. Aunt Nettie could help her sort this all out. Back on the road, her car plowed through the snow on the road. Finally, she reached home.

ર

Her aunt sat in her recliner, the soothing rhythm of her clicking knitting needles a drastic contrast to Ally's state of mind. She looked up, fingers not missing a stitch. "That was fast."

Ally pulled off her boots and put them on the tray by the door before flopping onto the sofa. "I had a moment of reckoning."

"Sounds serious."

"It is."

"Well, reckon away."

Ally blinked a few times. She took a big breath before speaking. "I went to camp and Will wasn't there. But his phone was on the desk. I looked at it and saw two missed calls from Sarah."

"And that worried you?"

"Exactly. Why would that stress me out? What's wrong with me?"

"You tell me."

"I guess deep down I'm afraid of another failed relationship. And in Will's office something dawned on me—that's why I've gone crazy with the newspaper job."

"You could have found a less stressful form of employment with the same pay, like, say the camp cook's job."

"Guess I was trying to prove something to myself. But what?" She stood and thrust her hands into the back pockets of her jeans. "And then I started a catering company. I must be nuts."

"Losing your house and job in California was difficult. I understand it's not fun to be poor."

"The losses made me crave security even more."

Aunt Nettie's ball of yarn slid off her lap and rolled onto the floor. Ally stood and leaned over to pick it up as her aunt continued. "Will loves you. But he doesn't want to play second fiddle to anyone or anything. I really haven't wanted to butt in
..."

"Please do."

"You sure?"

"Please."

"You were given a second chance, a divine do-over when you almost drowned. That doesn't happen often. And remember the word you told me you kept hearing?"

"Trust."

"If ever you needed to trust God, it's now. Maybe you and Will aren't supposed to be together. But whatever the outcome, God loves you and wants the best for you and your family."

Ally nodded.

"And another thing."

Ally bit her lip. "Go ahead."

"Don't take Will for granted." Aunt Nettie put down her knitting needles on the small table next to her. "Will has been very patient while you run all over God's green acres interviewing the whole town and baking up a storm. And only a tender-hearted man can love another man's children. Throw a special needs child into the mix, and a man of lesser character would have been long gone."

Ally blinked. "Don't make me cry."

Aunt Nettie stood and walked over to Ally. Wrapping her arms around her shoulders, she gave her a kiss on the cheek. "I'm not trying to. But tears can heal. They're good for the soul."

❧

Will pressed against the glass double doors and headed toward the airport's baggage carousel, the building's heat blasting him in the face. He surveyed the area and spotted Sarah, her back to him. Her familiar blonde hair trailed down her back, her petite body engulfed in a black down parka.

"Hey there." He tapped her on her shoulder. She jumped, pivoted, flashed him a wide smile, and threw her arms around him. "My dear friend. You're always ready to help." She gave him a peck on the cheek, and he caught a whiff of her favorite gardenia perfume, a smell that brought back memories.

He stepped back and bowed. "At your service." She pointed to a small black suitcase. Will leaned over and seized the handle, lifting it over the revolving carousel. He rolled it out the front door, and they headed to the parking lot, dodging the busy traffic.

"Do you mind stopping for something to eat? The flight from Mexico City was long. Nothing but peanuts on the plane since L. A."

He looked her over. Her face seemed thinner than when he'd visited her orphanage camp in Mexico last spring. He held up a finger. "I know the perfect place where we can find you a decent meal. It'll bring back memories."

Around the corner from the airport, Burgers and More was bustling from the noontime crush, but the waitress seated them quickly in a booth by the door.

"Really good to see you, Will," said Sarah. Her body brushed against him as she scooted into the booth. A faint flicker of the old attraction spread through him. Boy, he didn't need that.

"Sorry about your dad. I'll run you over to the hospital after lunch," said Will. He looked down at his menu. "I've been told the chili's great."

"You always loved chili, especially around football season. Our senior year all you ate was chili and *hamburgesas*, err, I mean hamburgers. Hard to switch back to English."

"Chili fueled me for quite a few touchdowns, senior year." He chuckled. "We really tore up the football field after homecoming. Remember?"

"Do I ever. Got grounded for coming home at 1:30 a.m., but well worth it."

"Good times."

She tilted her head to the side, her pink lips turned up in a perky smile. *Oh, why did she do that?* Will wiped a sweaty palm on his jeans. *Okay, Grainger, level with her.* He needed to give her an update. She had no idea how his life had changed. He wasn't the greatest communicator, and it usually didn't matter. He settled on small talk instead. "Glad your father is stabilized. When will they release him?"

"They're putting in a couple of stents, so he might be laid up for a while. But then again, he's a fighter. I hope you can come see him."

"Sure." He was picking up some strong vibes that weren't exactly platonic. Well, she *had* been a part of his life for a long time. "I'll try." He poured more cream than he needed into his coffee and swirled it around, the spoon clinking against the cup. "How's your camp coming along?"

"Thanks again for helping out with the orphanage's camp last spring. Probably helped your Spanish too."

"*Claro que si*. Of course."

"We had three hundred kids during the summer season, and they had a ball." She leaned toward him. "I could still use some pointers. We need to get our aquatic program going. Very few of the kids know how to swim, and your program is the best." She reached out and touched his hand. He flinched.

"Oh, sorry. Habits die slow," said Sarah. She pulled her hand back, and with her other hand she grabbed a lock of her hair, twirling it. He remembered she always did that when she was nervous.

"No, that's okay, just weird seeing you again."

"Why?"

Will opened his mouth to explain. Then he glimpsed a familiar face coming toward him, Don from camp. *This is awkward*. He wasn't doing anything wrong, only picking a friend up from the airport, but still Will's ears burned when Don stopped at the table.

Don glanced toward Sarah and then shot Will a curious look. "Hi, Sarah. I heard your father had an operation. How's he doing?"

Sarah, full of smiles and animation, said, "He's doing great, considering." Then she filled Don in on her father's condition.

"You seem glad to be back in town," said Don.

"I miss Michigan."

"I'm sure you do."

Will motioned toward Sarah. "I picked her up at the airport. She's headed to the hospital after we eat."

"Well, hope your dad recovers quickly," said Don. "Had to pick up some parts for the furnace on this side of town and thought I'd grab some lunch." They chatted for a few moments. "Oh, they just called my number for pickup." He nodded at them and left.

Will cleared his throat. "Um, we'd better get going."

"What for?"

He paused. In spite of the enticing smell of garlic, onions, and tomatoes wafting from the steaming bowl of chili, he'd lost his appetite. He took a deep breath. "We haven't been in a lot of contact for months."

"That's true. We've only had a couple of short talks on the phone. With running the orphanage full time, I'm way behind on my emails."

Her eyes had a familiar look. The two of them had been friends long before they became engaged. He'd pretty much grown up with her. Sarah was the reason he'd purchased the gray cottage he now owned. A lot of memories flooded his mind, good ones.

CHAPTER TWENTY-SIX

Ally battled the growing late afternoon storm and drove back to the newspaper's office, thankful for the talk with her aunt. She could depend on her to speak the truth, no matter how hard. She'd have to wait to talk to Will, but it would keep. There was a lot to tell him—if he still wanted her.

Russ dashed up to her desk at work as she booted up her laptop. "Hey, do I have good news!" He did a drum roll on the edge of her desk, acting like Christmas had come early. "You won the Headliner contest! The judges loved the article you submitted about the young man who found his mother and discovered she'd been his kindergarten teacher. Are you hearing me? They loved it!' He pumped his fist in the air.

"What? Really?"

"We're all celebrating. Dinner at Spumoni's this Saturday night. My treat! And a raise for you, my dear."

"Uh … thanks."

"You came through, Cervantes." He clapped her on the shoulder before heading back to his desk, humming.

Ally stood, her mouth agape. Her mind whirled with two conflicting emotions, excitement and disappointment. She had dreamed of winning the prize, and now that it had happened, the thrill wasn't there. Why? What was wrong with her? She turned back to the computer to concentrate on an article, but all she could do was pick at a hangnail.

"Nice job, colleague." Ally looked up to see Janice smiling at her.

"Must have been all those lessons you gave me on punctuation and formatting. Got me up to speed on the Associated Press rules," Ally said.

"Yes, you did have a lot to learn. Still, well written," Janice said. "Even with all your personal problems."

Ally swallowed hard. *And just when I thought we were getting along, you had to insult me.*

"Say, what does it look like for your winning the grant money?"

Janice lowered her brow and pushed her lips into a firm line. "If you must be such a stickybeak, the town decided to go with the music department's plan." She scooted back to her desk.

"Sorry." How could she ever make peace with this prickly woman?

❧

After work, Ally pulled into the camp parking lot. She turned off the ignition and closed her eyes, trying to gather her courage before walking into Will's office. Her heart ached, but she had to confront him about the journal entry and the phone calls to Sarah. She wanted God's best—for her and the kids—even if it meant letting go of Will.

The door was open, and his head was down, working on some paperwork with Don. She slipped back behind the doorframe and listened.

"It's not what you think," said Will.

"Just surprised to see you with her," said Don. He mumbled something else Ally couldn't decipher.

"We grew up together. You know that." Will paused. "We share so many memories."

Fighting against a sudden wave of nausea, Ally knocked on the doorframe. Her legs shook uncontrollably, but she needed to face him head on. "Jesus, give me courage," she whispered.

Both heads popped up.

"Hi, Ally," said Don. He glanced at his wristwatch. "Oops, gotta call a plumber about a … a … broken faucet in the kitchen." He scooped a pile of papers into his arms and bolted out of the office.

Ally closed the door behind her. "Do you have a minute?"

Will stood and came around the front of the desk. "Sure. What's up?"

Ally took off her coat and draped it onto a wooden office chair by his desk. Then she turned back to him. "Something has been bothering me." She swallowed. "So, when I was at your house this morning to pick up the folder …"

"Yeah, thanks …"

"I read a few pages of …"

Will held her at arm's length and raised an eyebrow. "Of what?"

"Your doubts about us. I know I shouldn't have, but I did, and I'm not ashamed. You wrote pros and cons on marrying me, concerns you had, like if you could make a commitment to me, or if I would be married to my job, if I could be flexible, and that I might be too independent and—"

Will threw up his hands, trying to contain a laugh. "Hold on a minute. Where did you read this?"

"If you don't want to marry me, I'll let you go." She glared at him. "And stop laughing."

"What? Where was this?"

"In your journal. You left it out."

"My journal?" He blew out a long, sustained breath of exasperation, his eyebrows knitted together in irritation. "And you *had* to read it. Did you notice the date of the entry you *accidently* read?"

Ally lowered her head. "No," she muttered. *He must think I'm a nosy, prying, neurotic woman.*

"Try two years ago. That was all about Sarah. You know we had major differences. I reread it to see how far *you and I* had come."

"But what about the calls? You know, to her."

"What? You checked my phone?"

"Embarrassing to admit, but yes."

Will sighed and shook his head. "Well, if you need to know, she called to tell me about her dad's heart surgery."

"But all those other missed calls?"

"Wanted help with her new camp."

"But Kylie said you were really involved in a conversation with Sarah when you picked her up at the burger place one night, and you even stepped out of the car so she couldn't hear."

Will slammed his fist down on the desk. "That's an outright lie. Kylie made that up."

Shock, relief, and humiliation circled through her mind. She wanted to crawl under the desk. She deserved the gold medal for jumping to conclusions.

"As a matter of fact, Sarah flew in today, and I picked her up at the airport. At lunch …"

"You had lunch with her?" Jealousy flared, and she tried to tamp it down.

"Yes, and had a good visit on the drive to the hospital. Sarah's a good woman."

"She is."

"But she's called to work with orphans in Mexico."

"She's so dedicated, so strong in her faith."

He locked eyes with her. She couldn't turn away if she wanted to. "But she's not the woman I want to marry. Al, I love *you*. Don't you get that?"

"I do."

"When are you going to get it through that crazy brain of yours that you're the woman for me? It's a done deal." He put his hands on his head, pretending to pull out his hair. Then his face clouded, and he slammed his palms down on the desktop. "If you want to poke around for problems, that rooting around will only make our relationship harder. Dig down deep enough around a bush's roots, and you'll kill the plant." A loud sigh escaped through his lips. "Don't look for trouble."

Ally reached for his hand. "I feel so foolish."

His face softened, and he reached out for her hand. "Ah, babe, we're all a bit foolish. But you have to trust me. Promise?"

"Promise."

"On your honor?"

"So now I'm a Boy Scout? Okay, on my honor, I will try to …" She put up her two fingers in the scout pledge. "Okay, that's the last time I snoop, except …"

"*Al* …"

She hopped up onto his desk and leaned in close. "I'm not finished."

"Oh really?" A wicked smile spread across his face.

"Not that. I'm serious. Confession time. I realized something about myself today."

"And that is?"

"In the back of my mind, I've stashed away a plan B."

"A what?"

"In case you and I didn't work out. I crave security—for me and the kids. I figured if I worked hard at the paper, started a cake business, I'd be okay if things between us fell apart."

His eyes rolled heavenward. "Oh, babe, why would you think that?"

She slid off the desk. How could she make him see? "You don't realize how failing at a marriage shakes your confidence. Throw in a job loss, and I became a slippery, tangled mess of a human being."

"But …"

"No, let me finish. When you left in November and when Kylie started to create friction between us, I feared deep down things wouldn't work out. I didn't ask the Lord for help, just tried to manage this relationship—and parenting—on my own."

Will ran his hands though his hair. "Maybe I haven't assured you of my love often enough."

"Now shush. This is me apologizing to you. And I've had a change of heart."

"Not sure what you're saying."

"Burned brownies and dry hamburgers, yes sir, my specialty." Ally threw herself into his arms, sobbing. "I've missed camp. Here I've won this great award …"

"The Headliner Award?"

"Yes, I won it."

"You won it?"

"Yep."

He let out a whoop. "Babe, that's great. I'm so proud of you." He enveloped her in a giant bear hug.

"Stop. I can't breathe!"

"Sorry."

He backed off a few inches, and she reached for his hand, studying it. He had strong fingers, red from the physical work he had done all winter. They were honest hands. Kind hands. "Funny thing, when Russ told me about it today, my only thought was, 'Meh, that's nice.' There was no thrill. None. Even when he gave me a raise. Instead, I thought back to camp and cooking for two hundred campers. One of the most rewarding times of my life. The kids, the singing, the dinner talks. Something different than I've ever experienced, and I miss it."

"Really?"

"I guess winning the award showed me how writing, as much as I love it, isn't what I want. Aunt Nettie says, 'Life is short, spend it on others.'"

"I didn't want to push you, but I'm happy to hear you say that. I've always wanted to do this together." He leaned over, tugged open the bottom drawer in his desk, and pulled out some white folded material covered with faded stains. He unfolded it. On the top of the garment was embroidered, "Head Cook." Her old apron. "Welcome back!"

Ally swallowed a lump the size of Lake Michigan, as joy bubbled up inside her. "You saved it!"

"Never lost hope."

She took the apron from him, fingered the strings fondly, and held it under her neck. "I didn't realize how much I love this apron."

"We'll be on a very tight budget this year."

"Just call me Stretch. Watch what I create and be amazed."

"I'm already amazed."

❧

Saturday morning, Ally sat on her bed, sorting out her closet to take unwanted clothes to the Goodwill store. She looked up when the door opened.

"Hey, sweetie."

Kylie stood in the doorway, streams of black mascara running down her cheeks.

"What on earth?"

"Mom, I just watched the saddest movie about a girl whose mother was killed in a car accident. It was awful, and this girl had to figure out life on her own without a mom." Kylie wiped a tear with the back of her hand. "I thought about how you almost drowned last fall." She rushed into her arms. "Don't ever die."

"Think you might need your mom, eh?" Ally motioned her to sit down next to her on the bed and rubbed the small of her back. "I'll be around for a long time." An idea brewed in her mind. "I've hardly been anywhere except work and church this week. Let's hit Cherry County Coffee for a caramel macchiato and some girl time."

"Okay."

Ally expected more enthusiasm from her daughter, but she'd take what she could get. Something told her Kylie needed some serious reassurance and an outing would help. She slid off the bed and picked up her purse hanging on the doorknob. "I'll see if Aunt Nettie can watch Benjie."

They settled into two brown, overstuffed easy chairs at Cherry County Coffee, cups in hand. A back wall created from old barn siding sported several framed posters of past cherry festivals. Ally lowered her eyelids, savoring the aroma of her drink. When she opened her eyes, she noticed Kylie hadn't touched her drink. Instead, she had a faraway look as she fidgeted with a hole in her jeans.

"Awful quiet for the Kylie I know. You started to talk in full sentences at eighteen months, and you've never been at a loss for words."

"I have to tell you something," Kylie said, chewing on her thumbnail.

"Okay."

"Remember when I told you how Will was in the car talking on the phone to his old girlfriend, and he made me stand outside?"

"Yes," Ally leaned in, wondering where this conversation was headed.

"Well, I lied about that. I wanted to make you feel bad and break up with Will."

"Kylie, why?"

"I know. I feel real bad about it, especially when Will was the one who rescued me from that party. I'm really, really, really sorry."

Ally shook her head. "That caused me a lot of hurt. I'm glad you decided to fess up." She seized her daughter's hand and squeezed it. "All is forgiven."

"Thanks. And I've been thinking."

"Glad to hear that."

"No, I'm serious." A couple of teenaged boys walked by their table, one slowing down to catch her daughter's eye. Kylie flipped back her hair and acknowledged him with a wave before she continued. "Can we speed up this wedding?"

"Excuse me?"

"It's taking too long."

Ally threw back her head and laughed. The mirth rippled through her body, giving her a delight she'd missed for a long stretch. She and Kylie weren't fighting; they were enjoying each other. "Where have you been for the last six months?"

"I'm tired of us fighting," said Kylie.

She reached out her arm and squeezed her daughter's forearm. "Me too. Glad to have my daughter back. You've grown up a lot in the last few weeks, what with helping Aunt Nettie around the house and babysitting your brother."

"Guess I've been mixed up this year."

"You'll find new friends. I promise."

"Anyway, I want you guys to get married soon."

"We are. Now I need to ask you something. Do you want to be in the wedding?"

"Mom! Why would you say that? I love Will!"

Ally shook her forefinger at her daughter. "You and Will haven't been getting along—"

"Oh, that's in the past. He's different than I thought." Kylie smashed her Angelic Pink lip-glossed lips together. "Mom, I need to say this." She took a deep breath. "I'm sorry. I know I haven't treated him right."

"Maybe you can tell him that yourself. You owe that to him."

"I already did. I called him last night."

Ally raised her eyebrows as she eyed her daughter. She wasn't a young girl anymore. She'd be twenty before Ally blinked. How did that happen? "Well, since it's confession time, I also have to say something. I haven't spent enough time with you the last few months. I know you miss your father, and I was so busy I wasn't clued in to your feelings. You've had a lot to adjust to, and I've let you down."

"No problem, Mom." She drained the last bit of her drink and set the cup back on the table. "So when can we go shopping for a dress for the wedding? Can I wear a strapless one? Can I pick out the color? Can I wear heels?"

"You'll have a chance to choose—within reason."

"I saw an epic dress downtown. I mean, it's the cutest dress ever. Can we go see it tomorrow? What is Benjie wearing?"

"Probably navy blue pants and a white shirt. I just bought him a blue-striped clip-on tie."

"I love ties on little boys." Kylie picked up the cookie Ally had bought, took a big bite, and swallowed. "Are Grandma and Grandpa coming?"

"Probably. Mom sounded a bit hesitant to travel. Dad's arthritis makes it harder for them to fly. I've begged her over the last few months to come see us. But yes, I hope they'll come."

"Why wouldn't they?"

"She may still be mad at me. My decision to marry Will dashed any hope for her and Dad that we'd return to California. I haven't told you, but she's been pestering me to move back. I'll always love my native state, but our life is here, snow and all." She pinched off a piece of Kylie's raisin-nut cookie and popped it in her mouth.

"Mom, you're eating it all!" Kylie stared at the small remaining bite left. "Anyway, what did Grandma do to pressure you?"

"First of all, she kept sending me job descriptions from companies looking for editors in the Bay Area. Then when I didn't bite, she sent me all kinds of real estate listings to show me there were still, according to her, affordable houses I could rent. She even talked to a friend about a job opening in his publishing company."

Kylie giggled. "Wow. Grandma's so weird. She doesn't call much, but then she tries to convince you to move back."

Ally swallowed another gulp of her coffee and rested her chin in her right hand, her arm propped up on the table. "I hope you will settle into Lake Surrender, because this is your home."

"If you'd asked me right after the party, I'd have begged to go back to California. But things are better at school. I'm hanging with Kennedy and Chloe, and they're cool because they don't just sit around and play with their phones. They do stuff. Chloe's family lives on the lake, and she and I are going to go paddle boarding this summer, and Kennedy wants me to room with her during the counselor-in-training program. Her daughter's eyes lit up as she talked about her friends, a sight Ally hadn't seen for months. "And her brother, Cody, is super cool."

"Mm-hmm." Ally pressed her lips together to stifle a smile. *Will had better shine up his shotgun to scare off overly friendly young males.*

"Hey, Mom?"

"What?"

"How old do I have to be before I can date? Because I'm pretty mature for my age."

Ally thought about reviewing the last six months with her daughter but decided against it. Instead she said, "Twenty-one, and that's final."

She crossed her arms. "Come on."

"Nope."

Kylie shrugged her shoulders. "So one last question."

"What?"

"Will asked you to marry him last summer. Why have you guys waited so long?"

"Did you really say that?" Ally scrunched up her face in surprise and chuckled to herself. She started to answer when Kylie's eyes darted to a table across the room.

"I'll be right back. I want to say hi to Josh." Kylie stood and meandered over to the table where the two boys who had walked by earlier were sitting.

Ally face-palmed her head. *Here we go.*

CHAPTER TWENTY-SEVEN

"Got a breakfast meeting. See ya at lunch!" Russ jerked open the front door as a burst of gusty March air swept into the office. The door slammed with a bang, leaving only Janice and Ally to lay out tomorrow's edition.

"Did you submit that ad for Cherry County Coffee?" Janice asked, looking up from the page she was designing. "I don't see it."

Ally took off her coat and positioned her purse strap on the back of her chair. She rolled her chair away from the desk and plopped down into it, taking a deep breath. "No, remember you said you didn't need it until next week, in time for the pre-Easter issue."

With a groan of exasperation, Janice shot up from her desk and placed her tastefully manicured hands strategically on her hips, a move Ally had seen numerous times. Janice spoke slowly, like she was talking to a child. "I specifically requested it for today. Looks like working, parenting, and planning a wedding are a bit too much for you." She stretched out the "bit" to make a point.

Janice's gaze announced a showdown. *Well, by George, she was going to give her one.* Ally clenched her teeth, ready to jump into the ring and fight. Instead, she mustered all the self-control she could and swallowed hard. "I believe you remembered incorrectly."

"I don't *do* incorrect. This is a newspaper office." Janice took a couple of high-heel strides toward Ally's desk. "Listen, I understand this wedding business has put you on overload, but we still have deadlines."

"No, Janice, you specifically told me in last week's meeting that you needed the ad for the pre-Easter issue." Ally's cheeks burned, but she tried to keep her voice on an even keel while Janice walked over and stood in front of her desk.

In a softer voice, which suggested Ally could confide in her, Janice asked, "What is it? Problems at home?"

"What?"

"Employees often bring their personal problems to work. You may need to talk to—"

"That's ridiculous. Will and I are fine."

"Is your daughter in trouble at school? Is Benjie acting up again?"

Ally's cheeks burned. *This woman wouldn't give it up.* Anger brewed, like a saucepan bubbling over on a stove. *How dare she meddle in my business?* "What is it that you don't like about my son? Yes, he has behavior problems, but we're working on them." She clenched her fists to calm her body but couldn't still the trembling.

"I'm sure he is. It's just you seem so"—Janice closed her eyes for a moment—"so scattered." With that, she turned on her heels, but Ally caught her arm.

"You don't like me, do you?" Ally stared eyeball-to-eyeball at the woman with the elegant swooping eyebrows and perfectly applied lipstick.

Janice blinked in surprise, shocked by Ally's bluntness. "Why, I—I don't know why you would say that."

"Because every day I've been in this office, you've found plenty of ways to criticize me. Shall I list them? The way I interview someone on the phone, don't use perfect AP grammar, or can't drive in snow. The way I don't seem to discipline my son or the way my daughter is rebellious. Pick one, any one."

Ally's voice's volume rose to an ugly screech. *Who was this wild cray-cray woman set loose? Get a hold, Ally.*

But it was too late. Janice's eyes widened, and her face turned two shades paler as she backed away from Ally. She fled to her desk and crumpled to the surface like a marionette puppet at the end of its performance. A mop of dark hair covered an agonized wail. A succession of heartbreaking sobs followed.

Ally's anger subsided as she tried to compose herself. "I'm sorry. I didn't mean to lose my temper." She walked over to Janice's desk and slipped her arm around the office manager.

Janice shrugged off her arm. "No, it's not you. It's my fault. I had this coming for a long time." She raised her head as flesh-colored driblets of foundation streamed down her face and onto her starched white blouse. "Excuse me." Janice fled down the hall to the restroom, slamming the door behind her.

Ally stared after her. Should she follow Janice or go back to writing and let this whole thing blow over? She was on deadline to finish a piece on one of the newspaper's biggest advertisers, Apple Blossoms Wedding Venue.

I know what to do. She slipped into the kitchen. She twisted the knob on the old gas stove and listened for the clicking before placing a kettle of water on to boil. Once heated, she poured it into Janice's teapot. Then she rummaged around in a cabinet and found her china cup. After a few minutes of steeping the fragrant Earl Grey tea, she positioned the lid on the top of the container. She found a tray and placed a small pitcher of milk, a sugar bowl, the teapot, and cup.

When Janice returned to her desk, Ally placed the tea tray down in front of her. "Thought this might help ... a spot of tea works wonders."

A glimmer of a smile touched Janice's face as she reached to pour herself a cup. "Spot of tea? Thank you." She added cream and sugar, then sat back, sipping the steamy liquid. "I owe you an explanation, Ally."

Ally plopped down on top of Clay's nearby desk and sighed. "Not if you don't want to."

"But I do." Janice poured more cream into her cup and stirred. She let out a long breath before sipping the hot brew. "You and your son, Benjie, remind me of a very sad period in my life."

"Oh?" Ally reached for the tissue box on her desk and passed it to her.

Janice pulled out a tissue and blew her nose. "I haven't been truthful. You must think I've had a very glamorous life, and I have. My achievements in London were the type that many graphic designers could only dream of—such as working at *Tattler* magazine. Later, I had full artistic control for *British Vogue* in London. I was about thirty, and my career was flying high." She pulled out a periodical from a file folder in her desk drawer. "It may seem silly, keeping this all these years, but it shows what I did in a past life."

Ally thumbed through the glossy issue of *British Vogue* Janice handed her, amazed at the top models and fashion designers she had worked with.

"My husband and I took trips to the south of France and Africa. Life was fabulous until it crashed. When we returned from a two-week trip to Lisbon, Portugal, I noticed I had no energy. Worse still, I couldn't keep food in my stomach. To my surprise, I was pregnant."

"That wasn't your plan?"

"It wasn't on our—as you say—'bucket list.' But I braved a brutal pregnancy, with morning sickness for eight months. Finally, early on June eighth, my husband raced me to the hospital, and after twelve hours of labor I gave birth to a boy, Trevor Andrew. He was born at 8:45 p.m. But something was terribly wrong. Several doctors raced into the delivery room, consulting with each other in whispered tones." She picked up her teacup and took a sip. "Whispering doctors are a bad omen. A nurse whisked Trevor away. I felt hurt and confused. Why couldn't I hold my son?" Janice dabbed at her eyes.

"What was going on?"

"Trevor was malformed. His head was hydrocephalic, very enlarged with water on the brain. His limbs were tiny, and he was missing a foot." Janice gripped the teacup handle so tightly her fingers turned white. "His birth turned into a hideous nightmare."

Ally cleared her throat. "You don't have to tell me anymore."

"No, I need to share this." Janice continued, placing her cup on the desk. "When my husband and I finally visited Trevor in the newborn nursery, he was covered with feeding tubes, breathing tubes, and beeping alarms. Nurses hovered over him for hours, doctors came in constantly to check on him. I picked him up, but he was too delicate to hold for very long.

"Martin insisted we never bring him home. I protested for a few days. Finally, I gave in. Two months later, when we should have had a tiny bundle in our nursery, we signed the papers for him to be institutionalized. I never saw him alive again. He only lived three more months." She gingerly placed her teacup on the desk as if its fragility reminded her of Trevor.

Ally leaned over and squeezed her hand. "I'm so sorry."

"So that's why I've been snippy to you. My lands, at least you still have him. My boy is gone, and when I see your son, he brings back painful memories. Oh, how I wish I'd tried to take care of my baby at home."

"How could you have?"

"I didn't even visit him. Not that he would have known I was there." Janice mopped more tears from her face.

Poor woman. Filled with a guilt that had shackled her for years. *This woman, whom I've sparred with and whose arrogance I hated, has a real heart. I judged her, not knowing her own struggles. She's in the deep end.* Ally walked to the kitchen to refill the teapot with hot water and poured Janice another cup of tea. While she poured, she offered up a silent prayer for God to give Janice peace.

Blowing her nose, Janice nodded a thank-you and lifted the cup to her lips. "Tea helps."

"Guilt is a cruel taskmaster. Believe me, I've been there," Ally said as she returned to her desk and sat.

"His short life still haunts me."

Ally put her fingertips together and bent her head down for inspiration. What could she say? Suddenly the words came. "I can relate to you more than you know."

"What do you mean?"

"I didn't physically give up my child, but in other ways I did. I spent years neglecting Benjie while I pursued a prestigious career in publishing. No, I never put him in an institution, but he had a boatload of babysitters and therapists who watched him afternoons, evenings, and weekends. Sure, I had to work, so he became low on my list of priorities. I'm ashamed to say I didn't try very hard to connect."

"But from what I see, you're so good with him."

"Now, yes, but the first six years of his life I wasn't Mother of the Year by any stretch of the imagination. I threw myself into my work, as did my ex." Ally covered her eyes for a moment. "I had been dealt a difficult hand in life, and I didn't want it."

"Go on."

"I had to first forgive myself for my selfish attitude. I didn't want to admit I wasn't the perfect mother. When I became a single mom and had to take the responsibility of raising Benjie and Kylie pretty much by myself, I had to learn fast. And one of the things I realized was that my son—as difficult as his behavior was—had value."

"Value? I have a hard time believing that."

"He was created by God, and even with all his disabilities and quirks, he was born for a reason. I don't think I'd be able to hear God's voice clearly in my life if it weren't for Benjie's sweet spirit in our everyday lives. He's a gift to our family."

Janice blinked a few times but didn't say anything.

Ally continued. "Your life has been hard too. But your child wasn't a mistake. Every life has purpose. You couldn't have taken care of him by yourself. No one could. But don't ever think his life was an accident, not for a minute."

"I never thought about it that way. I didn't want him, so I felt God was …"

"You have to forgive yourself. God forgives you." Ally rolled her chair next to the office manager's desk and wrapped both arms around her. Silently, they rocked back and forth. "Never forget that."

Janice looked up at her. "Thank you … friend."

"His life was precious. And so is yours."

CHAPTER TWENTY-EIGHT

"What do you think about lemon filling for the wedding cake, Aunt Nettie?" Ally looked up from her computer on the kitchen counter where she was checking her caterer's website. "The wedding's in a month, but I'm so glad we moved up the date to April."

"If you like it, I like it." Nettie's phone rang, and she picked it up. "Why, hello, Detective Whittaker. Yes, I'm fine. Thanks for asking."

Ally smiled to herself. Her aunt's voice sounded more cheerful than usual. She scrolled through Tasty Good Catering's website.

"Painting? Yes, I'm working on a project right now." Another pause. "Glad you're finally retiring. What's up?" So like Aunt Nettie to get right to the point. She didn't believe in chitchat.

Suddenly Nettie's voice became firm. "Did Ally put you up to this?" She turned and frowned at her niece before turning her attention back to the conversation. "Yes, we did have a good time when we went out." Her aunt listened for another moment, shuffling a pile of bills on the counter and then making a shooing motion. Ally took her laptop into the family room to check her email.

She heard her aunt hang up the phone and saunter into the room, parading back and forth like she'd won a beauty contest.

"Let me guess. You won the Publisher's Clearing House Sweepstakes, and you're taking us all to Europe. Or, the furniture shop accepted your new designs," said Ally.

"No."

"Kylie did all the laundry for us?"

"Better. Got a date for the wedding. And this weekend." She clapped her hands together.

"Awesome. Let me guess who."

"I'm sure you heard, Detective Whittaker. You know, from the soup kitchen."

"Make sure he doesn't take your fingerprints."

"Just lip prints."

Ally let out a whoop. "I can't believe you said that. Sounds like I need to chaperone you two." Her phone rang. Will.

"Hey, can you jet over here ASAP? It's Friday night, and two staff members are stuck in that freak snowstorm down south. I have fifty school superintendents coming in two hours and nothing cooked for dinner. Al, if they cancel, we lose a lot of money, and the camp needs every extra penny this year." His voice sounded rattled.

Ally ended the call and cupped her hands to yell for her kids upstairs. "Guys, hop in the car. We need to rescue Will."

&

"Fastest thing to feed a crowd is my Rustic Spaghetti. Guaranteed to bring rave reviews," said Ally as she threw on her old camp apron and pulled the chef knife out of the drawer. Her heart raced. She could do this. She loved a challenge.

"I don't care what you cook, as long as it's edible." Will raked his hand through his hair. She'd never seen him so stressed.

"Also salad and garlic bread. And I've ordered three large pans of tiramisu from Spumoni's. They gave me a good deal, and they'll deliver in an hour." Ally hacked off both ends of an onion and started to chop it. "It will all turn out great, trust me."

Kylie raced up to the counter with a big stainless steel bowl. "Mom, I tore up all the lettuce. Where are the tomatoes?"

Ally pointed to the walk-in refrigerator and turned her attention back to the onions. After she chopped the entire bag, she looked up to see Benjie coloring. *Oh good, he's staying put.* She breathed a prayer of relief. The last thing she wanted to do was chase him all over kingdom come.

Kylie washed off the tomatoes and chopped them into small pieces, adding them to the salad bowl, and then pulled out a stainless steel cart loaded with silverware, plates, napkins, and salt and pepper shakers. "Benjie, help me put these out. You are the shaker man."

"Shake, shake, shake." He stood, then danced around waving his hands above his head and jumping up and down.

Kylie scooted over to her brother and dragged him by the hand. "Hurry up. No time for dancing. We have lots of people who need to eat dinner tonight, and we have to help Will."

"Help Will."

Will sauntered over to the stove and stirred the spaghetti sauce. "You guys are awesome." A couple of small SUVs pulled into the lodge parking lot, and someone honked their horn. "They're here," said Will. He beat out a staccato drum rhythm on the edge of the stainless steel counter. "I'll meet them and show them to their cabins. Yahoo, it's show time!"

"TV?" Benjie asked. They all laughed.

❧

Aunt Nettie zoomed into the kitchen, her shirtsleeves rolled up and ready to work. She hauled out a large pasta pot from underneath a shelf of one of the stainless steel counters. Filling the pot with water, she dragged it to the stovetop and turned on the burner.

She turned to Ally. "Got a minute?"

"Sure. I've done most of the prep." Ally took the corner of her apron and wiped her eyes, stinging from the onions.

"Wanted you to hear it first. I dropped out of the Magnificent Maple contest."

Ally put down the chef knife. "What?"

"I drove over to the store this afternoon and compared the two designs. I looked at Janice's submission and suggested to them that though they looked comparable, I could see some differences. But between you and me the designs weren't that different."

Ally shook her head. "Did she think no one would notice?"

"Jack said he had a hard time deciding between the two and was planning to take a vote at the staff meeting on Monday. I told him to choose Janice's, I was dropping out of the running."

"But why? You're so talented."

"As is Janice."

"I hope you're not giving in because of my trouble at work with her. Things between us are better, but I need to fight my own battles. Anyway, you deserved to win."

"Not sure about that."

"But she got the idea to enter when you came by that day. She wouldn't have even know about the contest if she hadn't seen your design."

"That thought occurred to me when I came over to your office, so I slipped out quickly. I could already see the wheels turning."

Ally crossed her arms. "I still think you should win."

Her aunt lowered her head and picked at some peeling polish on her thumbnail. "Janice wants to win more than I do. In the long run, giving up a reward is sometimes the greater reward."

Will stormed into the kitchen. "The guests are settling in, and I told them to come to the dining room in twenty minutes. Are the salads plated?"

"Lined up to go."

"Like domonos, in line," said Benjie.

Will tousled Benjie's hair. "You and your dominoes."

❧

Ally surveyed the rustic dining room, a catch forming in her throat. Was the wedding really tomorrow? So much had happened in the last eight months. Even with spring's arrival, the air had a chill. She saw the stone fireplace, now lit, reflected in the floor-to-ceiling windows that looked out on the lake. This room would soon house all of her and Will's family and friends, gathered to celebrate their love. "I'm a blessed woman," she whispered.

Ally's mother had come through with her quintessential touch, finding the freshest flowers and renting elegant dinnerware for the event. Even though she'd had doubts about her daughter marrying a camp manager, her change of heart was obvious. Will now could do no wrong in her mother's eyes.

The cedar-paneled eating area, usually decked out with red-checked oilcloth-covered tables, had been transformed into a stylish venue. Covered with pale lemon-colored linens, each round table displayed a generous arrangement of paperwhites, daffodils, white tulips, and purple hyacinth in terra-cotta pots. A white china plate with a gold rim anchored each place setting. Filmy fabric illuminated with miniature lights hung from the ceiling beams and created an ethereal tent, while yellow Chinese paper lanterns emitted a soft glow.

Ally savored the flowers' aroma as she heard footsteps come up behind her. Will pressed his sturdy frame against her back as they surveyed the magical room together, his hands gliding around her waist. He nibbled on her neck.

"Mom did a great job."

"I wasn't sure they'd come."

"Neither was I," said Ally.

She pivoted to look at the man who would become her husband tomorrow. The twinkly lights made his deep-brown eyes glisten. Were those tears she saw? "God answers prayers," she whispered into his ear. "And He gives the best gifts."

"Yes, He does." Will dug in his back pocket. "I have one for you and wanted to give it to you when we were alone. Sit down for a minute, my lady." He pulled out chairs for both of them at one of the tables. "Now close your eyes." Ally lowered her lids. "Okay, you can open them now." He put a small object into her hands, a gift clumsily covered in white tissue paper and tied with a green ribbon.

She yanked on the ribbon, and the bow released.

"That's a special ribbon. It's the same color as the dress you wore the first time we went out on a real date."

"You remembered the color?" *And I think he doesn't notice.*

"I know. I don't usually pay attention to clothes, but I remembered that color. That night took me back to the young girl from so many summers ago. The girl who dug holes with me to find buried treasure and who threw pop in my face when I tossed her Adidas into the lake. I could almost see that face superimposed onto your grown-up face that night."

Ally found his hand, resting on the table. She took it and traced around his fingers.

"You left a piece of yourself in my mind," he said. "Those summers I tormented you when you'd come out from California, I never in my wildest dreams thought we'd end up together. But our relationship started long before you showed up at camp two years ago."

Ally caught a twinkle in his eye.

"Go ahead and open it."

Ally undid several pieces of tape, and the wrapping fell off. She gasped. Will had found an old photo of them at ages ten and twelve, in front of the lake's old General Store, and had it enlarged. The camera captured a ten-year old Ally licking an ice cream cone. In the photo, Will's cone was dripping down his hand while his eyes focused on her.

"Dad took it. Do you remember why we were eating those?"

Ally said. "I bet you an ice cream cone that I could put a worm on a hook and catch something before you did, and I won." Her hand stroked the side of the picture frame. "And me, a squeamish city girl."

"Even though all you caught was an old piece of an oar."

"You let me win? All this time, I thought I'd beat you."

"I didn't let any girl win in those days. You were different—always put me off balance. I think that's why I liked you."

She chuckled. "I once watched you chuck a baseball from Aunt Nettie's beach to three lots over. I never told you, but I was impressed." She looked around the room. "And then, the first day I came here, I followed you into your office to interview for the cook's job, and I thought, '*Where* have I ended up?' I mean, the sparse dining hall, your congested office, and that ancient kitchen. What I didn't know was God was wooing me down a different path." Ally slid onto Will's lap, wrapping her arms around his neck as she studied his face. "Oh how I love you, Camp." She ran her fingers through his thick unruly hair.

He took the ribbon and tied it around her wrist and cocked his head to the side. "This seals the deal. You're my Always Girl."

She tipped her head up. Her mouth met Will's as their lips melted together. *Oh, thank You, God, for this man.* The man who balanced her impulsive, overreacting personality with calmness, steadiness, and an unflinching faith.

The pounding of feet on the bare wood floor jerked them apart. "Hey, Mom, save that for tomorrow," Kylie yelled as she zoomed into the room, dragging her brother behind her.

Will jerked his head away. They looked at each other, and Ally giggled. He turned to Kylie. "I'll kiss your mother today, tomorrow, and the rest of our lives."

❧

"Let me show you our room," said Linda as Ally followed her mother back to her hotel after dinner. Her father had left to find a drug store, so the two of them were alone. Always the picture of efficiency, her mother unzipped her suitcase and pulled out a couple of pair of pants, hanging them up in the small mini closet before putting her cosmetic bag on the bathroom sink.

Ally followed her mother into the bathroom and studied their similar reflections in the mirror as Linda organized her toiletries and applied her lipstick. Linda gave her hair another swipe with the comb before turning to her daughter. "You're sure this is the one?"

Their eyes met in the reflection. "As sure as I've ever been about anything or anyone. There aren't a lot of Wills in the world."

"I just hope you two can live on your limited camp salaries."

"If not, we'll live on love."

"Ally, the impractical one." She sighed. "But you two will make it work."

"With help from above."

"I suppose. Well, we'd best be off." Mom glanced at her wristwatch. "Your sister should be here about now."

As they walked through the door, as if on cue, a small figure scurried down the hallway toward her. Ally screamed and ran to meet her sister. Georgia's blonde hair pulled back into a ponytail swung back and forth as she ran to meet her. They hugged.

"I wouldn't miss this for the world, Ally. Can't believe you're marrying that crazy kid we used to play with."

"I know. Who would have thought? You look great, by the way."

"So do you. What a wild year you've had. I was about to put my house on the market and move here. You need looking after, Sis." Georgia poked Ally in the side with her elbow.

"I survived." She poked her back.

Georgia reached over and squeezed Ally's hand. "I knew you would. Just hope you can survive Will. He's in the lobby going over the catering bill, and he looks nervous."

❧

"Nice to see you on such a marvelous evening." Janice nodded to Nettie as she took Nettie's elbow and steered her toward the church choir room. "Wanted to have few words with you before the service."

She pushed open the door and turned on the light. "Come in for a moment."

"Only a moment. I'm needed in the parlor."

The two women walked into the room and found a couple of chairs. "I will make it quick. I didn't win the grant. But I did win the logo contest."

"Good for you."

"I'm only telling you because I decided to contribute my award monies toward the wedding. I've decided to pay for Ally's caterer. I'm keeping it a secret but wanted to let you know. Your niece really helped me in a time of great distress. I will forever be grateful."

"That's very kind of you."

"It's the right thing to do. I will be talking to the caterer. Here's what I need for you to do. Please let Will know the food has been paid for so he can enjoy his special day. It's the least I can do for my friend Ally. But don't say who."

"Happy to give him the good news." Nettie stood to leave.

"And Nettie, your logo was fabulous. Very similar to mine."

"I noticed."

"Well, you know what they say about great minds thinking alike."

CHAPTER TWENTY-NINE

Ally stood in Lake Surrender Community Church's private parlor off the sanctuary—a cozy room with aqua walls and up-holstered couches, especially for brides-to-be—and arranged flowers in her hair. So different from her first wedding. More intimate. Not such a big production. When her mom and aunt entered, the door cracked open just wide enough for her to pre-view a blur of suits and evening dresses. Snippets of animated conversations filled the candlelit hallway as guests hurried to their seats in the church's sanctuary.

"Honey, we're about ready." Mom looked like an older ver-sion of Nettie, a tad grayer and with more pronounced wrin-kles around her eyes, although their personalities couldn't have been more different. Ally wasn't sure if the glow on Nettie's face came from her new pale green suit or the detective waiting out-side. Nettie drew Ally close and pressed a tissue into her hand.

"Where are Kylie and Benjie? They were just here," said Ally.

"They'll show up." Mom said. "Anyway, they're already dressed, and if Kylie is with Benjie, he'll be fine." She surprised Ally by taking both of her hands in hers. "Would the rest of you mind if we had a private moment?"

Nettie nodded and motioned to Georgia, their father, Betty, and Wilma—who had all come to say hi. They filed out.

"Come, sit here." Ally's mother dropped her hands and waved her arm toward a cream-colored brocade loveseat.

Sounds of Jorge's classical guitar music drifted into the room. Ally clutched the edge of her long lace skirt, lifting it up an inch before taking baby steps toward the loveseat. Her new too-tight heels already pinched her big toe. Seated, she fiddled with an unruly curl that had escaped a hairpin.

"Oh, stop fussing and listen to me," her mother said. When Ally turned to her, she cleared her throat. "You know I wasn't in favor of you running off to Michigan after your divorce and moving in with my sister. I thought you were throwing away your whole future in the publishing world."

"Mom, do we have to—"

"Now, hear me out. You've always been determined to go your own way, and I was mad at you for leaving California. At first, I didn't see things working out with Will."

Ally bit her lip, determined not to argue with her mother on this special April night. It couldn't be more perfect, with a silvery full moon in the sky. When she looked away, Linda's thin hand touched Ally's voluminous skirt, as she absently smoothed it out. "But now I can see you're happy, thanks to Will. You are well-suited to each other." Her mother paused to swallow. She saw in her mother's eyes a very proud woman admitting she was wrong. "Seeing the joy on your face the last few days has convinced me you've been given a gift—a new start in life. You're a brave young woman, and I'm proud of you." She withdrew her hand from Ally's knee. "There, I've said it. Now go get married." She stood.

Back to business. That's Mom, and I wouldn't have it any other way. Ally stood, biting her lip so she wouldn't cry. She wanted to frame this moment full of unexpected words from her mother. The frozen tundra between them had melted. Ally threw open her arms and squeezed her mother's torso.

Linda laughed. "Stop, I'm about to burst the buttons off this too-tight dress, Ally." She arranged the folds of her skirt and applied a fresh coat of coral lipstick. "Now we'd better find those kids of yours, so you can marry the man of your dreams."

❧

All month Benjie had studied April the thirtieth on Aunt Nettie's calendar. Mama had told him that was the day she would marry Will. Every day before breakfast he'd jumped up to touch the circled date. Often he did it ten or twenty times before Mama told him to stop and get ready for school. But he couldn't help it. He liked to think about the wedding.

Finally, the day arrived. Benjie sat on the side porch of the big church, building his rock trail, while Kylie watched him. He knew there'd be a big, tall cake, and Mama would wear a pretty, long dress. And best of all, his best buddy, Will, would start living with them. Mama said they'd have to move to the gray cottage, but that was okay, because he could look out the windows and see lots of deer. And Mama said he could take his button collection, his rock collection, his dominoes, and his stuffed toy squirrel.

Benjie wondered if his daddy would be watching today. Kylie said probably.

"Hey, we should go inside." His sister reached into her backpack and pulled out something wrapped in a paper towel. She held it in her hands for a moment and then put it back. "We need to talk to Dad today. Would you like to stop at his grave? It's just over there." She pointed to some pine trees behind the church.

Benjie nodded. He hoped Daddy would be proud of his fancy wedding clothes—blue pants, white shirt, and the special blue-striped tie that clipped onto his collar.

"Come on." Kylie reached out a hand to help him up.

The wind blew chilly, a reminder of the long winter. They crunched silently along the graveyard's gravel road dusted with the last spring snow, their gait slow to avoid slipping on a few frozen puddles. The lane was lined with tiny lights. Benjie counted the number of lights, twenty-six. He loved counting and numbers. He also loved Daddy being right next to the church. Maybe he could walk by with Kylie after Sunday school and visit him.

"Remember, it's in the back." Kylie pointed to the far corner and led him through the cemetery to a small granite stone laid flat against the sod, located between two small birch trees. She brushed off the snow so they could see the writing.

"Bryan Cervantes, 1/12/1978–3/13/2014, then 2 Corinthians 4:17–18," said Kylie. "See all the numbers? You are so good at numbers." She took off her coat, placed it on the wet ground, and then kneeled down. Benjie kneeled next to her. "Hey, Dad, came to say 'hi.' We miss you more than you can imagine, but we're glad you're hanging with Jesus."

A wild goose honked overhead, headed back from its winter hiatus down south. Benjie looked up in the sky as his sister paused. He wondered if his father could see the birds.

Kylie cleared her throat. "Dad, I wanted to let you know Will is a good guy who will take care of us. I was kind of mean to him for a while." She rubbed her hands together to stay warm. Spring in northern Michigan took a long time to show up. "Guess I treated him bad because I didn't want you to think I'd forgotten you. You'll always be my dad. But I love Will too. I hope that's okay."

Benjie thought he should do something too, so he leaned over and patted the stone.

Kylie turned to him. "Do you know what the stone says?"

Benjie shook his head.

"It says 'For our light and momentary troubles are achieving for us an eternal glory that far outweighs them all. So we fix our eyes not on what is seen, but on what is unseen, since what is seen is temporary, but what is unseen is eternal.'"

His sister bent over the grave, her long hair almost touching the ground. "Dad's not gone forever, just for a few years until we go to heaven. But we still live on earth, and we will have a good life." She put her opened hand out and caught a lone snowflake. "I believe that, don't you?"

He wasn't sure what that meant, but he nodded. Of course he believed her. He trusted everything his big sister said. If she said it would rain tomorrow, or they would have chocolate cake for dinner, he trusted her. She always told him the truth.

Kylie unwrapped the object in the paper towel she'd been carrying. He recognized the two twigs she had lashed together with twine at camp last year and fashioned into a cross. She piled up a remnant of snow above the marker and stuck the homemade object in it. "There, now Dad can look down and see we remembered him today."

Benjie looked up into the darkened sky. One large, fluffy cloud hovered above them, bigger than his school bus. Maybe his father was inside the cloud. Probably. Just in case, he waved to him.

His gaze then trailed back toward the church where he caught sight of Will and his mom racing toward him.

"What on earth are you two doing?" said Mama. "Benjie, your shirt is filthy, and your shoes are soaking wet."

"Sorry, Mom," said Kylie. "I wasn't paying attention. I forgot how much he loves mud."

Will shook his head and chuckled. "Back to reality," he said to Mama.

"But what a beautiful reality," Mama said.

She grabbed my hand, and we all ran back to church.

THE END

Where her journey ends, the lake begins.

Available from ShopLPC.com
and your favorite retailer.

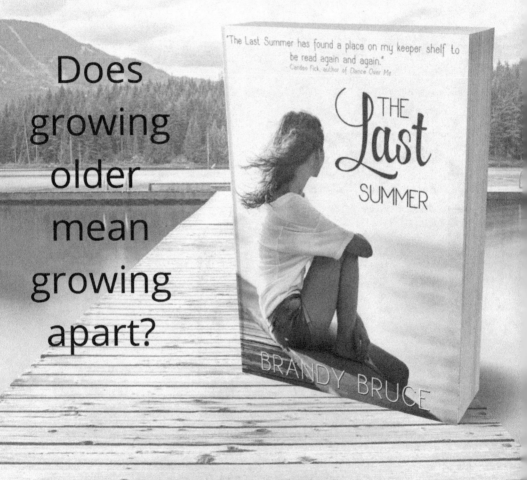